Hey Dennis, I hope you enjoy my mental wanderings. Pleased you care.

Patrick Phinn

Two Trails to Judith

Dexter C. McPherson

authorHOUSE®

AuthorHouse™
1663 Liberty Drive, Suite 200
Bloomington, IN 47403
www.authorhouse.com
Phone: 1-800-839-8640

©2009 Dexter C. McPherson. All rights reserved.

No part of this book may be reproduced, stored in a retrieval system, or transmitted by any means without the written permission of the author.

First published by AuthorHouse 9/9/2009

ISBN: 978-1-4389-7159-9 (sc)

Printed in the United States of America
Bloomington, Indiana

This book is printed on acid-free paper.

Contents

DEDICATION		ix
NOTES		xi
ACKNOWLEDGMENTS		xiii
PREFACE		xv
CHAPTER 1	INFATUATION	1
CHAPTER II	TRAGEDY & TRANSFORMATION	21
CHAPTER III	FOUR, THREE, TWO	38
CHAPTER IV	AND THEN THERE WAS ONE	50
CHAPTER V	GETTIN' ACQUAINTED	70
CHAPTER VI	THE ROAD HOME	80
CHAPTER VII	TOUGH WAY TO MEET	94
CHAPTER VIII	REALITY & MATURITY	110
CHAPTER IX	SURPRISES	136
CHAPTER X	THE TEST	160
CHAPTER XI	BIRTH OF A DYNASTY AND A CHILD	172
CHAPTER XII	THE CLEANSING	183
CHAPTER XIII	CLASH OF CULTURES	193
CHAPTER XIV	SHADES OF RED AND SCARLET	202
EPILOGUE		234

Illustrations

Montana Terr. 1879	xvii
Clayton McMahon	xviii
Shoshone Pony	20
Pauline	37
Bryce Girouard	108
Hoodoo Pony	109
Viola Millin	134
C-Bar-M Ranch	135

Photographs

Moccasin Town	4
Buffalo Town	26
Maiden Town	62
Judith Basin Homestead	98
Shawmut Town	165
Gilt Edge Town	209
Utica Town	227
Judith Mountains	229
Thunderstorm and Sunset	231

DEDICATION

This work is dedicated to all the descendants of pioneer Montanans, in memory of the hardships, heartbreaks, and also the loves and joys experienced by their ancestors as they guided the Territory of Montana into statehood and prosperity.

I further dedicate this book to the few brave people who still cling to, and fight for, the concept of family unity and see it as a desirable and successful social structure.

NOTES

Although the author devoted countless hours to research into historic, geographic, and cultural background, some names, places, and times have been altered to accommodate the story line.

Most of the names herein are composites of old family names. Any similarity to persons living or dead is by purpose and proudly rendered by the author in fond memory.

Other names are strictly fictitious and any similarity to persons, living or dead, is purely coincidental.

ACKNOWLEDGMENTS

I am forever grateful to my son-in-law, Vern Nickelson, for his tireless efforts in the editing and transcription of this text , and his wife, eldest daughter, Wendy, whose sharp eye and grammatical expertise corrected many an error therein.

Also, talented daughters, Linda, Jill, and Dana, for their wonderful artistic depictions of characters and scenes.

Also, daughter Susan and sons, Neil and Stuart, who unknowingly contributed to the characters of the young ones in the story through my memories of them all as children in a large and modest, but loving family.

Also, my lovely wife, Jean, who first introduced me to her home state of Montana and to those crusty old relatives who inspired my formation of characters with their hilarious tales of the past, related in old west lingo. I also thank Jean for her patience in the privation she endured as I wrote and roamed the states of Montana and Wyoming researching history.

Also, I am grateful to all the rest of our large family for their support and inspiration.

My thanks also go to my cousin, David Ross, and his dear wife, Joy, who provided so much of the family history incorporated herein.

I am grateful to Joyce Massing of the Upper Musselshell Museum, Kathy Frost of the Harlowton Public Library, and Karen Salinas of the Livingston Public Library for their patient assistance in my research of early Montana history

PREFACE

During twenty-four years of annual vacations in Montana, I became more and more captivated by the beauty, grandeur and vast lonesome reaches of that state. So, it was with little resistance, upon retirement, that I yielded to my wife, Jean, whose wish was to move back to her childhood hometown.

From our new home in Livingston, I began to explore that huge and remote area east of the Rocky Mountains. Each new ghost town, old mining camp or long-abandoned homestead piqued my interest and in intense yearning began to burn within me to know how these early pioneers survived, lived, loved, and grew to be successful ranchers, proprietors, railroaders, etc.

As each new piece of historical panorama unfolded, I found myself mentally and emotionally living back in those days, experiencing the many events that would epitomize the life of a late-1880's pioneer rancher. It was as if I had lived this life at another time and I was often startled upon arriving in a new ghost town to find it almost identical to the picture I carried in my mind. From this abstract feeling of belonging, it became natural and easy to construct a tale of that decade and to tie it to a plot and story theme I had been harboring in my mind for years.

The characters are largely built on the foundations of my own early ancestors. My father's mother, Sara Viola Millay (McPherson) did exist, did grow up in Bogard, Missouri, did teach elocution at Chillicothe Normal School, did perform on the stage, did write poetry, did teach elementary school, and did leave Bogard, Missouri for the west after marrying my Grandfather, Doctor Samuel Preston McPherson.

Upon their arrival in Chewelah, Washington around 1900, my Grandfather became medical officer for the Colville Indian Agency and remained as such until the agency was moved to the town of Colville. The young married couple then brought the old agency building, living in it where my two aunts, Rowena and Alice, my father Joseph, and my uncle Preston, were born. A generation later, I was born in this same cabin of hand-hewn logs. The old Indian Agency building still stands and is registered as a National Historic Site. My Grandmother, Sara Viola, was the ultimate educator and I often sat spellbound as she read from Nathaniel Hawthorne, National Geographic, and other publications. She always accented with her voice and facial expressions, but also lent much time to explanations and expanding my understanding when necessary.

This tiny Welsh actress would also line her grandchildren up on the old straight-backed chairs with horsehide seat cushions and perform skits from her repertoire of characters, which included Little Orphant Annie, and ran the gamut to the operatic Florence Meadowlark. A truly dear, intelligent, and talented lady, you will see her character in Sandra Viola Millin (Girouard) in my story.

Grandmother Viola was a cousin to the famous poet, Edna St. Vincent Millay, and she also possessed a great command of the English language. I have worked two of her poems into the story line.

I found it extremely easy to weave these ancestors into my story about the Judith Basin country of the 1880's.

As I haunted libraries, museums, historic sites, and picked the minds of old-timers, I found some incredible stories of tragedy, privation, courage, and success. These were remarkably persistent people. I've come to believe that the great westward migration of the American people and the rapid settling of this raw and wild country is one of the great under-storied sagas of world history.

Dexter C. McPherson

Montana Terr. 1879

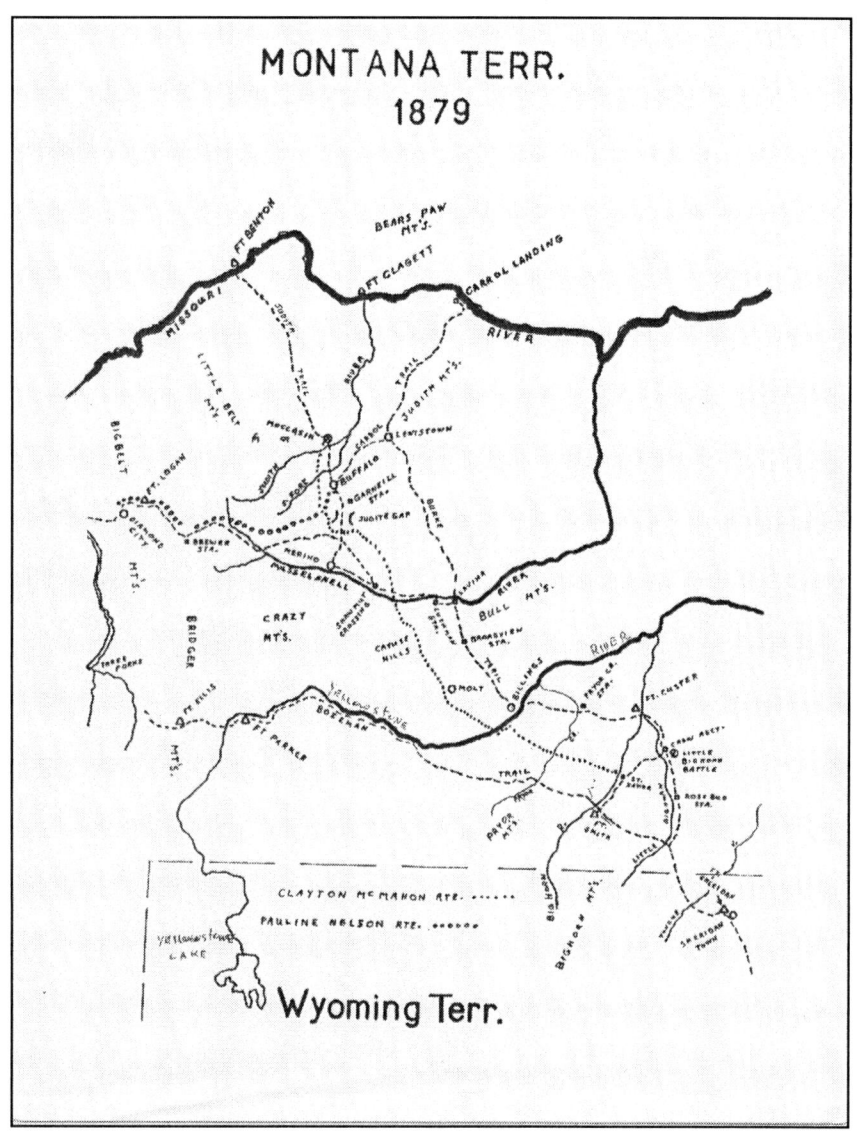

Clayton McMahon

CHAPTER 1
INFATUATION

Crude, disrespectful laughter jolted Clayton McMahon from his reverie.

Clayton idly walked his mount down the dusty main street of Moccasin, pulling abreast of the Blue Bull Saloon. Three men lounged against a railing in front of the weathered board-and-batt exterior. Now, eying the men from beneath the lowered brim of his Stetson, he could plainly see that the raucous laughter was, indeed, directed at him.

As he turned to face them, the two in shabby range garb leered back in obvious contempt. The third man, dressed in a neat black suit with pant legs tucked into shiny riding boots, was familiar to Clayton. The dark-haired man turned to his two seedy companions and spoke sharply, but inaudibly, whereupon the three turned and entered the saloon, one of the men looking over his shoulder, sneer still in place.

The Stetson shaded Clayton's rusty hair, which crowned a lithe six-foot frame. Deep blue eyes squinted in concentration as he rubbed a hand across his freckled and sunburned nose. Wide shoulders erect as he rode easily astride his sturdy pinto, he pondered the unusual confrontation.

Just troublemakers wanting to push an unarmed man into a fight? It didn't make sense. There were many sheep men, miners, and sodbusters who frequented Moccasin, Montana daily as they went about their business and pleasures. Why single out an inconspicuous cowboy to taunt today?

Clayton could not rationalize the strange behavior. He had seen the well-dressed man around town several times during the past week.

Marvin Quessing had told him the man spent most of his time at the poker table and seemed to do well, winning steadily from many of those who played against him, including Marvin, who said the talk around town was that the man cheated but no one had caught him at it.

Clayton had met the man face-to-face only once as he entered the bank to see Bonnie. Bryce, as he was known, had looked Clayton straight in the eyes as if curious, but there didn't seem to be any animosity or recognition. The black eyes, set in a handsome, dark-skinned face, seemed questioning in their directness.

Was the man someone from the past also struggling to place Clayton McMahon? Clayton searched his memories. Someone from his rowdy days as a young man in the Dakotas; his brief fling as a deputy sheriff in Rapid City where he had dogged a wanted killer south to Texas? In a showdown, he had outdrawn and killed that man.

The systematic track down of the outlaw and Clayton's courage in facing up to a known gunman had made him a hero in Texas—so impressive that the fledgling Texas Rangers had offered him a job with the agency. He had spent five years as a ranger. Now he sifted through the many faces of outlaws, cattle rustlers and killers for some resemblance to the man or his two sidekicks. Nowhere in his past could he recall the three.

Clayton knew the possibility of someone with an old hatred recognizing him as one who had wreaked justice on a miserable soul and would want revenge, but he had resigned himself to living with that. He always carried a carbine in his saddle scabbard but had laid aside the gun belt and pistols over a year ago. He did sometimes wonder how he would react if challenged at close range. Still, a peaceful rancher should not have to carry a sidearm, Clayton reasoned.

Returning to more tender and pleasant thoughts, he savored the warm satisfaction that comes to one who has finally reaped a return from years of hard labor and difficult times. The sale of the first beef shipment had gone well and prices had been good.

Bonnie had bestowed a look of pride upon him as he cashed the check and made the deposit, all but enough to pay off faithful old Curly and a little cash for supplies. Maybe now he could convince Bonnie she needn't work at the bank any longer and should move out to the

C-Bar-M for good. His heart ached so for her those five days a week she stayed in town, coming out to the ranch only on weekends.

His lips still burned from the emotional kiss they had shared outside the bank doors as he left. He did not recall any kiss like that in their brief marriage of six months but Clayton reasoned it was a good sign that things were looking up.

Many a young lady had been attracted by Clayton's good looks, easy manner, and ready smile, but he had always been able to slip from their grasp, leaving them heartbroken, although still friendly. What was it about this dark-haired, olive-skinned girl that had suddenly captivated his heart above all others?

He had first met Bonnie when he went to the bank one day, immediately stunned by her beauty and grace. Dark laughing eyes set in a lovely face; full, expressive lips below high cheekbones, all framed by shining black hair that fell in soft waves below her shoulders. Clayton was sure Bonnie was the most beautiful girl he had ever seen or would ever see again.

Haunted by this beautiful girl, Clayton knew he must see her again soon. The next day he moped around, accomplishing little meaningful work. By noontime he knew he just had to see her again. He idly announced to Curly that the gate hinges he had ordered should be in so he might as well ride into town and maybe just stay for the Friday night dance.

Curly looked up curiously from his plate, surveying Clayton intently and shrugged. "Well, you just as well bein' you ain't getting' nothin' done around here anyhow, but what's the damn rush? Those hinges won't run off on you."

"I know, but I'm just not in the mood to ante in today. Maybe a couple days off will do me good, huh?"

"Hell, I don't know, I ain't been your age for a long time but as I recall, I always worked my ass off just to keep my belly from collapsin'. Didn't have much time to go dancin' and that kinda' crap, but I guess things is different now."

Not another word was spoken as they finished their meal, but as Clayton got up to leave, he took a glance at Juanita standing in the kitchen door and the knowing smile on her face told him she had a shrewd insight that her husband lacked.

Moccasin Town

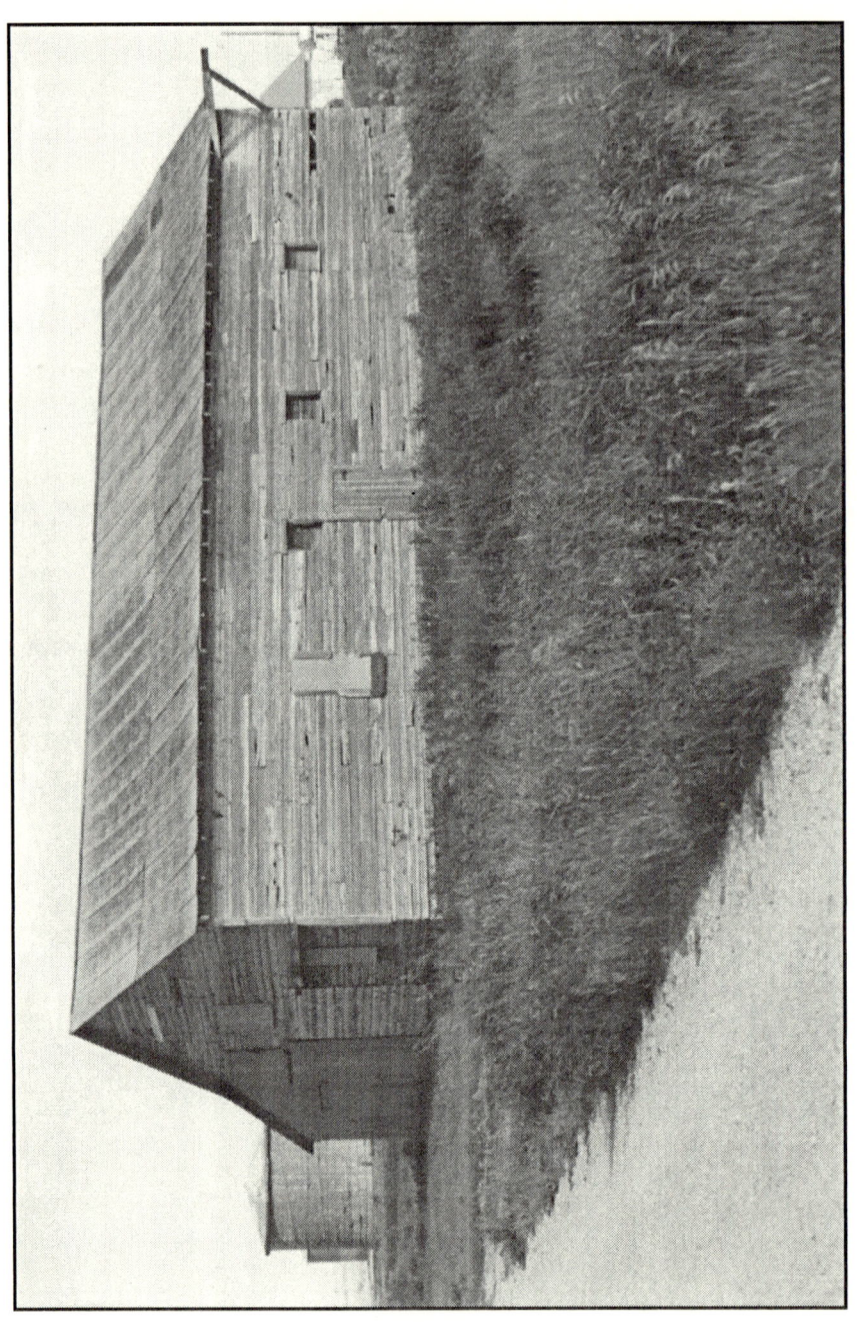

As he headed for town, Clayton didn't try to hold Shoshone back as the spirited pinto cantered past neighboring ranches—where he usually stopped for a chat—and right into the main drag of Moccasin.

He went directly to the bank and Bonnie's window on the a pretense of drawing out some cash. His face burned as he found the courage to invite her to the dance.

To his amazement, she accepted, making him the envy of all the bachelors as they danced every dance. His head reeled in silly giddiness as he smelled the light fragrance of her hair and felt the lithe slenderness of her body against him.

The courtship had been short and sweet with Clayton floating on air when she said "Yes" to his proposal. He rented a buggy that day and she visited the ranch for the first time.

Bonnie seemed delighted with the ranch in general but said, "That house needs a lady's touch and I'm just the one can do those things."

When Clayton gently explained to her that all those changes she planned would cost money they didn't have, Bonnie pursed her lips in silence. That was when she announced she could stay on at the bank for a while and save her income for the new curtains, chiffonniers, bed, and other items on a long list.

Juanita looked sharply at Bonnie in a way Clayton had never seen before. Although they both had the same kind of dark beauty and there was even a similarity in the soft slight accent of speech, he felt the older woman did not approve of Bonnie, but as in the way of a man in love, Clayton assured himself that it would all change once they were married and both living on the ranch. How could anybody not love this beautiful creature, given time to know her?

Curly maintained a patient aloofness throughout the courtship, even though Clayton's attentions in town had shifted more of the workload on the old man. He made only one comment after the wedding, "Mebbe' we'll get some work done around here now, but it'd be a shuck better if'n she was here all the time to help with the cookin' and ..." He dropped the subject in mid sentence as he caught the glint of resentment in Clayton's blue eyes.

Clayton had known Curly was right and that he had been forced to, more or less, take over management of the C-Bar-M once Clayton had lost his heart to Bonnie. Because of this, the resentment was short-lived and Curly had never volunteered any other opinions on the subject.

Juanita, who had longed to have children of her own, quite openly treated Clayton as a son and he also developed a warm love for the kind and doting lady.

She remarked once, "I guess old numb nuts came down in the wrong way too many times while breakin' broncs and just couldn't make babies no more. It wasn't cause we didn't try though."

Juanita accepted Bonnie's weekends at the ranch cordially enough but Clayton had noticed how she studied Bonnie at times as if trying to recall a person from her past. He also noticed, when she was unaware, a look of worry on her face from time-to-time.

It brought back memories of a similar look on another woman's tired face when, as a young lad, he had announced he was leaving home to find a life in the west. Sometimes at night the hurt in the eyes of both ladies returned to awaken Clayton, trembling and aching inside.

Those times he would get up and dive into chores with wild abandon. Such recollections, coupled with the ache in his heart to have Bonnie near, made further sleep impossible. An early breakfast, coffee and work often helped ease such frustrations.

As Clayton resumed his way out of town, the memory of Bonnie's touch and kisses, and how she would yield her warm, searching body to him when they were together as man and wife, rendered him completely oblivious to the riders, wagons, stores, and bars he passed. Those hot, moist tissues and soft eager hands that guided him into the union that made them as one for the first time sent imagination reeling wildly. The coming weekend with her at the ranch promised to be exciting, indeed, and his heart pounded in anticipation.

There would also be a time to talk about her becoming a fulltime ranch wife and leaving the dull little room she rented from Mrs. Calahan.

As he neared the edge of town, Clayton reined Shoshone to a halt as a buxom lady, gray hair braided into a bun, waved and called from the door of a small shop.

"Yoohoo, Mr. McMahon, hold up a minute."

Clayton turned his spirited horse to the cramped boardwalk and swept the battered Stetson from his head with a flourish. "Afternoon, Mrs. Byrd. You're lovely as ever."

"Now you stop that foolishness, Clayton, this is business. That pink satin you picked out for Bonnie's new dress is here and I'll get started sewing right away. Bonnie won't need to know about it because I can use Kalee, the Blackfoot girl who works for me, as a model. They're just the same size and build, but I still don't see why you spoil her with such a dress for a six-month wedding anniversary present. Heavens, any woman should be happy with less than this, even after a year. I hope she appreciates it."

Startled by the woman's sudden harsh voice, Clayton looked down into her clear blue eyes that seemed to reflect worry, then quickly softened to a look of affection as she said, "Don't worry, I'll have it done by Thursday and you can pick it up then."

Clayton quickly forgot Mrs. Byrd's harsh words as he pictured his wife in the new gown. The vision of her young, firm breasts filling the bodice, long black tresses spilling down the open back over olive skin sent his mind wandering again to manly needs when he pictured her dark eyes flashing with delight as she came to his embrace.

The sun was just sinking behind the Little Belts as Clayton drew abreast of the Q2 ranch. The Quessing boys had been good neighbors and they seldom passed each others spreads without stopping for a chat.

Rob was the most business-like of the two Quessings. Of course he had a jovial wife, Doreen, to keep his mind at home. He stayed pretty much on the spread and tended to ranching, while younger Marvin, although hard working when things needed done, was not beyond a drink or two or a good poker game when he could get to town.

As he turned the pinto into the Q2, Clayton could see Doreen's smiling face peering between two polka dot curtains and then turn toward the living-room where he knew she would welcome him at the door with a big hug.

"Clayton McMahon! What are you doing headin' home so late? You're sure lucky you've got Curly and Juanita to look after the place while you're gone. What you need is a woman who'll stay with you and help make a home for you. Say, just when *is* Bonnie going to quit that piddling job at the bank and join you on the C-Bar-M? Soon, I hope."

Knowing Doreen as a big hearted, but extremely frank woman, who would not purposely hurt anyone, least of all him, Clayton replied, "You're just like all these country gals, Doreen, you just got to have your man right under your bossy nose all the time or you're insecure. Nosy too, so I just as well tell you. I'm going to convince Bonnie this weekend on our anniversary, six months that is, to quit the bank and move to the ranch. No need for her to work anymore. We got a good bank account and a good crop of yearlings comin' on. Ain't no reason we can't live like you'd want us to now."

"Well, glory be, I'm sure happy for you. Now you just set down while I pour some coffee and then I'll go holler for Rob. He's out around the feed shed somewhere."

A lanky redhead with a big smile, Rob Quessing popped Doreen on the rump as he entered the kitchen to grab Clayton's hand. "You must have done good on your herd from the smug look on your face. We're all done with roundup and are gonna' have some good stock to market too. We'll run 'em in next week if Marvin will get his butt back here in time. He and the others lit out for town as soon as we was done cuttin' and brandin'."

"If you need a hand, let me know Rob. Me an Curly can help. Glad to lend a hand anytime."

"Yeah, might do that. This is the biggest bunch we've ever had. Fat and sassy and wilder'n hell."

Although the Quessings always made it painful to leave them, Clayton knew he had best return to the C-Bar-M. It was now dusk and the four miles yet to go would be largely a ride in the dark.

A ride home in the dark was not uncommon for ranchers in this remote area of Montana but Clayton wanted to get the pay owed Curly and Juanita to them as soon as possible. Tomorrow would be their day to do shopping in Moccasin and he'd have to be up early to feed and turn out the riding stock, feed chickens and milk the old Durham cow Juanita kept for milk.

Clayton was extremely grateful for the warmth the old horse wrangler and his charming wife had brought to an otherwise ordinary cattle ranch. Just to be in their presence was like backing up to a red, potbellied stove on a cold winter day.

Curly had started as a boy in Missouri and slowly worked his way west to Texas, always near horses, finally becoming a top-rate bronc buster and remuda boss. He met Juanita, as a beautiful French-Mexican girl in Austin and promptly won her hand.

When the trail drives started north from Texas to Kansas, Dakota, and later to Montana, Curly and Juanita became widely known for their individual skills—she as an excellent trail cook and baker, Curly as a wrangler, remuda boss and later as trail boss, but as the years and miles piled up, they longed for roots and a home.

They both fell in love with Montana and the endless miles of waving grass, where, Curly opined: "Longhorns grow fat as Swedish milk maids, while in Texas they have to pick shit with the chickens." When they had occasion to deliver the first small herd Clayton had purchased for starter stock, the meeting turned out to be a God-send for all.

Not having ready cash to pay his new employees, Clayton had offered a house of their own, a small monthly income and ten percent of each sale of beef, half in cash and half in shares in the ranch. Curly and Juanita cheerfully accepted—an agreement Clayton was increasingly grateful for.

Curly would brush off questions about their last name with a wry smile and the comment that, "He wasn't borned, he was hatched on a stump in the sun." Taking Clayton into confidence one day, Juanita whispered that their last name was a rather embarrassing Wilphart and Curly had absorbed so much ribbing about it that they no longer revealed it except on legal papers. Clayton vowed never to use or reveal their secret and Juanita smiled broadly.

The pinto pricked up his ears as they neared the rushing sounds of Wolf Creek. He knew those sweet, clear waters and Clayton always allowed time for the sturdy mount to drink his fill. They were now on C-Bar-M range. The stars spangled across an immense expanse of sky and a soft warmth filled the fresh air as Clayton turned the pinto through the gate towards the lights of home.

The indescribable beauty and fertility of the area he had selected for the C-Bar-M never failed to awe and impress Clayton, even after five years. The grasslands spread into the foothills of the Little Belts, fingers of pine and fir bordering green benches and gentle ridges. The western reaches of the C-Bar-M extended up to pure stands of timber on Big Baldy Mountain where large herds of elk showed mornings and evenings at timberline.

Mule deer were plentiful and regular additions to the larder that Juanita turned into delicious table fare. While whitetail deer were found in the brushy creek bottoms, they were difficult to approach and Curly scorned Clayton's attempts to sneak up on them.

"You can't hunt them little bastards that way," he would say. "Back in Missouri we kilt 'em all the time but you can't go bargin' in the brush like a horny, old bull. You gotta' sneak in quiet like and find their trail. Then you climb a tree and jest sit there 'til one comes along. They don't ever look up so you jest pick the one you want and bang, you got 'em. But shootin' down you'll miss if you jest aim like on the level. Overshoot ever time."

Clayton tried Curly's method once but the boredom and thousands of mosquitoes soon abated his taste for whitetail venison. He vowed then if he couldn't hunt from horseback, he would eat beef.

Clayton led the pinto into the barn as Curly came running with a lantern. "Christ amighty, you come in later ever time you see that woman of yours. Hell, you might as well jest stay there and come out here on weekends," he admonished.

Patiently, Clayton unsaddled his horse ignoring Curly's remarks. "Tell Juanita I had dinner at the Q2 so don't go fixin' something for me. As soon as I get Shoshone rubbed down, I'm gonna' hit the sack. Oh yeah, here's your share of the sale and Bernie's got your stock in the ranch all drawn up. I signed 'em today, so you can pick them up at his office tomorrow."

Clayton wearily headed for the ranch house and another lonely night, but that would soon change.

A full-to-bursting bladder roused him from a deep sleep and he swung his feet over the side of the bed. Painfully bending over his bloated belly, he groped for his high moccasins and quickly slipped them on.

Sounds of rain beating on the roof only magnified his biological needs as he muttered, "Jesus!" and headed for the door. He stepped out onto the stoop under the shelter of the lean-to roof and quickly relieved himself, gazing out into the darkness.

He saw no sign of daylight, which would come late this day. Curly and Juanita would find it tough going into town in the morning. Rain such as this quickly turned all trails and roads into hells of sticky gumbo mud. There was no way they could traverse the road in the ranch wagon. They would have to stay on unbroken range land off to the side. It would make for a long, slow ride to town.

As Clayton rolled back into bed, lightning flashed and thunder pounded almost immediately, indicating the storm was directly overhead. "I sure hope this blows over by daylight," he muttered to himself, knowing all the ranch chores would be his responsibility that day.

Pulling the blanket up over his head and rolling from one position to another did not bring the return of sleep and shortly Clayton found himself reliving those bitter childhood days again. After his father had been killed, his tired old mother had worked her fingers to the bone to keep food on the table for three hungry children and see that they were properly educated.

He remembered the cold empty feeling inside when he received sister Estelle's letter informing him of their mother's death, and yet again when another letter told of little brother Daniel's death at Appomattox. He wondered where Estelle was now and if he would ever see her again before she, too, was gone. He knew that some day he must return to Ohio and locate his family. It had been so long.

Thinking he had put disturbing thoughts to rest, Clayton again sought slumber but suddenly found himself pondering his bride, her beauty, his loneliness and something else he could not identify. An inner dread gnawed at his mind. An unknown feeling of impending disaster.

Past experience with these nighttime mental wanderings led him to again swing his feet out of bed, don the moccasins and start pulling on clothing. With a, "Piss on it," he groped for matches to light a lamp.

Clayton began feeling better after turning the wick up to light the room with its golden glow. He picked up the old two barrel alarm clock from the night stand. Four-thirty in the morning was not too early to get up, he reasoned. Cook a good breakfast, drink a few cups of coffee and it would be daylight, time to get started on the chores.

The part he hated most was milking Juanita's old cow. He'd discovered that big, muscular hands used to fencing, building, roping and other heavy work just didn't please a persnickety old Durham cow used to small, soft, agile hands.

The old cow always gave Clayton a bad time, stepping around, sometimes on his left toes, splattering runny manure all over and then switching a shitty tail across his face. He dreaded the job but admitted to himself it was a small price to pay for the honor of having Curly and Juanita on the ranch.

Clayton loafed around over his coffee longer than intended and didn't even realize the storm had passed until he heard the creak of wagon trees and realized his partners were leaving for town. With a sigh he pulled off the moccasins and reached for his boots.

The fall sun warmed his back as he completed the morning chores and busied himself repairing corral rails damaged during the roundup and branding. He glanced up to see steam rising from the wet grass and far out towards town a rider approached at a gallop.

He climbed on the corral fence for a better look, recognizing the big, blaze-faced, chestnut that Marvin Quessing rode. In awe of the way Marvin was pushing the big horse, Clayton sprinted towards the main gate.

He swung the gate open just as Marvin pounded through and slid the chestnut to a stop.

"What the hell," Clayton started, when Marvin yelled, "We've been wiped out. Banks been robbed!"

"What are you talking about?"

"God dammit, Clay, they cleaned the bank out last night. Every last dollar."

"Who's they?"

"That Bryce bastard and his two gun slingers. Early last night, Marshal Garwood says."

"How does he know that?"

"Cuz, there ain't no tracks. All washed out and it didn't start raining until about midnight."

"What's Garwood gonna' do?"

"He's gettin' a posse up. Every rancher around here lost their stake and they all let Garwood pick his posse from the hands that was in town."

"I got faith that the marshal will get 'em. At least with no money and no bank business, that probably means Bonnie doesn't have a job now. It'll make it easier for her to move out here to the ranch."

Marvin stared intently at Clayton, stammered a bit and then finally said, "Well, that may not work out for you, Clay."

"What the hell do you mean?"

"Well, Bonnie's left town. Oh shit, I hate to have to tell you this."

"Bonnie's gone? Tell me what?"

"Garwood says it appears Bonnie was involved in the whole thing and that she left with those guys."

"What?" Clayton grabbed at Marvin's stirrup, a cold spasm wrenching his stomach. "What the hell do you mean? She wouldn't do that," he blurted, feeling his face blanch white.

"I'm sorry as hell but I'm just repeating what I heard. Course I left right away to come out and tell you. It could all be wrong."

"Damn right it's wrong. Help me saddle up and I'll get to town and prove it wrong."

Marvin kept his eyes from Clayton's distraught face and said nothing more as they saddled Shoshone and led him out to the gate where Marvin had ground hitched his big chestnut.

"C'mon," Clayton said as he leaped astride the pinto and turned its piebald face towards town. He dug in the spurs and bolted out the gate at a gallop.

"Hey, hold up, Clay," Marvin yelled, "my mounts rode out."

But Clayton just continued his full gallop, not looking back.

"Well, Buddy, I guess you and I had just as well head for the Q2 and let that dang fool find out for himself. Damn nice guy, but a dang fool."

Shoshone Pony

CHAPTER II
TRAGEDY & TRANSFORMATION

Clayton spurred the sweating pinto down the main drag and didn't slow down until he was abreast of the jail and Marshal Garwood's office. Sliding to a stop, he threw the reins over the hitch rail and bounded up the steps to the boardwalk in one leap.

"Where's Garwood?" he rasped as he entered the small office and confronted deputy Griffing.

Griffing, an older, lean-faced man looked up in surprise and said, "Well, he's out looking to pick up the trail of them bank robbers. He left as soon as he rounded up a posse."

"What's this bullshit about my wife, Bonnie, leavin' with them. She wouldn't do that. They must have kidnapped her."

Griffing's gaunt face softened as he saw the anguish in Clayton's eyes and he gently replied, "Well, son, we have pretty sure facts that show Bonnie was in this from the start. Maybe even was the one who planned it. Now hold up, Clay. I wish you would talk to a few folks around here who can tell you what you didn't know was going on. Why don't you start with Mrs. Calahan, then banker Sutherland and Mrs. Byrd. Then come back here so we can have a heart-to-heart talk."

Clayton stumbled from the steps not noticing the air of excitement in the town nor the eyes cast his way from the small group standing in the street. Some were curious or aloof, but most showed sympathy for a deeply wounded young man who loved too much and too sincerely, if blindly.

As he passed the pinto he felt a soft hand on his shoulder and turned to face Curly's concerned face. "I'll take Shoshone to the livery and rub him down for you."

"Yeah, okay, thanks," Clayton murmured as he started to turn up the street.

Curly's hand on his shoulder tightened. "Me and Juanita gotta' talk to you before you leave town. We'll be over at the hotel, you hear me?"

Clayton nodded as he pulled free and started up the street towards Mrs. Calahan's rooming house. The confusion in his mind ebbed, to be replaced by cold anger and a determination he had not experienced since leaving the Texas Rangers. A determination to solve and prevail that had made him one of the best and most successful officers in the Rangers.

He entered the rooming house and was met in the foyer by plump little Mamie Calahan.

"Clayton, how nice. Come on in. I have a pot of new-made coffee on," she fussed, obviously trying to make the best possible of an uncomfortable situation.

She led him to an ornate but comfortable settee, moved a coffee table closer, then quickly waddled into the kitchen.

Clayton found himself in grim control of his emotions as she returned with two cups of coffee and a plate of cookies.

He asked, "What is it I should hear from you about Bonnie?"

Nervously, Mrs. Calahan sat down beside Clayton and taking his rough, callused hand in hers said, "This is difficult, but it seems your wife had a side we didn't see at first and I guess you didn't see at all. Not to blame you though, as much as you adored her the way you did."

"What kind of side, Mamie?" Clayton asked quietly.

"Now you just relax and drink your coffee and I'll tell you when I first started wondering."

"She was writing letters to someone starting right after she came here and received at least a couple back from someone. I figured some kin folk but I noticed she burned them as soon as she'd read them."

"What's so strange about that?"

"Now just hold on and I'll get to the rest. She was late to work one day so she asked if I would take a letter down to the stage station so it would go out that morning. I said yes and you know I'm not nosy, maybe curious, but not nosy. Anyway, I see it was addressed to a Bryce Girouard in St. Louis and I thought that was a coincidence because Bonnie's last name is Girard, isn't it? Just spelled a little different?"

Clayton's heart had skipped a beat when Mamie said the name Bryce and the few unusual meetings he'd had with the man flashed quickly through his mind as he replied, "Yes, please go on."

"Shortly after the last letter she sent, this Bryce guy shows up in town. I put two and two together real quick and when I caught him leaving Bonnie's room one night, I didn't know what to do. I wanted to tell you, but you was so much in love I know you would've just told me I was crazy. I wish I had, now, though."

Mamie buried her face in her apron. Clayton could see she was falling apart, sobbing uncontrollably. He felt a sudden tenderness that breached his own pain as he reached out and pulled her to his chest.

"Now, don't you carry on so, Mamie. Let's finish our coffee and have a cookie, then we'll be able to make some sense out of this. I'm okay now, so you needn't feel bad."

Mamie Calahan wiped her eyes and gave Clayton an unsteady smile as she lifted her cup with a shaking hand.

"I went right up to Bonnie's room and told her I wouldn't stand for any of that goings on. Not in my rooming house. She just laughed and said Bryce was an old friend and he wouldn't come to her room no more. So I just left it at that."

"Yes, Mamie, what else?"

"I didn't see any of this, but she went out to dinner almost every night and I heard she was seen coming and going from this Bryce's room at the hotel. Mrs. Byrd done told me and she says it's the truth."

"What about last night?"

"As far as I know, she didn't come back here at all last night, Clay. When I went up to her room this morning after news of the robbery, I seen most of her clothes and personal stuff was gone. Just her dress up clothes and fancy stuff was left. Her riding habit's gone."

"I see."

Clayton was shocked to find his mind clicking methodically, putting facts and rumors together into a reasonable picture of what had transpired, just as it used to when working as a lawman. He knocked on the door of Mrs. Byrd's, seemingly closed, little dress shop.

The door opened a crack and two eyes, dark as pools, looked out at Clayton.

"Is Mrs. Byrd in?"

"Yes, yes," the slender Blackfoot girl responded as she opened the door to Clay, "She want see you."

Wilma Byrd was obviously distressed as she welcomed Clayton into a small office in back of the shop. Kalee, the Indian girl, followed them in.

"Now, Wilma, Mamie says you know Bonnie was seeing this Bryce Girouard in his hotel room at night. How do you know that?"

"Kalee here, saw her going up the back steps of the hotel and then saw her in this Bryce's room several times. Kalee lives in that little shack in back of the hotel with her mother, you know. She said she saw them embrace once, even."

Fighting back his emotions, Clayton swallowed. "Kalee, did you hear anything that was said between them?"

"I heard girl cuss hell out of one of bad guys Bryce man had with him."

"Yes?"

"Well, she go upstairs as two bad guys come down and the red faced guy grab her and try to kiss. She slap him and call him son-of-bitch and said, 'You touch me again and Bryce will kill you.' She say, 'I'll be glad when this over so we can kick your ass down road.' That's all I hear."

Clayton left Mrs. Byrd and Kalee to stride rapidly towards the Moccasin Stockman's Bank where he hoped to find the banker, Roy Sutherland, and more parts to this puzzle. He was no longer an easy-going, hard-working rancher. He had transformed into a grim, calculating, solver of riddles and man hunter again. A throwback to years past he thought he had left behind forever.

Clayton found Roy Sutherland standing in the middle of the bank with a lost look on his face. He reached out for Clayton's hand and squeezed it between both of his.

"I sent everybody home and I can't even keep busy. No money, no business in banking. She fooled us all, you know."

"Tell me about it."

"She's shrewd as anyone I ever met. She had to have planned this robbery herself. My guess is she rounded up those three guys, probably old accomplices, just to help her pull it off without a hitch, but she planned it all right."

"Why do you say that?" Clayton asked testily.

"Because she somehow stole a key to the back door of the bank, or had a copy made and the vault wasn't blown, it was opened by someone who had the combination. Only I and the head teller, John Cyrus, had the combination and that was in our heads. The only written copy is kept in a safety deposit box at our main branch in Billings."

"How could she get the combination then?" Clayton could not quite control his indignation although he knew that his wife appeared more and more to be the accomplished thief others believed her to be.

"I trusted the girl and on several occasions she was with me when I opened the vault. It's hard to do, but a real quick minded person could listen and pick up the clicks. She could easy watch and see which way I turned the dial and, Clay, she's an incredibly intelligent girl, a natural mathematician and best teller I've ever seen. She could count out cash and make change quicker than anyone I've ever seen and all the time talking to the customer too. I realize now she is one of only a few people that could have planned this robbery."

Clayton grimaced and said, "Okay Roy, so she was in it up to her neck. How much did they get?"

"All the negotiable currency, including $16,000 in gold and silver bullion. All told about $85,000. I'm figuring up the exact amount now."

"Jesus, that's a lot of bulk to be carrying on horseback. Wouldn't it take all four with saddle bags loaded to haul it?"

"Well, no, I suppose two or three on horseback could carry it all but you can't run away from a posse loaded down like that. I'd say that's why this job was planned with four. Bonnie knew just how much weight was involved."

Buffalo Town

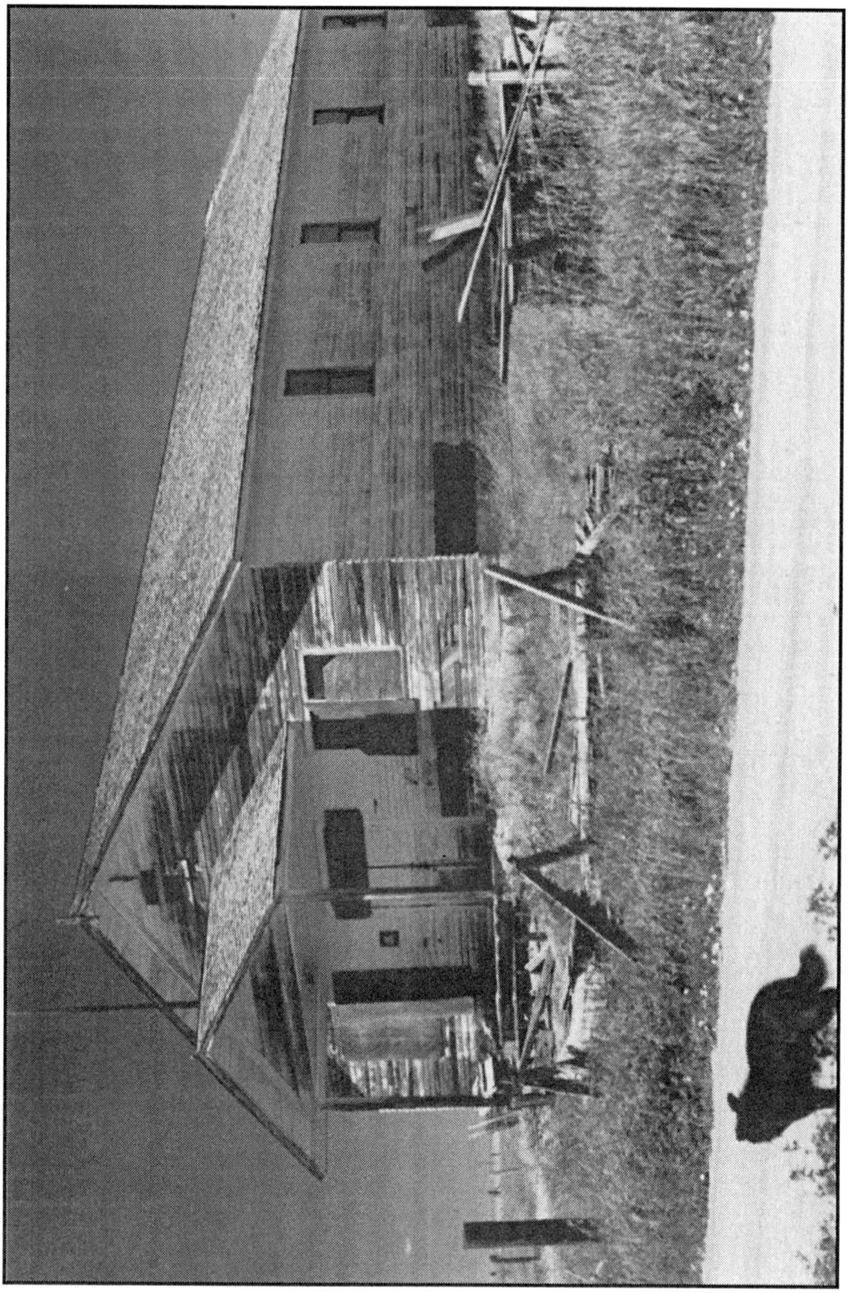

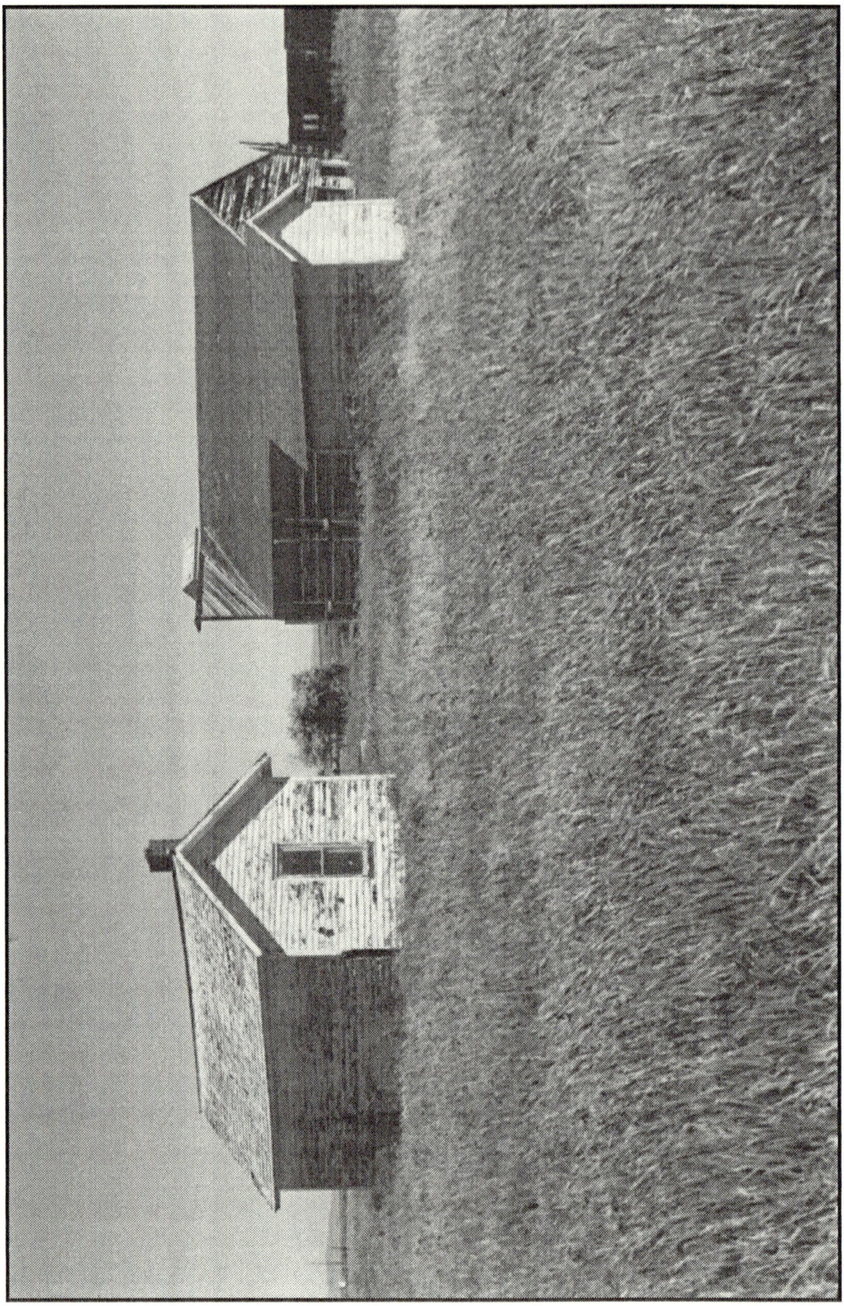

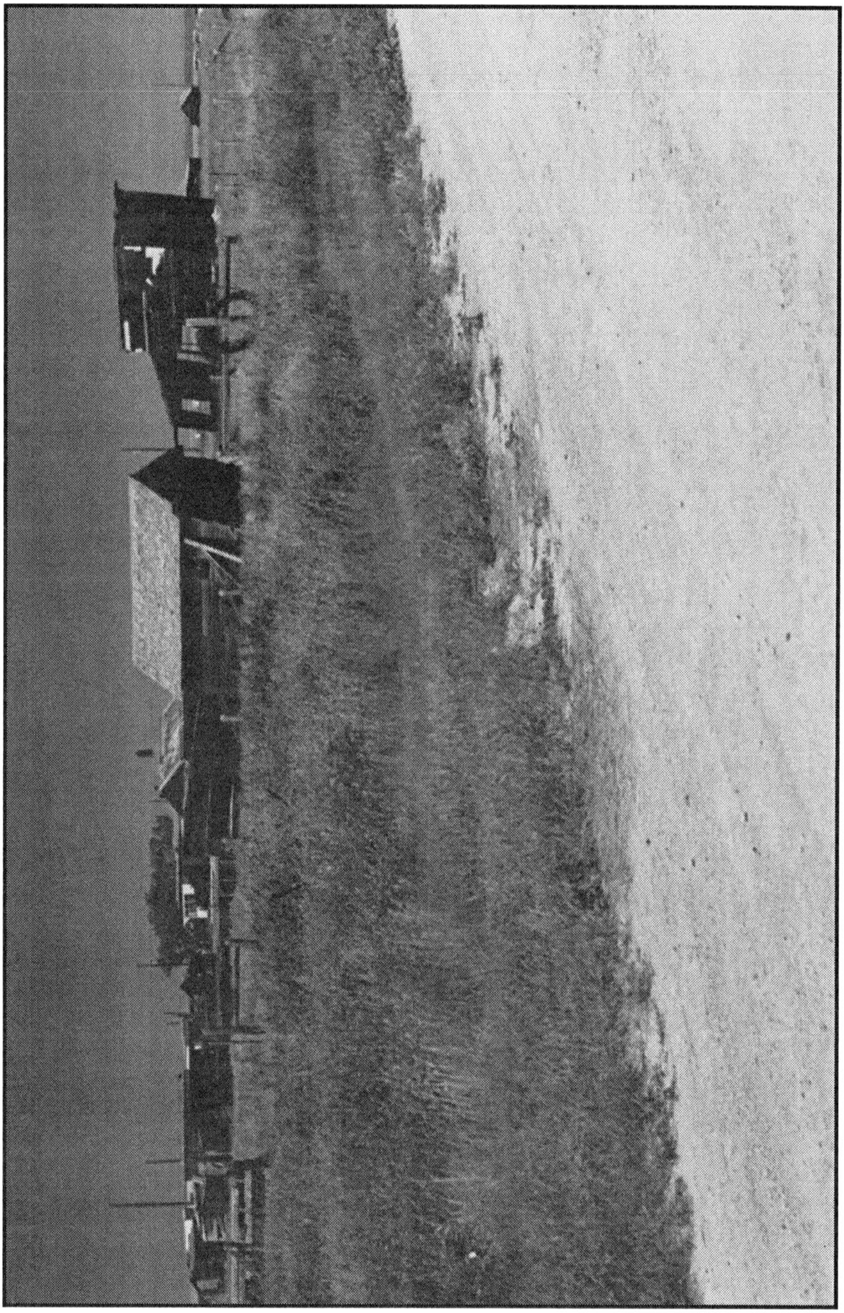

As he strode across to the marshal's office, Clayton calculated what the thieves would do if there were less than four or a posse got hot on their tails. They'd have to cache it somewhere and come back later if they got away. With that thought in mind, he re-entered the modest jail office and sat down opposite Howard Griffing.

"How much lead do you calculate they had on Garwood, Griff?"

"Spencer and the posse didn't get out of here until about 9:30 and if they pulled this thing off about 10:00 or 11:00 last night, that's, let's see, oh, about ten or eleven hours."

"Why does Garwood think the robbery occurred that early last night?"

"Because it started raining about 11:30 and their tracks was all washed out. Couldn't pick up a sign."

"How in the hell did he know which way to go lookin' for them then?"

"Now calm down, Clay, he didn't just go sashaying off, you know. We talked to some of the guys at the Blue Bull and they said that Bryce guy was French and Indian so they must have come from somewhere in Eastern Canada country. That loud mouth bully, Curt, that rides with Bryce, once told the barkeep this stuff when he was all canned up."

"So which way did the posse head?"

Griffing looked at Clayton with poorly concealed annoyance and said, "We're only about a hunnerd miles from Canada, you know, so we figured they'd beeline that way. Spencer and the posse headed down the Judith towards the Bears Paws. They'll pick up fresh mounts at Judith Landing on the Missouri and figure they should be able to catch up with them somewhere in the Bears Paws. Those robbers probably won't stop for fresh mounts unless they steal 'em from some rancher and there ain't many ranchers up that way."

"So Spencer figures they'll cut tracks somewhere out there where it ain't rained?" Clayton ventured.

"Yeah, that's it," Griffing answered. "You know Garwood's good at that stuff."

Clayton started at a fast walk toward the livery stable, suddenly remembering that Curly and Juanita were waiting for him at the hotel.

He opened the heavy oak doors with their etched glass insets and strode into the lobby. The scrawny little desk clerk nodded towards the dining room.

Clayton found Curly and Juanita sitting at a back table just finishing the last of their meal.

"Set down, Clay," Curly said, "And have yourself a bite."

"Haven't got time. Got to try and catch the posse. I've got more than a bank account stake in this, you know."

"Now why would you want to go a chasin' them fellers up north for?" Curly idly asked. "You ain't et nuthin' since mornin' and you can't think and figger' good on an empty belly."

Clayton had to admit that, along with other things, hunger was gnawing at his insides, so he nodded as he gazed at Curly curiously.

"Why shouldn't I try join the posse, Curly?"

"Cuz, mebbe' them outlaws didn't go that away."

"Deputy Griffing says the Girards or Girouards, whichever, are French Canadians with Injun blood and that's the most logical way they would go to escape. You know there isn't any organized law in Western Canada and once they cross the border it will be almost impossible to catch them," Clayton replied.

The waiter brought Clayton a platter of steak, spuds and gravy with pan fried toast on the side, then silently turned away. As he started eating, Clayton watched Curly. He knew from experience the old man would say what was on his mind when he felt good and ready.

Juanita watched Clayton wolf down the food with a motherly smile on her face and gently said, "There are other French crossbreeds, you know, Clay, and I'm one of them."

Clayton didn't respond as she continued, "I knew where Bonnie hailed from as soon as I heard her speak. You see, she has the same accent that's in my past. Just like my kindred used to talk. My father came out West and married into Spanish stock so I grew up with a different way of speaking but I've never forgotten how Papa's family talked."

Between bites, Clayton asked, "So?"

"You see, many French settled in the lower Mississippi Delta—Bayou country they called it. Some were pirates and many are their descendants. Like all French seem to be, they interbred easy and intermarried with most any female they could get next to. Usually Indians. Some Caribs, but mostly Cherokee, and even Africans at times. Some of those French/African/Indian people are beautiful folks. They're called Creoles and Mulattos. Pure French call themselves Cajuns.

With his belly full and on his second cup of coffee, Clayton was more eager than ever to get started after Bonnie and the others.

"So, what are you leading up to?" he impatiently asked.

"What we're a sayin' is, if that's where they're from, they're gonna' light out to the southeast of here and they ain't gonna' slow down until they're at least in Colorado Territory. That's a hell of a long piece from here and communication what it is around here, they're gonna' be damn hard to find," Curly said.

"My guess is they're headin' for the Louisiana country and that's where you should point your nose, Clay," Juanita gently suggested.

Clayton considered their advice as he sipped the last of his coffee and rose to his feet. "Okay, I trust you two more than anyone I know. I'll saddle up and head out."

"Wait, just a minute," Curly said, "You'll need a fresh mount and a lot of other stuff to pull this off. Why don't ya rent a horse from the livery, ride out to the C-Bar-M and get your gear? When you get back, ole Shoshone will be all rested up and ready to go. Juanita and I will get back to the place in time to do mornin' chores."

Tears welled in Clayton's eyes as he shook hands with Curly and gave Juanita a bear hug. Why should he pine over a beautiful but unscrupulous wife when he had a loyal and loving family such as this?

Late that evening, equipped with what he calculated he might need for a long time on the trail, Clayton swung astride his big pinto and headed south out of Moccasin.

His mind engrossed, he weighed the various options. The robbers were about twenty hours ahead but would go cross country to avoid all towns and ranches. Clayton had to decide. Should he ride on established roads where he could make better time and try to intercept tracks further ahead or should he take the cross country route the pursued would surely take, hoping to meet someone who may have seen them? Al least it would assure him that they had been right in assuming the four would head straight as possible for Bayou country.

Clayton decided on the latter as he bypassed the little town of Buffalo where a few dim lights flickered to his left. He knew this country well, having ridden it several times on business trips to Billings, but once south of the Yellowstone River it would all be new to him.

As he headed towards Judith Gap, he concluded that this low and gentle pass could be crossed anywhere over a wide area on either side of the little town of the Ubet. As Clayton tried to think as a fleeing robber would, he suddenly became aware that the pinto had pricked up his ears, looking to the east where a low line of brush barely showed in the dim light.

He pulled to a halt and put his hand over the pinto's nose to keep him silent. Listening and looking revealed nothing, but then he suddenly caught the faint smell of wood smoke.

Who would be camped out here, away from roads and other humans? Surely not the people Clayton hoped he was trailing, but it could be someone who had seen the four. They had to be many miles beyond here by now.

He slipped from the saddle and pulled off his spurs, hanging them on the saddle horn, loosely tying the pinto to a sage bush. He again put his hand over Shoshone's nostrils knowing the intelligent animal would remain silent until he returned.

Walking silently into a gentle wind, Clayton found the smell of smoke leading him towards the low bushes he had seen when mounted. He continued until abreast of what appeared to be a row of scrub juniper. Then he saw it.

Just the slightest flicker of a flame showed through the juniper boughs below him. He pressed carefully forward until he could finally see a small fire reflecting against what looked like the side of a weather beaten wagon. Someone wrapped in a large blanket leaned against one wheel.

He pulled the boughs to one side and saw golden hair spilling onto the blanket and what appeared to be a child nestled close under a woman's right arm. A woman and child out here? Were they alone? Strange.

Clayton reasoned he should leave well enough alone. Still, she may have seen or heard something he should know. He could faintly hear the stamping and grazing of horses but nothing else. It appeared the woman was asleep.

Rising to his feet, Clayton called, "Hello, the camp. I mean no harm. Can I talk to you, ma'am?" The blanket exploded as Clayton found himself staring into a big-bore rifle muzzle. Holding the huge gun was a slender woman with long blonde hair. A small tad of a boy clung to her side, peering in Clayton's direction.

"Hold it, lady, I mean no harm. My name is Clayton McMahon and I'm a cattle rancher from these parts. Can I come to your fire and talk to you?"

After what seemed an eternity, the muzzle lowered and Clayton parted the brush to slowly step into the wash and walk up to the fire. It was then he realized how thoroughly frightened the woman was. Her slender body trembled.

Squatting by the fire, in a way he hoped would ease her fear, Clayton asked, "Are you lost? You're three miles east of the main wagon road. It's pretty rough going out here with a rig like that."

"Please, Mr. McMahon," the woman finally spoke, "but we don't mean to trespass. We're just trying to get to Fort Benton. I'm afraid to travel on the main road, a woman alone and with Tommy here, so we've been traveling aside the roads and camping out of sight at night."

"First," Clayton said, "You're not on my range. Maybe nobody's land and, second, you're traveling right where them that don't want the law to see them will travel."

"Oh, I didn't think of that. I guess I've made a number of bad decisions since Steve was killed," the woman quietly stated. She laid the old buffalo gun aside and pulled the blanket back over her lean shoulders.

She appeared haggard, with straggly, honey blonde hair. Her face was lined with worry and concern showed in her deep blue eyes, eyes which clearly mirrored a determination that contrasted with her overall appearance.

Clayton guessed the young lad at about eight years old. He seemed to show no real fear as he studied Clayton intently with the same deep blue eyes of his mother.

"Steve the boy's father?"

"Yes, and my former husband."

"What happened? If I'm not intruding on painful ground," Clayton ventured.

"No, I've had to put Steve's death behind me, which I know he would want me to do. I'm trying to get Tommy out of this horrible, wild country and back home to Ohio. I have a sister and brother-in-law there."

"What are you doing heading north like this," Clayton queried.

"I heard if I could get to Fort Benton, maybe I could sell the team and wagon for enough to book passage on a paddle wheel down the Missouri to St. Louis. Steve was a lieutenant in the Cavalry and we ended up at Fort Logan when the Indian problems died down. They trimmed the forces down then and rather than be transferred to Arizona, Steve decided to resign and try his hand at mining."

"Steve loved Montana and we moved to Diamond City where he mined for gold. It was a growing town and Steve did pretty good until the tunnel caved in on him. I sold the claim but didn't get much since it was all caved in, but I did get enough to buy a team and this wagon with a little left over for supplies. Do you think I'm doing the right thing, Mr. McMahon?"

"Please just call me Clayton, Mrs. —?"

"Oh, I'm so rude and so sorry. I'm Pauline Nelson and this is Tommy." She pulled the boy to her and kissed him softly on the hair.

Clayton smiled at the boy and said, "To answer your question, I can't fault you for what you're doing. It took a good deal of courage to start out the way you've done but there's no way you'll be able to book passage with the money you'll receive for your rig. Paddle wheel rates have gone way up since the Indian problems are over. People are flocking up the Missouri to Oregon and Washington Territory in droves. They save a month or two of tough going in a wagon train by steaming up the Missouri as far as Fort Benton."

"Oh dear," Pauline uttered, her voice trembling, "What can I do, Clayton?"

Clayton wondered why he had investigated the smoke. He had an extremely difficult search ahead of him and didn't need any other problems. Remembering the reason for his contact with the woman and boy, he remarked, "Pauline, maybe we can help each other. Do you recall seeing or meeting four riders, one a woman, heading south last night or early this morning? They would have been moving fast."

Knitting her brow in thought, Pauline finally replied, "No, I didn't see anyone but I heard some riders traveling fast to the south this morning just as we were ready to pull out. We just laid low in a gully till they passed. Does that help any, Clayton?"

"It may be very important. Now tell me, where were you camped?"

"Just south of that little pass back there."

"Were you east or west of the stage road over Judith Gap?"

"West, I guess. We had crossed the Musselshell and I was following the foothills kind of northeast. We never crossed any roads."

"Thanks, Pauline," Clayton said, "That may be very important to me. Now, maybe I can help you out if you will trust me. You are safer on the main road than you are out here, so you head east from here till you hit the main road, turn north and stay on that road. The first town you'll come to is Buffalo. Go straight to the town marshal, Hick Jenson. Hick is a friend of mine, so tell him I sent you and he'll find a safe place for you to stay overnight."

"The next day you continue to Moccasin and look up Mamie Calahan. She has a rooming house there and will put you up for the night. I'm partners in a ranch west of there where Curly and Juanita are runnin' things while I'm gone. I'm sure they could use help and the ranch house is empty. You and the boy will be more than welcome there. They can figure out a way to get you home if anybody can. Just trust Juanita and Curly. They are top of the heap folks."

Pauline fought back tears as she tried to express her gratitude. Clayton meanwhile twisted the thongs on his buckskin vest in embarrassment.

Borrowing a pencil and paper, Clayton quickly scrawled out notes and instructions to Marshal Jenson, Mamie Calahan and Curly, with a special line to Juanita about cleaning up the mess he had left behind in the house.

Bidding the Nelsons goodbye, Clayton returned to his mount. He patted the patchwork neck and let Shoshone nibble at his hair a bit before mounting and heading south towards Judith Gap.

Pauline

CHAPTER III
FOUR, THREE, TWO

A golden strip of dawn showed faintly on the eastern horizon as Clayton neared Judith Gap. The black bulk of the Big Snowys arched upward to merge with still onyx skies to the northeast, telling Clayton he was leaving the Judith Basin country and would be dropping down into the Mussellshell Valley.

Through the gap and down the south slope, he searched for Pauline Nelson's last campsite. Her directions had been good and just as dawn broke, Clayton quickly found the campsite in a brushy draw where wagon tracks and a fire ring barely showed.

Searching to the west where Pauline had heard the riders, Clayton carefully scanned the hard ground covered with dying brown grasses. At last he found what he was looking for.

Tracks of horses moving at a trot to the south. Two, no three, and then off to the side, the fourth. The tracks of the newly shod horses gouged deeply, indicating they were heavily laden.

As the morning sun warmed him, Clayton felt a deep weariness and, although the drive to continue was strong since he had cut tracks, he knew he and the pinto needed rest.

Now that he had found the trail, the stubborn doggedness that had enabled Clayton to excel as a lawman came into play. He knew that speed was not of the essence right now. Let the bank robbers exhaust themselves and their mounts. Eventually Clayton's relentless pursuit would overtake them. He never doubted that.

Turning back to the secluded draw, Clayton unsaddled the pinto, rubbed him down and fed him a handful of oats before turning him loose to graze. He had watered Shoshone early in the night and knew he'd be fine for another four hours.

He laid out his bed roll on a soft sand bar in the lee of a sharp bank, stretched out and was sound asleep in just a few minutes.

Back astride the pinto in early afternoon, Clayton followed the quite visible unwavering tracks as they turned southeast towards the Carrol Stage road. He mulled over this change in direction, calculating where it would lead. He knew old Hans Shawmut had constructed a bridge across the Mussellshell, where he charged a toll to cross, and further east, Charley Cushman operated another toll bridge. Ranch wagons and teamsters routinely used these structures but those in the saddle could safely cross at a number of places, which surely fleeing bank robbers would choose to do.

Clayton reasoned the four he pursued would avoid both toll bridges and cross some place where they could remain unseen. They had no way of knowing Marshal Garwood and the posse were searching for them north of the Missouri.

Clayton found no sign that the thieves had camped or even stopped for a rest. They and their mounts had to be extremely tired. Still, they had a substantial lead and Clayton estimated it could be as many as four days before he could overtake them and by then they could be well into Wyoming Territory, country that was strange to Clayton.

Abruptly, he lost the tracks and started a careful swing to circle back, suddenly on track again. The tracks veered off to the south, then stopped in the lee of a small knoll. It was obvious the four had milled around in this place for some reason.

Far to the south, Clayton could see a row of Cottonwoods where the Mussellshell wound its way through the barren land. He rode to the top of the knoll and could see the reason for the fugitives' indecision. The cattle trail from Shawmut Crossing to Judith Gap lay below. Possibly they had seen some traffic on the trail and were waiting out their passage.

Unraveling the confusing tracks took some time but Clayton soon found where they skirted the knoll on the north and headed directly to and across the trail and turned back southeast.

The tracks continued through Deadman's Basin and across the Mussellshell, but the riders were traveling at a walk now and Clayton could see that their mounts were kicking up sod as they scuffed their toes in fatigue.

The trail continued up into some low foothills covered with scraggly pine. Clayton knew they were nearing the Cayuse Hills. Then he found it—the first camp since the four had left Moccasin with their loot.

He left the old campsite as it turned dusk. Clayton knew he had gained at least four hours on his quarry. Possibly more, as tired as they and their mounts had to be.

Vowing to continue into the night as long as he could follow tracks, Clayton hurried on as he noticed something strange. Two sets of tracks had become inseparable. These two tracks were always in single file, a big shod, slue foot always in the rear.

"They're leading one horse," Clayton reasoned. "Now why do that?" Possibly one rider, maybe Bonnie, was too tired to work the reins, but that didn't make sense. They were all riding top quality mounts and all a tired person need do was tie the reins to the horn and hang on. The horse would keep up with the others. No need to lead.

Clayton continued trailing after dark, relying on judgment as to where the tracks would go. Now and then he dismounted and searched by match light until he was sure he was still on the trail, which continued in a general southeast direction, taking advantage of shallow draws, swales and occasional benches, slowly climbing into the hills.

This time Clayton noticed it first and reined in the pinto at the smell of smoke. The wind blew gently in his face and the smoke seemed to come from straight ahead.

Seeing nothing, Clayton eased Shoshone ahead and traveled some distance before stopping again. He not only smelled smoke, he could faintly hear laughter and raucous voices.

As he dismounted, his boots rattled in loose rock and he knew just removing his spurs was not enough. Clayton dug in a saddle bag and pulled out the Apache moccasins and made the switch.

He moved silently, easing along towards the sounds as they got louder. Soon he could see the glow of a fire and hear someone splitting wood. He peeked over a rocky ridge. Before him lay what appeared to be a mining camp and a shaft in the opposite slope, a pile of loose rock tailing down hill below. Near a brightly burning fire stood an old Army style tent. Two men sprawled by the fire talking loudly as another still chopped somewhere out of sight.

Just some damn miners, Clayton thought to himself. Why get mixed up with them? He had started to back away when one of the men said something and Clayton froze.

"I can't blame the guy for trying to lay down that gal. By God, she was sure a looker."

"Yeah, but you saw what happened to the redhead for trying to screw her. You want the same medicine?"

A third man walked into the light with a load of wood, dumped it by the fire and asked, "Is that really why he killed him? You sure?"

"Well, that's what the black-haired guy said. He said that fancy fella' in black shot him for messin' around with the girl," a gray-bearded miner offered.

"He done a hell of a good job of it," said the wood splitter, "Right through the heart. One shot, pow!"

"Well, anyway, that's the easiest hundred bucks I ever made," said the third miner. "Brand new hundred-dollar bills to each of us. Jest to bury a dead man? But it's mighty suspicious that they told us to keep quiet about it."

"Hell, man. that's murder. But I guess no one would fault a man for protectin' his woman. Especially one like that dark-skinned beauty. Did you see that long, black hair? Whoohee!"

"You know what that rounder told me?"

"About what?" asked an older-appearing miner with a long, handle bar mustache.

"About how that guy in black kilt the redhead."

The two other miners waited in silence.

"He said they faced off and the redhead pulled iron first. He never cleared leather before that guy in black had put a hole through his heart."

"Jesus, he must be some kinda' slick gunman."

"Yep," the older miner agreed. "That's maybe why they was in such a hurry. Probably wanted by the law up North."

Having heard enough, Clayton eased away toward where he'd left the pinto. Now he knew why they were leading one horse; they had one pack animal and he had lost his advantage in the pursuit. They could either load most of the loot on the spare mount or take turns riding it to spell their own tired horses.

Clayton decided they would do the former as no two persons' saddle tastes were the same and they wouldn't take time to switch rigging.

He mulled over the redhead's killing and what he had heard about how it was done. He was up against a top gun, maybe two. Although the thin-faced, dark man named Curt had never pulled leather on anybody during the short time he was in Moccasin, he certainly pushed a lot of innocent folks around, seemingly trying to provoke a fight.

It had been over two years since he had been forced to draw in a gun fight and he had to be rusty. Now it appeared he would be coming up against two gun slicks when he finally caught up to them. He needed practice.

Quietly circling the miners camp, Clayton again headed out in the same southeast direction as before, knowing he could pick up the tracks again in daylight.

Deep in thought, Clayton rode through the darkness and suddenly realized the land was dropping down a little, even though still broken and scattered with small pine.

"Must be over the Cayuse and dropping down toward the Yellowstone," he mused aloud.

From here they could drop down anywhere to a river crossing. Clayton decided to call it a night and get a good rest. Tomorrow he could hit it hard and gain some distance on his prey.

He awoke from a sound sleep and raised his head to look about. A low sun cascaded golden rays across a landscape sparkling with frost. The back side of the ridges, shadowed and dark, showed eerie patches of ground fog. He rolled out of his bedroll, shivering as he pulled on his pants and boots.

Shoshone nickered softly as Clayton stretched into his old range jacket and looked around. Before him, to the south, lay the wide shadow of the Yellowstone Valley, but it was the sight beyond that caught his breath.

The huge bulk of the Beartooth Range soared skyward, peaks and crags bathed in rosy pink light. To the southwest, the magnificent

Absaroka Mountains were also bathed in soft light, the glaciers and snow fields in north and northeast facing basins shining back at him. He was in the midst of some of the most beautiful country the world had to offer. He also knew that now, in September, the first snows would soon be coating these lofty peaks of up to eleven thousand feet in sterile whiteness. Such sudden storms could make tracking either impossible or extremely easy depending on when and how deep.

He would just as soon find his quarry and get this thing over before Mother Nature had a chance to cast her odds, he decided, as he downed a cold breakfast of hardtack and jerky.

He had left so hastily that he needed supplies badly but the only sure source he knew of was in Billings, too far to the east. It would cost him several days. The bank robbers had to be in the same fix, yet they seemed to know where they were going. Maybe they knew of some source of supplies he did not.

There was a small settlement called Columbus on the Yellowstone where some sod busters had started to farm the rich river bottom land. There was a small general store some distance to the southeast, but Clayton calculated the fleeing bank robbers would probably give Columbus a wide berth.

Cutting along the south-sloping side hills, he found no tracks leading to the river from the west, so he turned around and headed east. He had gone only a short distance before he caught the tracks, surprised to find the trail traveling almost due east. He was sure they were the right tracks for they had become intimately familiar to him, the hoof prints of the slue foot easily recognized.

Riding as hard as he believed his pinto could go and still carry him into darkness, Clayton followed the trail to the east into more flat, benchy land. It was rather barren and littered with crumbly, pink and white shards of rock that looked like sandstone.

Clayton thought it was sterile, unfertile land until he caught sight of flat grasslands ahead from the top of a gentle rise. Still desolate, but at least there was grass growing there.

The trail headed almost due east as it dropped into a rocky gully where a small stream of milky-colored water ran. He tasted the water before letting Shoshone drink and although the water did not taste bad, he pulled the pinto away before he had his fill. What he didn't need now was a sick horse.

Riding easterly, in mid-afternoon he topped a rise and stared down at a small town in the valley below—if a cluster of maybe ten buildings could be called a town.

Wracking his brain, Clayton muttered, "Molt, that has to be Molt."

He had never been there but he had heard of Molt, a small farming community of German wheat growers. They raised good quality, red top winter wheat that they readily sold in Billings. The seed, from Russia, reportedly came with the German immigrants, and hard red wheat flour made the best bread in town, it was said.

The trail dropped down into a small basin where the three riders had set up camp. He circled to the south and picked up their trail heading towards the Yellowstone. That didn't make sense to Clayton. They obviously had spent some time in the campsite. Why, other than to pick up supplies in Molt? Circling to the east proved this to be true as he picked up the tracks of a lone rider heading directly towards Molt and further north, the same tracks returning.

Clayton turned his mount towards the town at a gallop, spurring his mount directly between the meager row of modest, but neat buildings. In the middle of the town he approached the largest building on the street and saw he had picked correctly as he read the small sign over the door.

Kramer Brothers General Store and Mercantile was surprisingly well stocked and Clayton saw he would be able to purchase everything he needed.

Behind the counter, a large man with a well endowed belly and a large mustache smiled and asked, "Yah, can I help?"

Clayton started naming the items he felt he would need and noticed the storekeeper writing it all down in neat letters that Clayton could not read. "In German," Clayton said to himself.

The storekeeper stacked all the supplies on the counter, seemingly oblivious to the fact that Clayton was a stranger. He placed each item in a burlap sack as he wrote down the price in a neat column. Having finished, he skimmed his finger down the long column of figures and placed the total at the bottom in a matter of seconds.

Mathematical German mind, Clayton thought to himself as the roly-poly man said, "Yah, dot seven dollar and twenty-six."

Clayton paid the storekeeper and asked, "You must be Mr. Kramer?"

"Yah, I be Wolfgang. My brother is Conrad. He goes to Billings today."

Wolfgang stuck out a big ham of a hand as Clayton introduced himself.

"Did you sell supplies like I just bought to someone else in the last few days?"

"Yah, skinny-faced man two days ago. You his friend?"

"No, as a matter of fact I may have to kill him," Clayton said without smiling.

"Mein Gott in himmel, you must hate dot man bad."

"No, Wolfgang, I don't hate him but he's a bank robber and he probably won't surrender without a fight. In that case I'll have to kill him."

The old German folded his hands over his belly and looked at Clayton with wide eyes. The only sound he made was a tongue clicking, "Tsk, tsk."

Clayton rode the Burke Stage Road out of town, noticing the well-maintained school building with neat manicured grounds. The last building he passed was a white church, a sign, in English, proclaiming it to be of Congregational faith.

As the stage road turned east towards Billings, Clayton continued south. His hunch was right as he shortly found the four horse tracks. He turned to follow again as they headed steadily southeast.

The trio chose a crossing at a wide gravel bar above a deep pool. Shoshone trotted across daintily, the water never over ten inches deep, and clambered up the south bank. The water was at its lowest this time of the year, otherwise passage would have to be made by rope-pulled ferry rafts at either Columbus or Billings.

Clayton crossed a lush flat to the base of a rock bluff, the tracks intersecting the well-used Yellowstone Trail. He stopped for a moment to cogitate, reasoning that the bank robbers would travel east on the trail down the Yellowstone until they could find a niche in the rock wall. They would undoubtedly then continue their southeast heading.

He followed the trail, keeping an eye to the rock wall for passage until he spotted a dry draw and a notch in the wall. A large game trail followed the bottom of the draw as the horse tracks turned away from the river and into the notch.

Clayton had just started to follow when Shoshone gave a snort and wildly leaped to one side. He caught a glimpse of a huge rattlesnake coiled beside the trail. Instinctively, his hand flew to his pistol and he drew and fired in one motion. The snake flipped end over end and landed writhing on the ground.

As he calmed the wide-eyed pinto, Clayton felt a warm satisfaction with the involuntary way his hand had reacted. He had been practicing drawing the last few days, the hammer falling on spent shells to save ammunition, but he had not been concentrating on aim.

There are two kinds of gunmen—one who outdraws the rival and one who outshoots the other. Clayton had been one of the former and he knew aim was not as important as speed. In such gun fights, the opponents were so close that the first one to shoot could hardly miss. Clayton had heard of a sheriff in Arizona who was the other type. Wyatt Earp used a long barreled Colt 45 and he was careful to choose his spot. Drawing from a great distance and aiming carefully, he had shot several dangerous gunfighters between the eyes as they blazed away wildly.

Over time, Clayton had become a combination of both types of gunfighters. He had a lightning draw and was blessed with naturally superior reflexes which enabled him to also shoot accurately. He had practiced hours on end at shooting while in motion. On horseback, as when he shot the rattler, or on his feet where he would dive to one side shooting while in the air, then roll over and back onto his feet.

The roll and shoot trick had saved his bacon several times and Clayton planned to brush up on this skill until he felt he had the function of drawing down pat.

He rode up the wide game trail until it broke out on top of rolling land studded with more scrubby pine. The tracks left the game trail and headed again to the southeast.

"Entering Crow country," Clayton muttered to his pinto, who didn't seem to care as he now had a belly full of fresh oats, water and good forage.

The Crows were generally friendly, even helping U.S. Cavalry forces against their old enemies, the Cheyenne, Sioux and the Blackfeet, but there was always the chance of running into a group of young bucks who would like to make coup. They also were master thieves, stealing anything not tied down. He would have to keep his eyes open in all directions now. A lone rider was at a distinct disadvantage.

Clayton was disappointed that now the bank robbers had an extra mount, he was not gaining on them at all. He would have to change tactics or they would have to make a mistake before he would have a chance of overtaking them.

The old Apache scout who had given him the high legged moccasins, had once said, "Never catch Cochise, he run faster'n horse."

What he had meant, when questioned, was that the Apaches would ride their mounts until they started failing and would then dismount and dog trot for miles, leading their horses before remounting. They literally ran the Cavalry mounts to exhaustion.

Clayton had used this tactic several times when riding with the Rangers but he was younger and better conditioned then. Still he saw no other alternative and knew he had to try it.

Pushing Shoshone harder, Clayton rode him through some very broken ground until the tracks broke out onto a flat grassy benchland. No better time than now, he thought as he pulled the moccasins from the saddle bag.

Clayton trotted along ahead of his pinto, beginning to realize how much he'd softened up. Still, he resolved, I can toughen up if I just keep it up.

Trotting a ways and then walking to catch his breath, he found he had covered considerable distance before the trail dipped down into a wide valley. He could see the tree line of a stream below.

Clayton remounted and followed the trail-side hill to the valley floor. Continuing across gently sloping grasslands, he came to a lively and clear-running stream.

He scanned the area while allowing the pinto to water up, noting an old camp in some Cottonwoods. For some reason, his quarry had camped after covering less ground than usual.

Were they, or maybe one, sorely tired and in need of rest? If so, it would be Bonnie. She had ridden frequently on her visits to the C-Bar-M, but she was obviously not an experienced rider and definitely not in condition for the ordeal she was now experiencing.

Reckoning that he had gained at least another half day, Clayton pushed on, riding in rough ground and trotting ahead of Shoshone on level terrain.

When he reached a narrow but steep draw, Clayton remounted and spurred the pinto down where the others had descended. Slipping and sliding, the sturdy mount reached the bottom and started up where the tracks reached a narrow ledge angling up a steep side slope of crumbly rock imbedded in the hill side.

He dismounted, deciding it was better to lead his pinto up this area than take a chance on a mishap. An injury to either he or his mount and Clayton knew the chase was over.

He had begun to make the climb when he glanced down and saw something unusual. Loose soil had been sloughed from the ledge and trailed down to the floor of the draw. The imprint of an impact was visible in the soft material at the base of the slope.

Clayton led Shoshone up to level ground, tied him to a bush and slid back down into the draw. It appeared clear now that a horse had lost its footing and tumbled to the bottom of the draw

As he studied the signs, it was also apparent that several men in riding boots had milled around the area as if picking up scattered gear. Money and possibly bullion?

The horse must have survived unhurt or it would have been shot and left to the buzzards. As he puzzled over this, Clayton spotted something else on the boulders in the dry stream bed. It appeared to be blood stains.

He turned cold inside as further investigation proved this to be true. One of the three he pursued was injured or possibly dead. It did not take a lot of imagination to reason which would be the most likely victim.

He continued on the tracks, nursing an ache deep inside. All the events of the past year coursed through his body in a mad rush and he suddenly felt sick inside.

Why, oh, why had fate throw he and Bonnie together? Why the wild infatuation for this beautiful girl, now his wife, and obviously a devious thief?

Clayton slid from the saddle, knelt on the ground and buried his face in his hands. He now knew the fallen rider had to be his wife.

The sensation of his faithful pinto, Shoshone, nibbling at the now long hair on the back of his neck, steadied Clayton. He fought back his emotions, remembering that others loved and cared for him. Right now the pinto, but there were those back in Judith Basin who cared also and understood his pain.

The emotional collapse brought the humbling realization that he was not the tough, resolute manhunter he had pictured himself to be. Surprisingly, he did not feel shame or self pity over this new realization. Clayton knew that he had just reached another plateau in male maturity.

He had a job to do and it was time to get on with it.

CHAPTER IV
AND THEN THERE WAS ONE

Knowing they were deep in Crow Indian Country, Clayton chose a campsite away from the tracks following a well-used trail. He selected a patch of golden aspens in a little basin on the side hill.

A small trickle of water ran into a sump, obviously man made. Flint chips and scattered bones made it plain it was an Indian campsite of long usage, but nothing recent showed so Clayton made camp.

He had downed a cold meal and then not only tied the pinto securely to an Aspen but hobbled him also. Fearing that after the days events he would sleep like a log, he did not want to take the chance of losing his mount. Legs, unused to the day's abuse, ached and cramped as he tried to drift off to sleep.

Clayton was suddenly awake! Then he heard it again. The pinto neighed harshly in the way he did when annoyed.

As he lay facing the horse, Clayton could clearly see two lean figures beside Soshone. One held the reins and the other was on his knees working at the hobbles.

Rolling to his feet, gun in hand, Clayton barked, "Stand right still, you thieving bastards. I'll kill the first one to move."

The figure on his knees quickly raised his hands and started crying out, "Sa na ko se, sa no ko se!"

"I'll sanakosee you, all right, if you so much as move a muscle," Clayton said, advancing slowly. In the bright moonlight he could now see they were but two skinny Indian lads.

The boy on his knees was still moaning softly but the other stood silently, hands in the air. Clayton could see a tightly strung bow on his back and another such weapon on the ground behind the moaner.

Clayton walked over and kicked the bow and quiver of arrows down the hill, bringing renewed moaning and chanting from the lad.

Likely they could not understand orders, so Clayton motioned them away from the pinto with his pistol and pointed to an open spot in full moonlight.

"Injun just want to look at horse of cloudy sky," the silent one suddenly said.

"So you can understand me, you little red devils!"

"Curly Coyote not devil, me Injun brave."

"Well, you were just about a dead brave. Where'd you learn white man's talk?"

"Me one smart Injun," Curly Coyote asserted, "Me go to white man's school." Pointing to the other lad, he said, "Long Tail, he dumb Injun. Don't know nuthin'."

"Where is a school around here?"

"St. Xavier School. Father Prando, he teach me much. I smart Injun. I know all about you. You damn tough fella', run like Injun."

"Okay, but I shoot much better than Injun. Didn't Father Prando teach you that horse thieves often die?" Clayton asked.

"We just want to ride horse of cloudy sky. We not steal."

"Yeah, in a pig's ass. Where you from?"

"We from Greasy Mouth Clan. Very brave Injuns. All our people."

"You been watching me for awhile haven't you? See any other white men come this way?"

"No," Curly Coyote ventured, "But we see two tough fellas' that come to St. Xavier."

"Two, only two?" Clayton asked knowing the Indian boy was right.

"Only two riding, they have another wrapped in blanket, tied on horse. They give dead one to Father Prando."

As he looked at the lean bodies, Clayton knew they must be hungry. Although the Crows didn't take part, since the massacre of Colonel Custer's forces on the Little Big Horn all red skins had been treated brutally. Stripped of their firearms, it made killing of the dwindling bison for food almost an impossibility.

Motioning for the boys to sit down, Clayton rummaged through his supplies and threw each one a chunk of hard tack and some jerky.

As they hungrily chewed at the tough food, Clayton asked, "You show me quickest way to St. Xavier?"

When they both sat in silence he added, "You want to ride horse of cloudy sky?"

"You bet, tough fella', we show you way," Curly Coyote responded with a smile. Long Tail sat in consternation, not knowing what was going on until Curly Coyote spoke to him in Crow. His eyes lit up and he also smiled for the first time.

As dawn started breaking, Clayton saddled up Shoshone and tied down his gear. Motioning to the young braves to pick up their primitive weapons, he turned to Curly Coyote.

"You tell Long Tail to light out for St. Xavier School. I'll lead the horse and you ride. We'll switch around later, Ok?" Clayton explained.

"You betcha', tough fella'," Curly Coyote said as he scrambled up into the saddle.

The Indian lad, Long Tail, broke into a trot heading in a southeasterly direction. Clayton painfully followed leading the pinto bearing Curly Coyote.

His stiff, sore calf and thigh muscles ached mightily as he tried to keep up but he had to slow to a walk periodically as the boy leading the way patiently paused and looked back. The stiffness slowly disappeared and Clayton soon loped along at a steady gait.

Mile after mile fell behind as they continued the pace. Clayton finally called a halt and indicated to the mounted lad that it was time to trade places.

"Long Tail not smart like me," Curly Coyote declared beating his chest, "He just fall off, better Curly Coyote ride horse of cloudy sky."

"If he falls off we just put him back on again until he learns to ride. Now get your butt offa' there and start trottin'," Clayton said with motions to Long Tail indicating he should get astride the horse. "And, he's a pinto, not horse of cloudy sky."

Long Tail smiled broadly as he climbed aboard and the procession again moved out. Curly Coyote set out at a trot repeating over and over, "Pin-toe, pin-toe, pin-toe."

As they continued across the softly rolling grasslands, small herds of horses began to appear. Each herd had an obvious dominant stallion who kept the group of mares and colts bunched until, with a snort and a nudge, he would urge them to a gallop and out of sight.

As Clayton stopped for a breather, he asked Curly Coyote, "Whose horses?"

"Injun horses," the boy replied, "Crow much rich with horses, many horses."

"How come you're walking with all those horses?"

"Only warriors and hunters ride horses. Me and Long Tail not warriors until we catch horse for ourselves," Curly Coyote responded.

"Or steal someone else's horse." Clayton offered, "Why don't you catch one? There's certainly not a shortage of ridin' stock out here?"

"Damn hard to do, Crow horses very smart and wild," the boy replied.

It dawned on Clayton that they had to run the horses down on foot, or trap them some way, with no help from the older warriors. Some kind of maturity test, he guessed. Or they make big coup if they stole a horse.

Near mid-day they topped a rise and Curly Coyote stopped, pointing proudly ahead. "Big Horn," he said.

Below lay a broad, shallow valley bisected by a sparkling stream that meandered through cottonwoods and hackberry groves. What a beautiful country, Clayton thought to himself as he gasped for breath and fought to still his weak and trembling legs.

Curly Coyote pointed again towards a clump of cottonwood trees on the east bank. "St. Xavier, my school place," he proudly announced.

The brown of a building, corral and some log out-sheds were barely visible.

Clayton pulled Long Tail from the saddle. "Okay, boys, now it's my turn." He painfully mounted and turned to Curly Coyote. "Well, now, do you Injuns think you can keep your hands off of white man's horse? Stay alive that way, Savvy?"

Both boys nodded vigorously, although Clayton knew Long Tail did not understand a word he said. He turned the pinto down hill towards the Big Horn and the building beyond.

Fording the cold, clear waters, Clayton headed at a gallop towards St. Xavier School and a painful meeting with the truth about his beautiful but now dead wife.

As Clayton rode into the neat courtyard, a group of small Indian children scattered for cover. They all found somewhere to partially hide as they peeked out at him with dark, frightened eyes.

Clayton dismounted at the hitch rail and turned to see a small, wiry man with silver hair approaching.

"Welcome, stranger. We are truly blessed to have you visit our humble mission," the little man said in a soft and slightly nasal accent.

Clayton took the small hand offered and said, "Father Prando?"

"Why yes, my friend, Father Peter Prando, that I be, and how may I help you? Oh, but such bad manners. Will you please join me in a cup of tea? I have much time to ask questions later."

Clayton nodded as the old man turned to a small log house beside a larger building, which Clayton took to be the school. He dreaded the questions he knew he must ask. Maybe a shot of tea would help. He would rather have had a shot of rot gut but he was willing to give tea a try.

As they entered the small but neat cottage, a slender Indian girl stood in a doorway which Clayton took to be the kitchen.

Father Prando said a few words to the girl in his soft, French/English accent and she darted back into the kitchen.

"My housemaid, Morning Rain," Father Prando remarked. "Her parents were both killed in a reprisal raid by Cheyenne warriors after the battle of the Little Big Horn. She's lived here at the mission since and she's surely been a lot of help to me. She's very bright and a hard worker too. She's learning English now and studies hard."

"Like Curly Coyote?" Clayton asked.

"Oh yes, so you've met my former student. He wants so to be a big, bad warrior but his tribal culture clashes terribly with white man's ways."

"So I found out," Clayton ventured, "But I think he understands now that it doesn't pay to steal white man's horse."

"Oh dear, did you hurt him?" the little priest asked, visibly shaken.

"No, Father, we just had a heart-to-heart talk," Clayton assured him. "Curly Coyote tells me you had three visitors the other day, two riding, one tied on."

Father Prando studied Clayton's face as the Indian girl brought hot tea and two cups. She shyly set them in front of the two and darted back to the sanctuary of the kitchen.

"Now, why would that Indian boy say that?" Prando asked. "You know how these heathens are, they like to make big stories to white man."

"I realize they asked you to keep quiet about this, Father, but I know they came here because I've been tracking them from the Judith Basin country. The dead girl was my wife, Father."

"Although she participated in a bank robbery up in Moccasin, we were husband and wife. I don't know why she did what she did but I've been trailing them for days. There were four involved in the robbery but there are only two left now and I'm going to catch them and return the money to the Moccasin bank," Clayton said.

"Well, not all of it I hope," Father Prando said. "The girl's brother left three hundred dollars with me to bury her here in our cemetery. They are Catholic, you know. French people, like me."

"Half French, anyway," Clayton responded. "Will you show me where she's buried?"

"Certainly, my boy and my heart is with you. What a beautiful girl. What a tragedy," the little priest exclaimed as he finished his tea with a shaking hand.

The priest led Clayton to a small cemetery behind the mission and pointed to a new mound of earth. Making the sign of a cross he then hurried away leaving Clayton alone at his wife's graveside.

When Clayton returned to the cottage, Father Prando had a meal of venison steak, potatoes, fresh baked bread and wine, waiting.

"Sit down, my son, and partake of our food, for the people you seek are far ahead of you and you will need much strength," Father Prando offered wisely. "You will need a death certificate you know, to dissolve this tragic marriage," he added.

"Thank you, Father," Clayton responded as he sat down. "How do I get a death certificate?"

"As an ordained priest, I can provide you with that, but first may we give thanks and enjoy this fine meal?"

As Clayton ate, his mind whirled in confusion. Brother and sister? That explains a lot. Death certificate? Have to pick that up when returning, if I return. No need for it anyway, if I don't return. Three hundred dollars just to bury the girl? Maybe it was more as a donation to the school.

"They paid you three hundred dollars just to bury Bonnie?" Clayton asked.

"No, that was to pay for a headstone, which I will have to order out of Billings." Father Prando said. "It will probably take as long as three months to have it engraved and sent here by stage."

"What will it say?" Clayton asked.

The Jesuit priest arose and going to an old roll top desk returned with a tablet which he handed to Clayton. "You see her real name was not Bonnie." he gently said.

Printed in immaculate scroll lettering was written:

Michelle Girouard
Beautiful girl who loved beautiful life.
Now beautiful girl graces our beautiful Heavens
3/16/1851 - 9/21/1882

Clayton knew that he could not improve on the inscription and silently handed the tablet back to Father Prando.

"Her brother was very upset over Michelle's death, Clayton. He openly cried as I spoke the final words. He appeared to be a thoroughly beaten and distraught young man. Not at all like the other man, who seemed only interested in moving on. She will have a nice home in our little cemetery here, my son," Father Prando said. "We hope to have a permanent mission and school here shortly, then we will keep a neat and orderly place of burial."

"How will you finance these developments, Father?"

"The Jesuit Order has promised to finance us. Father DeSmet is insistent that all the tribes be offered schooling and religion. At his urging, Mother Frances Xavier Ross organized an expedition by the Sisters of Charity to explore possibilities for missions in Indian country. A group of six Sisters passed through here in the fall of 1869 on their way to Helena and on their return, they recommended the Big Horn Valley as a likely site to serve the Crow Nation. Father DeSmet sent Father Urban Grassi and myself to investigate. We chose this spot, erected the buildings and started the school. Father Grassi is in St. Louis now, working on funding for the mission and Sisters to teach."

Clayton remained silent, so Father Prando continued. "These poor savages need help so badly. They have so much to overcome if they are going to survive."

"I'll repay the three hundred dollars if I recover the stolen money, Father. She was my wife, but her name is Bonnie Girard on our marriage certificates, how will the death certificate read?"

"I will put both names on the certificate, with Bonnie Girard as an alias," the priest explained.

Clayton wrote on the tablet the way their names were written on the marriage certificate and rising said, "I've got to get riding, Father, if I'm ever going to catch them. Did they say where they were going?"

"No, but they headed right south on the military road towards Fort Smith. They would probably turn east on the Bozeman Trail there and head towards Fort Sheridan and Wyoming Territory. There's quite a little town there now with a hotel, bars and stores."

"Why would they head that way?"

"Well, I heard the skinny faced one say he'd be glad to get to a good bath, bed and some liquor, as if they were heading for a town and that's the nearest town south of here. The next one is Buffalo, down where the Bozeman Trail takes off, but Sheridan is closest."

"Thanks for your hospitality, Father," Clayton said as they shook hands, "I'll pick up the certificate on my way back. Got to be moving now, though."

He and the pinto turned south on the military road and faded out of sight as the frail little priest gazed after them.

Clayton continued to the south on the military road. It was no longer necessary to constantly search for tracks as he rode with slack reins and the pinto trotted jauntily along as if very proud to be allowed his own judgment.

It also gave Clayton time to brood over past events and the realization that a page in his life was painfully over brought about a strange new feeling in him.

From the start of the chase he had intended to kill the three men involved, necessary or not. Now, though, a strange new feeling enveloped him.

Since visiting Father Prando, brooding at his wife's grave and reading the epitaph, the hatred he felt and the need for vengeance had, somehow vanished. The thought of further violence and death now repelled him.

He must have loved his sister dearly, Clayton mused. The epitaph he had composed spoke of such love and the determination to see that she had a Christian burial showed more concern for her than for his own safety.

Clayton decided then and there that he would fulfill his mission according to law. He would enlist the aid of any available law organization, local, territorial or military, if necessary and try to make an arrest.

He continued to Fort Smith and turned the pinto easterly as Father Prando had directed, the bulwarks of the military garrison showing to his right at the mouth of a deep canyon.

Riding over the rolling grasslands, Clayton saw more fine looking animals, others were scraggly and stunted, but he was amazed at how many feral horses there were.

Up in the Judith Basin country such horses would have been rounded up, culled, gelded and the good ones broken for use as ranch stock. Good saddle mounts were at a premium up north. Here, they just ran wild.

The road topped a final rise and dropped down into another lush valley where yet another sparkling stream wound to the north and intersected a well-traveled road paralleling the easterly bank.

This must be the Little Big Horn and that has to be the stage road to Billings, as Father Prando described it, Clayton thought. He crossed at a shallow ford where the military road joined the stage road and turned right.

After a night of sound sleep, Clayton continued southward, the road following the flat land near the river. He once passed a small family group of Indians who discreetly pulled off to one side and carefully eyed him as he passed.

Just after mid-day, Clayton met two freight wagons loaded to overflowing, each pulled by a team of four huge draft horses.

"We come all the way from Cheyenne on the Dry Fork Trail," the first teamster proudly stated. "First load of freight to reach Wyomin' by rail. They got the railroad punched through the Medicine Bows to Fort Steele and almost to Rawlins now. We can reach Billings with freight a whole month faster'n they can by riverboat and wagon from Fort Benton."

Asked how far it was to Fort Sheridan, the teamster replied, "You'll make it by dark if you keep at a trot, but you'll want to go right into town. It's busting at the seams now that them Injuns got their asses whipped. Good town, Sheridan is."

Just as the teamster said, Clayton rode by the gates of Fort Sheridan as the sun set behind the towering Big Horns, now crested with fresh snow. He waved to the sentries, continuing to follow the road as it turned east, crossing a small stream and ahead, on the east bank, he could see the cluster of buildings comprising the town of Sheridan.

Clayton rode down a wide main street, amazed at the activity. New construction was taking place in every open space and the street thronged with riders, wagons, and humans of every description.

"Almost as big as Billings," Clayton mused, "May be bigger soon, what with the Union Pacific just south of here now."

He turned into the first livery stable he came to and approached a stooped old man with a long beard. Without dismounting, he asked, "Did you have two men come in here the last few days? They was ridin' two and leadin' two."

Looking the long-haired and full-bearded man over carefully, the old livery spit a cheek-full of Red Star into the hay he was feeding and took his time in replying.

"Nope, I don't get much folks like that here. Mostly jus' cowhands and such being I'm down here by the cattle pens." He offered no more advice until Clayton requested it.

"Where else would a rider put up his mount around here?"

"Probably down at Johnson's, behind the Fetterman Hotel. Real close to all what's goin' on that way."

Clayton thanked the old man and turned Shoshone down the street. Patting the salt-caked neck, he said, "Just a bit further old boy and you'll get a first class rub down, water, hay and the best grain they've got. You've earned every bit of it and more."

The Johnson Livery and Stable was a huge building lined with rows of stalls, most of them occupied. Out back were rows of buggies and wagons and a large corral filled with some very good saddle stock and draft animals.

The livery keep was a young, enthusiastic man with a freckled face and a mop of red hair. "What can I do for you mister?' he asked, taking the reins Clayton handed him. "Almost full, but I do have a stall for your pinto if you're a lookin' to board him."

"Fine," Clayton said, "Give him your best and rub him down real good, you hear?"

"You bet mister, he gets the royal treatment, don't you worry none."

Clayton followed the man as he led the pinto down a long row of stalls, his eyes scanning the horses they passed looking for a big salt-and-pepper roan he knew to be the slue footed one—the one the red-faced "Romeo" had ridden.

"Do you get many strangers in here these days?" Clayton idly asked, as he continued to eye ball the many mounts in the livery.

"Oh yeah, they're comin' and a goin' all the time. More and more ever day," the redhead said.

"How about two dark haired fellas' ridin' two and leadin' two? One being led a salt-and- pepper roan," Clayton asked just as he spied a speckled face staring across at them from the opposing row of stalls.

"You must mean that big gray with the black spots, right across from us."

"Yes, that looks like him all right."

"Someone must'a shoed him bad once 'cuz his right, hind hoof kinda' turns out. Don't seem to hurt him none though, he gets around real good. Those guys friends of yours?" the livery man asked.

"No, and I don't want them to know I'm in town," Clayton replied, as he slipped a gold coin into the man's hand. "If they ask, you never seen me, okay?"

"You bet mister, ... mister?"

"Mister Faris. Now you keep this quiet and take good care of that pinto. It will be worth your while to do so," Clayton said as he picked up his saddle bags and walked out the door.

Clayton entered the rear door of the Fetterman and walking up the long hallway to the lobby, he asked a chubby little lady at the desk looking at him over eye glasses set on the end of her nose. "Gotta' room for a few nights?"

"Well, are you lucky, mister, a couple just left on the stage and I got one room left. Isn't fancy and on the top floor but it's clean. Chimney goes right through it so it's warm in the mornings."

"That's fine," Clayton said as he signed William Faris on the register. He took the room key, turning at the foot of a wide and ornate staircase to ask, "Where can I get a bath around here?"

"We have a bath house at the far end of the lobby, right out that door there," the clerk said, pointing. "We also got a barber out there and you could sure use one, 'cept he won't be in until eight o'clock in the mornin'."

Clayton found his room at the far east end of the second floor hallway. After stowing his gear away he was tempted to sprawl on the bed and let the world go to hell for awhile but thought better of it.

He hadn't located either of the men he was trailing and they might be tempted to move on at anytime. A hot bath would help ease the tiredness from his bones and a good meal couldn't hurt either.

Soaking in the steaming water, Clayton decided that the bank robbers undoubtedly would not recognize him with the long hair and bushy beard. They also had no reason to suspect him of trailing them. They would be more likely to avoid contact with officials of the law.

Maiden Town

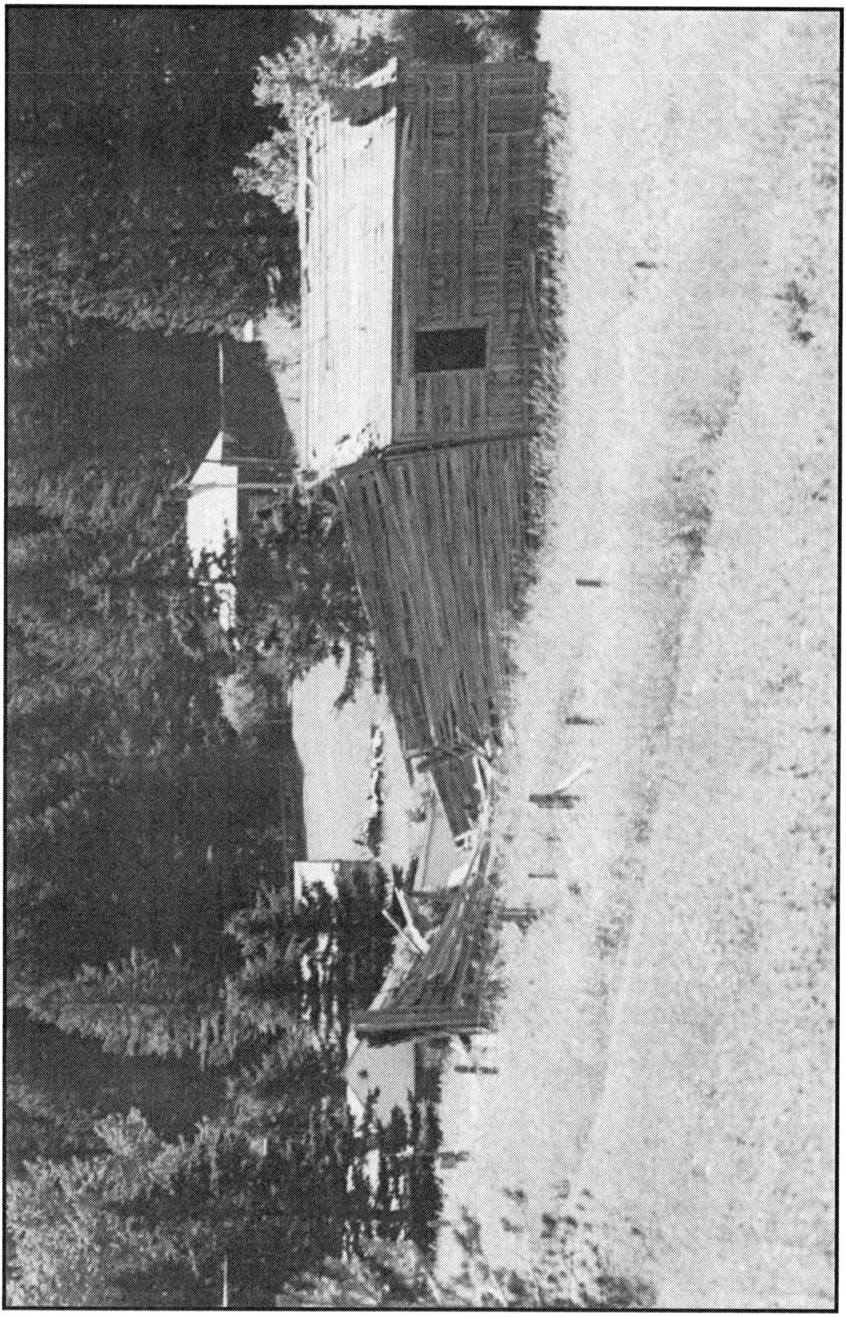

There didn't seem to be much in the way of law in this part of Wyoming Territory but possibly a town the size of Sheridan might have hired a town marshal. If not, then the Army was probably the only law and, depending on the Post Commander's attitude, may or may not intervene on his behalf. Anyway, the two men had to be located first.

He strode through the lobby, soiled trail clothes rolled up under his arm, salivating at the overpowering odor of roast beef drifting from the dining room. With a muttered, "Holy cow," Clayton turned that way and sat down at a table adorned with fancy silverware on a red-and-white checkered tablecloth, placing the roll of soiled clothing next to the wall. He anticipated the prospect of his first roast beef dinner in weeks and a steaming cup of black coffee.

His meal finished, Clayton lingered over a final cup of coffee as he flagged down the waiter.

"Where can I find a good poker game around here?" he asked. "One with some decent stakes."

"I would say, sir, that you should probably go to the Palace. The Emporium gets a lot of play but they've got a house betting limit and that's where most of the cow hands go. Can't get hurt too bad there." the waiter responded.

"How do I get to the Palace?" Clayton asked.

"Two blocks down on this side of the street, sir, and good luck. They play for blood down there and they're all armed." the waiter said eyeing Clayton and his lack of weaponry in disdain.

Clayton paused before entering the massive swinging doors of the "Palace" to check the movement of his six shooter in the holster and the position of the thong, now tied around his right thigh. He pushed his way into the smoky, noisy saloon, and moving among the crowded tables to the bar, noted that the poker tables were located against the far wall. Clayton moved on down the bar to the only open spot at that end.

A slick-looking, handle-bar mustached bartender slapped a bar towel across in front of Clayton and asked, "What'll it be?"

"Whiskey," Clayton responded without looking at the man, his eyes scanning the poker tables. It's still a little early and they may not be here yet, he considered. And then he saw him.

Bryce Girouard sat at the nearest table facing Clayton, his face shaded by his black, wide-brimmed hat. The man directly opposite, with his back to Clayton, had to be Curt Ellis. Yes, he was sure of it.

He turned back to the bar and sipped his whiskey, pondering his next move. Find out if there is any law in Sheridan and if there is, will they allow him to sign a warrant for the two men's arrests? More important, will they deputize him to assist in the arrests?

He gazed at his half empty whiskey glass, considering his options. A chair scraped loudly behind him and a harsh voice said, "To hell with you, Bryce. You're on another of your lucky streaks and I'm gettin' out. You can kiss my ass for all I care."

Curt Ellis kicked his chair across the floor and started towards the bar as the others at the table looked after the arrogant one with wide eyes..

Bryce Girouard sat impassively gazing after Ellis, a cold, disdainful look on his face.

Ellis lurched to the crowded end of the bar slamming his shoulders between Clayton and the man on his right.

"Bring me a drink, dammit!" the thin-faced man yelled, his features contorted with rage.

Clayton reasserted his place at the bar and said, "There's room farther down the bar, mister."

"Yeah, well why don't you move down there then. I'm drinkin' here," the bully said as he again slammed his shoulder into Clayton.

The back of Clayton's clenched fist caught the sneering face square in the mouth and Ellis reeled from the bar, drawing his gun as he pivoted in Clayton's direction.

Instinctively, Clayton threw himself to the right as a bullet slammed into the bar where he had been. As his shoulder hit the floor, he felt his own gun buck in his hand almost simultaneously and heard a solid thud that told him he hadn't missed.

Clayton rolled over on one knee, his six shooter already lined up on the poker table,. finger easing from the trigger just in time to prevent killing Bryce Girouard, who stood with both hands on the green felt, making no move to draw.

This was not the same person he had last seen face-to-face in Moccasin. The cold, calculating eyes were now, dull and sad appearing. He looked openly at Clayton in obvious understanding.

After a long silence, Girouard softly said, "No, Clayton, I'm not going to draw down on you for gunning Curt. It was a fair fight and that son-of-a-bitch has been asking for a bullet in the gut ever since we joined up. I always knew someday I'd have to do it if he didn't get himself killed first."

"All right, Bryce," Clayton said as he stood up, keeping his gun leveled, "then you won't mind lifting your gun out, ever so easy with your finger tips and place it, muzzle towards you, on the table."

The man calmly did as Clayton asked and slowly pulled back his jacket to expose a small Derringer, situated in an elastic sheath sewed to the inner lining where it could either be rapidly drawn or could be shot directly through the fabric at a person across the table. He carefully removed the trick firearm and laid it on the table.

After the first frantic bedlam as people lunged to get out of the line of fire, the saloon had fallen deadly silent. Clayton moved over to sit opposite Bryce and excited voices rose.

"Good God almighty, did you see that guy roll and shoot? Got him right through the heart."

"The bastard asked for it," another voice said. "He was spoiling for a fight every night and he finally got it."

Clayton remained silent as he slid the two firearms toward himself and carefully ejected the cartridges.

Bryce Girouard's face remained impassive.

Clayton heard the barkeep bellow, "Get the hell out of the way so I can get some sawdust on that blood, it'll raise hell with my floor. Barney, go see if you can find the marshal."

Clayton asked, "Why didn't you draw on me, Bryce? You had me dead to rights. I know how well you handle a gun and I didn't have a chance."

"I've never drawn on a man unprovoked and I've never killed a man except in self- defense. Besides, we're related. Brothers-in-law you know."

"How did you know I wouldn't gun you down, standing there like that?"

"I'm a good poker player, basically because I know how to judge character. Comes to me natural, I guess, and I knew you wouldn't shoot me if I didn't threaten you."

"You had a lot of faith that I could hold up my trigger finger. What if I couldn't?"

"You'd have missed me. At the last second you'd have shifted your aim. People of your caliber are like that."

"What do you know about me?" Clayton asked.

"More than you think, probably, although Missy didn't tell me much."

"Missy?"

"I'm sorry, that's what we've called Michelle since she was a little squirt down on the bayou."

"What did she tell you?"

"She said she heard you were some kind of lawman once but you must not have made much of a mark because you never bragged about it. She also said you wouldn't be no problem to us. Said you was too easy going to come after us. You see, she had her talents, but judging people wasn't one of them. I knew she was off the mark that day I met you at the bank and we looked each other in the eye."

Bryce continued, "I tried to talk her out of it but she was determined and I'd have had to shoot it out with those two bums she recruited to help carry all the gold and silver. I wish now that I had forced the issue, regardless of the outcome."

"Missy did plan it all then?" Clayton asked.

"This was the third robbery she'd pulled off. The first one, she cleaned out the safe on a paddle wheeler we were working on. I wouldn't join her in it and I thought I had her talked out of it but she did it anyway and pulled out on me."

"Where did she go from there?"

"I don't know, but about two years later I got a letter from her. She was in Abilene and said she was working at a bank under the name of Shirley Jacobs. She said she had a sure way to rob the bank and get away with it. Wanted me to join her in the job."

"Well, did you?" Clayton asked.

"I went to Abilene, not to join her but to try to prevent the robbery. I got there on a Friday night to find she had already pulled the job. She knew the loss wouldn't be missed until Monday, mid-morning, when the bank opened.

"I admit I helped her get away. What would you have done if it was your little sister? We were always very close and I loved her very much."

Clayton was aware that someone had approached the table as Bryce stopped talking and looked beyond him.

"Harrumph, Mr. Faris can I have a word with you?"

Clayton motioned to the chair on his left and a watery-eyed old man with a weathered face and scraggly white hair protruding from under his hat, wearily sat down.

"I hear that dead guy started the fight and drawed on you first so I ain't blamin' none, but I also hear you did some mighty fancy maneuvering and shootin'. Now a man don't learn that kinda' stuff punchin' cows. Why don't you tell me about yourself."

Seeing the star on the old man's vest, Clayton stuck out his hand and said, "Nice to meet you, Marshal —?"

"Norris Spangler," the old man said, "now, how about you?"

"Well, to start with Marshal, my name is Clayton McMahon not Faris, and I didn't know the guy I shot. I guess he just wanted to push somebody around and picked on the wrong one."

Looking at Clayton intently, the old marshal said, "Well, if you're the McMahon used to ride for the Texas Rangers when I was sheriffin' down on the Strip, he sure as hell did pick on the wrong fella'. But what's with this Faris crap?"

"Sometimes a guy doesn't want a certain lady to know he's around, you understand? No sense in advertising."

The marshal grinned broadly, then nodded towards Bryce. "What's this guy got to do with the shootin'?"

"Well, nothing at all," Clayton said, "I was mistaken and I'm giving him back his weapons now." He shoved the guns and ammunition across the table.

"Well, okay, McMahon but don't leave town without talkin' to me. Got a report to fill out, you know. I'm also gonna' check up on that guy and try to find out who he is. I'll betcha' he's wanted somewhere. Maybe a reward."

"Yeah, I'll do that," Clayton said as he turned to Bryce Girouard's questioning face.

CHAPTER V
GETTIN' ACQUAINTED

No one seemed interested in poker anymore so the two had the gaming section to themselves as Clayton and Bryce looked at each other, disbelief in Bryce's eyes.

"Well, brother-in-law, you learned something about my past, now tell me about you and Missy. I already know you're not full blood Cajun."

"No, our father was Cajun and married our mother when she and others of her tribe fled to the Bayou country to escape the southern cotton growers. Mama was Cherokee and the planters were killing them all off to claim their land for cotton production. Our Papa was a trapper, shrimper and fisherman. We had a cabin on the bayou and we lived a good life until he got bitten by a cottonmouth and died." Bryce paused, his expression sorrowful. "Missy and I were just little ones then and things were really tough until our mother took in a bachelor man from down the bayou. I don't think she ever married Yves, but he did provide food for us, although not like Papa did.

"Mama was educated in a French convent and worked real hard to see to it Missy and I were schooled. She was very intelligent and teaching seemed to be a natural skill with her. She bought an extensive library with her to the bayou and we children read constantly. She was a good woman, Clay."

"Did Yves treat you well?" Clayton asked.

"Well, no, he drank a lot and took to beatin' me when he was like that. Once, when Mama tried to interfere, he hit her in the mouth and knocked her into the water. I vowed then that someday I'd kill him for that. I did too!" Bryce said softly.

"How did you do that?"

"I knocked him in the bayou with a pirogue pole and then held him under with the pole until bubbles quit coming up."

"When was that?"

"Shortly after he hit Mama she got sick with smallpox and died in just a few days," Bryce continued. "Yves went on a tear and took off to the settlement to drink while we buried our Mama beside Papa."

"How old were you then?"

"I guess I was about seventeen and Missy was fifteen."

"Why didn't you leave then?"

"The only way to get around in bayou country is by pirogue and Yves had that. We were marooned, Clayton. No other way to cross those swamps full of snakes and 'gators. You got to have a boat of some kind."

"When did Yves return?"

"In a couple days, and he was all hung over and mean. He kept sittin' there staring at Missy in a nasty way. Then he grabbed her and started tearing at her dress. That's when I hit him and you know the rest." Bryce said.

"Except how you ended up a professional gambler and Missy a professional bank robber," Clayton added.

"Well, I got us a job on a paddle wheel boat. It was a big boat and had lots of wealthy business people on board all the time. I started out as a roustabout and Missy waited tables in the dining hall. The captain was a good man and he kinda' took a shine to us both, I guess. Anyway, I got to dealing cards and taught Missy how. Pretty soon she had men fighting to play at her table beings she was so beautiful. She was an expert dealer though. She could read cards and add figures faster than anyone I've ever seen."

"So I've been told," Clayton said, "So she ended up cleaning out the boat's safe, huh?"

"Yeah, and she never seemed to get over her craving for money and nice things after that. You know where it got her. We both know."

Clayton sat in silence not knowing what to say.

"For what it's worth, she truly loved you, Clayton. She never took up with any other man. You were the first one. She went to work at that bank planning to rob it right from the start and she'd never have let you interfere if she hadn't loved you like no one before."

Clayton sat staring down at his clenched hands.

Bryce added, "She just couldn't control her love for money and the fast life. You never stood a chance, Clay."

Clayton felt a twinge at the personalization of his name and realized there was, indeed, a brotherly bond between them, one that they might never experience in reality.

Both men sat in silence, each struggling with his own inner emptiness of a love now gone.

"There's still a matter of the stolen money, Bryce. I know you didn't bring it into town, so you must have cached it somewhere."

"That's right," Bryce replied, "We buried it behind an old shack just northwest of town. Now you realize the problem I had with Ellis, as a partner. He'd have shot me in the back the first chance he got. You did me a real service in gunning him down. I made up my mind after Missy got killed that I was going to return it somehow, but I had to contend with Ellis first. Course he's not a factor now. What do you suggest, Clay?"

Clayton pondered a bit and said, "Look, I can return that money if you show me where it is. I can stall a day or two while you make tracks, then I can take it to the Sheridan bank and have them ship the money back to Billings by stage."

"Would they do that?"

"Yeah, as long as the banks at Billings and Moccasin pay for the guards, which they will be glad to do. The parent bank to all those little banks up there is Stebbins, Post and Mund in Billings."

"Why was there so much gold and silver bullion in that little bank?" Bryce asked.

"That came from the bank at Maiden, which burned down. Most of the town burned, in fact, and they were just vaulting it for Maiden until they built a new bank or they could get it shipped east," Clayton replied

"That stuff makes it awful tough to move the funds around. Believe me I know." Bryce offered.

After some thought, Clayton said, "Look, why don't we find us a strong box tomorrow, go out with a wagon and load it up. I'll take it to the bank here in Sheridan and have them place it in a security vault. They won't have to know what it is. I can tell them it's valuable government bonds and papers or something like that. Then after you're gone, I can tell Marshal Spangler, blame it on Curt Ellis and have the bank arrange to ship it back."

"Why would you do that for me?"

"I could say, because we're brothers-in-law, but that ain't it. I'd do it because I understand how you got into this mess. I know you're no thief."

"I'll pay you that three hundred dollars we gave the miners to bury Thomas. That was the only money spent out of the robbery money. I paid the priest at St. Xavier out of my own pocket."

"Will you have enough traveling money?" Clayton asked.

"Oh yeah," Bryce said, "I took the money Missy had with her when we buried her. Would you believe, over five thousand dollars?"

"Where did she get that kind of money?"

"Probably left over from the Abilene bank job. Like I said, Clay, she just couldn't control that greed for money. Rightfully, it's your money as you're her surviving husband," Bryce added.

"I don't want any of it. I'd be obligated to return it and explain how I got it. Best let sleeping dogs lie."

"What about the three hundred dollars I took?" Bryce asked.

"Forget about the three hundred dollars," Clayton said. "She was my wife and I'll make up the missing funds."

"Much obliged," Bryce said, "How about us meeting in the hotel for breakfast and then I'll take you out to where the stuff is buried. I'm plumb pooped out now and can use some rest."

Clayton agreed and they left for the hotel together as the barkeep still scrubbed at the blood spot.

"Damn stuff will get to stinkin' like hell if you don't get it washed real good," he said. "Even then, you got to put creosote on it."

Clayton and Bryce walked in silence toward the hotel.

The two men had just finished a breakfast and were savoring a second cup of black coffee when the door to the hotel burst open and they heard an excited falsetto voice say, "Where's Mr. Faris? I gotta' find Mr. Faris."

Clayton looked into the lobby just in time to catch the eye of the redheaded livery man.

"Mr. Faris! Mr. Faris! There's a guy out there says he going to kill you. He said he's calling you out to prove he's a better gun than you," the young man stammered.

"Oh, for Christ's sake," Clayton said, "One gun fight and already I've got a challenge. There's too many young kids reading Ned Buntline these days. Who is he, kid?"

"I ... I ... don't know, Mr. Faris but he's wearin' two guns low and tied down. What'll I do?"

"Well, you go out and tell him I'll be out as soon as I finish my coffee," Clayton said.

As the young man turned wide eyed towards the door, Bryce asked, "You want me to take care of this one, Clay? I owe you one, you know."

"Thanks Bryce, but you can't draw any attention to yourself. I think I know how I can end this without anyone dying." Clayton said. "Would you just cover for me in case there is more than one? This may be a trap, so watch the roofs and high windows."

"Will do," Bryce responded as Clayton headed out the back door of the hotel.

Clayton turned up the lane by the livery and started walking up the alley behind the row of buildings when Marshal Spangler stepped out of a doorway.

"I tried to stop that young fool McMahon, but he said if I interfered he'd kill me too and I can't go up against a young gun no more. I just ain't fast enough these days.."

"Norris, have you told anyone my real name?" Clayton asked.

"Well, no, I didn't know if you was ready for that or not."

"Okay, now as far as you know I'm Bill Faris and let's always keep it that way, agreed?"

"Yeah, yeah, sure Bill," the wise old sheriff said.

By that time, Clayton was striding rapidly towards the next side street, which would put him a block and a half away from the hotel entrance.

Turning the corner and walking past a saddle shop, Clayton strode out into the middle of Main street. The street was amazingly vacant and Clayton could clearly see a young man crouched facing the hotel doors and plainly heard him yelling.

"I'll bet you're finishing your coffee, Faris. You're probably lookin' for some way to sneak out so you won't have to go up against a real gun. I'm not the caliber of that third rater you lucked out on last night. If you got any goddamn guts you'll come out here and face me."

"So you're a real fast gun, are you, kid?" Clayton yelled.

The young gunman turned around quickly and stared at the tall, relaxed figure, standing with his arms folded across his chest a block and a half away.

"You damn right I am. So you didn't have the guts to come out of the hotel and meet me face-to-face, did you?" the young man asked.

"I don't want to have to kill you, son," Clayton yelled, "And I am facing you, right now."

"At a mighty safe distance too, I see. Well, we can change that mighty quick," the hot-head yelled as he started up the street towards Clayton.

"Hold it right there!" Clayton yelled, "One more step and I draw on you. I'm going to draw on you anyway, but I want you to know when, so's it'll be a fair shake."

The young man stopped in disbelief. He'd never been put in a spot like this before and for once did not have an immediate retort.

Clayton yelled, "Okay, son, I'm going to draw on you now so you're fair warned." He drew so fast that his gun was leveled before the boy even cleared leather as he grabbed for both guns.

Turning sideways, Clayton took careful aim as he heard the boy's guns go off. A bullet whined by to his right and another plowed the dirt to his left just as he fired.

The young gunman's hat went flying off his head as he was propelled backwards to land flat on his back.

Marshal Spangler and Bryce Girouard both bounded out of the hotel and reached the prone figure before Clayton's long strides covered the more than a block distance.

The marshal kneeled beside the boy. "Jesus, look at the furrow on his head. A little deeper and he'd be stone dead."

Clayton heaved a sigh of relief and glanced down at his shaking hands. He had called the play and knew it was up to him to make it work. One little miscalculation and..... Thank god it was over.

"Better get him over to Doc Hindahl," the marshal said as he gathered up the boy's belt and guns. "Tell the Doc I got a cell all ready for him when he's well enough to move."

Clayton, Bryce and Marshal Spangler stood in the street as the crowd followed those carrying the limp body toward the doctor's office..

"By God, Clay, that kid didn't stand a chance against your draw." Bryce said. "You would of killed him for sure if you'd faced off with him."

"That's for dang sure," Spangler added. "Man, that's good long range shootin', Mr. Faris. Now, what should I do with the stupid little fart when his head clears enough so's he can think?"

"You might tell him how badly he was beaten to the draw and tell him he's lucky my partner here didn't come to face him. He's twice as fast as I am." Clayton said, nodding towards a grinning Bryce.

"Yeah, that ought to give him sumthin' to think about. If we scare him bad enough, maybe he'll give up this crap about being a gun fighter," the marshal said.

"All right, from now on I'm William Faris," Clayton said. "If he comes lookin' for Bill Faris someday, he'll find him hard to locate. As soon as I leave here, I'm Clayton McMahon. Okay?"

Both men nodded as they all entered the dining room to finish their morning coffee.

Clayton and Bryce left the livery stable with a wagon and team as the redhead gazed at Clayton in awe, his usual, non-stop dialogue stilled.

They rode westward on an old wagon road. Bryce had tied his mount, as well as Michelle's, to the tailgate. His mount was saddled with all his traveling gear tied on behind.

They bounced along in silence as a brand new strong box thumped on the boards behind them. In a short distance they were behind a low hill and out of sight of town.

"You know, Bryce, I'm positive I can convince Marshal Garwood that you tried to prevent the robbery and participated in recovering the loot by killing one of the robbers. We kinda' cooperated and I done in the other guy. They're getting all the money back so I'm sure the bank will drop charges."

"Why would you do that?" Bryce asked quietly.

"Because I'd like for you to come see us sometime with no ghosts in your past. You can't gamble all your life and there'll always be a job for you at the C-Bar-M."

"I'm askin' you again, why?" Bryce asked.

"Because we're brothers, damn it!" Clayton said. "In fact, you're the only brother I've got now."

They rode on in silence and soon turned off to the north on an even more indistinct road that snaked down a gentle embankment to a grassy flat by a stream.

"Must be the Tongue River," Clayton said.

"Could be," Bryce agreed.

They soon reached a small trapper's cabin. It appeared to have been long abandoned. Probably killed or run off by Indians, Clayton surmised.

Bryce guided the team around behind the cabin and pulled to a halt. He clambered down and walked to a pile of buffalo berry brush. Getting a good hand hold, he tossed the brush to one side and then leaped back, sucking in his breath.

A huge rattler lay coiled atop a mound of fresh-turned earth, feebly trying to rattle.

Clayton was shaking with laughter at the look on Bryce's face as he stared at the snake.

"Jesus, he's a big one," Bryce said. "Why don't he rattle?"

"Too cold. The nights have been freezing of late and he hasn't warmed up yet. If he don't get denned up pretty soon, he'll die from the cold."

Bryce broke into a nervous laugh. "I didn't know. Those bayou snakes are active all year. They don't ever change much."

Clayton got the shovel from the wagon and sliced the snake's head off with one swing. Picking up the writhing body with the shovel, he threw it to one side and began digging. He had dug only a short distance when the shovel hit something soft but unyielding. Scraping back the dirt, he exposed a tightly woven moneybag.

"Didn't see much sense in digging to China," Bryce said, as they started lifting out sack after sack.

With the money and bullion all stowed away in the locked strong box, both men looked at each other awkwardly.

"I guess maybe I will drop by to see this fancy spread of yours someday," Bryce said as he extended his hand.

"Great, we'll be lookin' for you," Clayton replied as they shook hands.

Then, involuntarily, they both embraced in a truly brotherly hug.

Clayton strode down the street towards Marshal Spangler's office. The strong box was safely in a vault and it was time he leveled with the old man.

After recounting the whole story, Clayton said, "Now you know why I used a false name when I came to town. Just as well leave it at that, considering that hot head you've got back there in a cell. How's he doin'?"

"Fine, other than a hell of a headache. I had a little talk with him and gonna' have some more before he gets outa' here. The little pissant ain't so tough now. By the way, where you headin'?"

"I'm taking the stage to Billings. I'll be trailing three horses as far as that new Crow Agency and then take a run over to St. Xavier School."

"Why're you goin' back there?"

"Father Prando is going to have a death certificate ready for me and I know a couple of Indian bucks there who will appreciate those two extra horses," Clayton explained.

"Why give them hosses to a couple of Injuns?" Spangler asked incredulously.

"Maybe keep 'em from gettin' shot. They're mighty poor horse thieves," Clayton answered.

"I'll have Stebbins, Post and Mund, in Billings contact this bank and arrange to have that strong box shipped north," he continued.

"Too bad the telegraph ain't through yet," Spangler mused. "It's supposed to be done from Cheyenne to here next month and done to Billings by next summer, if the weathers good and the Injuns don't keep pullin' it down."

"Well, if the bank asks about that strong box tell 'em arrangements are under way to ship it. Okay?" Clayton asked.

The marshal nodded his head. "You bet, Mr. Faris."

"I'm going to be ridin' out on the morning stage," Clayton said as he extended his hand, "So I guess we'd best say good bye now."

Clayton shook the gnarly, old hand, warmly.

CHAPTER VI
THE ROAD HOME

The stagecoach creaked to a rocking halt amidst a swarm of brown-skinned, dark-eyed children. Indian teepees clustered between the stage road and the Little Big Horn River, while on the right a group of military men labored constructing a building from sawn lumber.

"That's gonna' be the new Crow Agency building," the stage driver said. "Right over there in that draw is where Custer and his troops got shot to hell. Injuns insisted on puttin' it here. Kind of a sacred spot to 'em now."

Clayton nodded as he untied the three horses. "How far to St. Xavier?" he asked.

"Oh, I dunno', about 20 miles I guess. I ain't never been there," the driver replied.

"When can I catch the next stage to Billings here?" Clayton asked.

"Same time tomorrow night. We're runnin' one ever day now. Been real busy lately. Just don't be late 'cuz we'll pull out at 4:30 sharp."

"You bet. Thanks," Clayton yelled, already fording the river on the trail west.

He rode into the school yard just at sun set, the late rays reflecting in florescent gold from turning leaves of the huge Fremont cottonwoods. He stopped in wonder as the glow changed the bleached logs of the little school to a delicate golden blush.

As he gazed in awe, the voice of Father Prando rang out. "Clayton, my son, you made it back. My prayers were answered. I worried so about you."

"I told you I would be back Father. I've never forgotten the venison you treated me to. You knew all the time I would be back didn't you?" Clayton teased.

"Well, yes, my son, but I also knew you had a monumental job ahead of you and not without danger. But why three horses this time?"

"Do you still see Curly Coyote and Long Tail once in a while?" Clayton asked.

"Well, yes, they stop by here every couple of days, mostly to get something to eat, I believe. Things are real tough for those boys and winter's just around the corner."

"Do you think a couple of horses will help their situation, Father?"

"It will give them great prestige in the tribe, where they are now treated with scorn. They'll probably brag they stole them at great danger to themselves so they can claim big coup, but I don't know if it will help their hunting success or not. The buffalo are pretty much all gone now. But come, let's stable your horses, then we can go inside to talk where it's warm." Father Prando turned toward the outbuildings.

Clayton silently ate the hardy meal set before him as Father Prando beamed his satisfaction.

As the after dinner tea lay warm in his midsection, Clayton asked, "Father, what are these Crow people going to do to survive this winter?"

"The government says they will distribute food and blankets to those who stay in this area. They also say it will be a reservation belonging to the Indians but I don't know, they haven't given them any help yet."

"Is that why all those Crows are camped over where they're puttin' up that new agency building?" Clayton asked.

"Yes, they're waiting for the food and blankets like they were promised."

"Do they realize they've got a fortune in saddle stock running around these parts?" Clayton asked.

Father Prando thought a while. "They don't think in white man's ways.. They can't understand the philosophy of raising or capturing something and selling it for currency to buy what they need. They've always just shared whatever they have and only the horse they ride belongs to them individually. Those other wild horses belong to everybody, in their way of thinking."

"Well, they had better learn our ways real fast or they ain't gonna' make it. Do you suppose they could be taught to capture those horses, break and train them to sell? There's a ready market for good riding stock."

"I don't know," the priest said, "but how would they capture them?"

"When those Indian boys were leading me here, I asked them about the Pryor Mountains west of here and they said it was rough country with lots of canyons. That's what you need to corral those mustangs, Father," Clayton explained.

"Those wild critters would just run up those canyons and out on the top rim,.."

"No, no, you have to build a pole fence across a narrow part of the canyon and other pole gates you can swing in place once the nags are in the trap. A few crazy ones will jump over, but you can get most of them," Clayton explained. "That's the way we rounded up some pretty good mounts down in Texas, including Shoshone out there. The Shawnee and Shoshones learned to do it. These Crows could too."

"I don't know, my son. These braves scorn stuff like building fences, digging holes and such. That's traditional squaw work. They're used to just hunting and fighting. No menial labor you know," Father Prando said.

"Well, they're gonna' have to change their ways. Maybe starving through this upcoming winter will make them wake up. I know it's cruel, but they've got a mighty leap to make and it may be that's the only thing that will do it. If they just get to sittin' around on their haunches waiting to be fed and clothed, they never will learn to survive in our world. Do you think you could convince them that this is a good thing, Father?"

"I could try. Maybe the new Indian Agent would help get the government people in here to train them," the little priest said thoughtfully.

"They'd have to learn to cull, breed, geld, break and train them so they'd be saleable. The cavalry is always short of mounts. Listen, Father, if it doesn't work out, write me at the C-Bar-M in Moccasin and maybe I can find some way to help. My partner is one of the best horsemen this country has ever seen. I'll bet he'd come down and help. We could take some mustangs to pay for our time, if we wasn't breakin' some law by doin' it."

Father Prando studied Clayton's face a moment and then said, "My Lord, you mean it and it just may work too! But it's late and you must be tired. We shall talk about it tomorrow after a good night's rest. Come this way."

The priest led Clayton to the stables where a soft pallet of hay was spread in a roomy bunk.

"This should do you well, my son and I shall expect you for breakfast shortly after sunrise."

Father Prando hung up the lantern and with a "May God be with you," left Clayton alone.

Shortly after midday, Clayton bade good by to St. Xavier and Father Prando. With a last reminder to impress upon Curly Coyote and Long Tail that they must treat their new mounts with kindness and respect, he turned to the east and the Crow Agency.

The skies had turned gray and a cold wind whipped from the northeast as Clayton neared the Agency. He knew they were in for the first lash of winter and he wished he were back in his snug ranch home.

It had been almost a month since the robbery and he acknowledged he was homesick. Not much longer now and he would be in Billings.

He must contact Stebbin, Post and Mund's Bank so they could arrange for the return of the stolen funds and oh yes, he must record the death certificate at the Territorial Office.

It seemed so final, so coldly business-like, but that was the way these things were done.

The stage ride to Billings was cold and snowy, with a stop overnight at a dingy little stage station on Pryor Creek. Clayton was pleased to be checking in at a warm hotel at last. A good hot bath and hearty meal would make things better, but now that the long trek was winding down, the old loneliness began to creep back in and he found sleep difficult.

It would take a long time to forget the brief but intense love he had known.

Leaving Stebbins, Post and Mund, Clayton turned up the street towards the Territorial Office building. As he walked, he mulled over the many things that he knew must be done after he returned to the C-Bar-M. He was so deep in thought that he almost walked past the drab stone building that housed the government agencies.

A seedy little man with thick glasses took the death certificate, read it over and said in a nasal drone, "Yes, yes, it all looks in order Mr. McMahon. Please accept my condolences." He slowly turned away, heaving a sigh.

Clayton sat on a hard, but highly polished wooden bench as the Territorial clerk took his time making a copy. Looks like a hell of a lotta' folks have sat here on their butts and waited for him to get movin', Clayton thought as the little man laboriously penned away.

After what seemed like an eternity, the clerk returned to the desk.

"Now, Mr. McMahon if you will just proof read this for me to make sure it is a true copy, I'll assign a book and page number to the document."

After comparing the two documents to make sure they were identical, Clayton returned them to the clerk who stamped a big "COPY" on one and "ORIGINAL" on the other.

He applied another rubber stamp that said, "Notary," on each and yet another reading "Recorded, Date, Book & Page."

"Now, if you will just sign under Original and Copy on each document, I will notarize and record the documents," the clerk droned on.

Jesus, Clayton thought as he left the building, if that's an example of government efficiency those poor damn Indians don't stand a chance on a reservation. They damn well better learn to take care of themselves.

It was late in the day when Clayton returned to the hotel, his stomach uttering vicious sounding groans. He turned directly to the dining room and took a seat at a table.

After placing his order, he looked around the room, focusing on three men at a table to his left.

Damn, they look familiar, and that voice? Clayton searched his mind for a time and a place. Then it came to him as the one with a handlebar mustache said, "Let's just be patient, fellas, there has to be some decent horse flesh around here somewhere. I still say we can make more money raisin' and breakin' horses than we ever will a mining."

"Well, doggone it, Roy, here we got good money to pay and all anybody wants to sell us is their old nags. You can't start a herd of marketable saddle broncs that way," the gray bearded one said.

"That's 'cuz good ridin' stock is scarce out here, Hank," said the third and youngest of the three. "That's why we could do real good at raisin' and sellin' prime saddle broncs. 'Sides, I don't want to go back East with my tail between my legs. I like it out there, too."

"Bernie's right, Hank," said Roy. "We got those mining claims and they're better rangeland than mining ground. We got water, meadows, lots of grass, shelter in those draws for winter, and that big flat for corrals. We even got good timber for buildings and corrals."

"Well, I wish I knew as much about hosses as you do. Maybe I'd feel better about this," Hank said.

Clayton rose and walked to the table. "Pardon me gents, but may I join you?"

The older man, Roy, looked Clayton over and cautiously said, "Well, I guess so, but do we know each other?"

"You don't know me but I know you gents," Clayton said as he sat down. "I also know you've got three hundred dollars to invest in breeding stock."

"We earned that money fair and square," Bernie sputtered, indignantly, "'Sides, how do you know what we got?"

"No offense," Clayton offered and went on to relate the entire story and how he had spied on their camp that night.

The three ex-miners looked at each other, trying to communicate their thoughts, then Roy, cautiously queried. "And you want the three hundred dollars back so's you can return it to the bank, right?"

"No, you earned that money honestly. I'm more interested in making you a proposition that'll net you some good breedin' stock for your horse herd," Clayton said.

The three men looked Clayton over suspiciously as the waiter delivered his meal and refilled all the coffee cups.

Between bites, Clayton continued, "Roy, you're an experienced bronc wrangler from what I hear?"

"Yeah, Roy Kinne's the name. My old man was a horse trader and breeder back in Kentucky and I took over after he died. Did real well at it too until my wife up and died of diphtheria. I just couldn't stay there no more after that, so I turned the place over to the kids and lit out West. I always wanted to see this country and needed to forget. So I just did it."

"By the way, this is Hank Stryker." Kinne nodded to one of the man, "and this here's Bernie Ebert."

They shook hands around the table.

"You think you could teach a bunch of Indians how to be horse breeders?"

"Injuns? God all mighty, take a chance on loosen' our scalps?"

"These are Crow Indians down south of Billings. They never were hostile but now the poor bastards are going to starve to death if they don't learn how to use the resources they got," Clayton explained. "The government's going to make a reservation down there as soon as they quit fighting over boundaries. They're afraid they might give them some land that's worth something. Still, they owe the Crows something because they helped the army run down the Sioux, Cheyenne and Blackfeet. They're building an agency headquarters now on the Little Big Horn."

"They got lots of horses?" Kinne asked.

"They got lots of wild horses running loose all over the place down there, After the battles at Conner, Massacre Hill, Wagon Box and the Little Big Horn, there were surviving horses running loose all over and the Crows picked up the easy ones. Mostly cavalry horses and most still saddled. They'd walk right up to the Indians, wanting to get undressed and rubbed down. They just ignored the wilder Indian ponies."

"Why didn't they start breeding a herd from that stock?" Kinne asked.

"After the wars were all over, the army went around demanding all the cavalry stock back, plus any offspring," Clayton explained. "They said they would hang any Indians as horse thieves who didn't return the stock. That left the Crows with very little riding stock."

"What kinda deal you suppose we could make?" Stryker asked.

"If you can reach an agreement with the chiefs before the Bureau of Indian Affairs takes over, you could probably keep half of all the horses captured. Fair split as to quality, age, sex, and all that."

"What's the government got to do with it?" Ebert asked.

"After they take over, they'll want to approve any agreements and I'll bet they'd tell you to go to hell. They don't want 'em to be independent. Seems they want them to be reliant on the agency. Keep 'em beholden and always beat down that way. It may not work for too long, but I'll bet long enough for you to build up a good herd and long enough to teach them how to be horse breeders."

"What would we have to teach 'em?" Kinne asked.

"You'd have to show them how to round 'em up, cull, castrate the stud colts, break and train to ride and breed for better quality. They're not stupid, those Indians. They just don't understand how to adapt to our ways. No matter what you think of Indians, these are proud people and you'll have to treat them and their lifestyle with respect. You insult them and you're done. Think you can do it?"

"How we gonna' talk to 'em?" Stryker asked.

"Some of the young ones have been taught at the St. Xavier Indian School and can speak passable English. Father Prando is involved in this effort and he'll help you make contact and strike up a deal. I've seen many of those wild broncs and there's some real good ones out there."

The three men sat in thought as Clayton pushed his plate back and tackled the now tepid coffee before him.

"I'll write you a letter to Father Prando so he'll know you've talked to me and are sincere in this thing. He has a great deal of compassion for the Indians and wants to help them. He's a good man."

"Let us talk this over, McMahon, bein' we're partners in this, you know. Can we meet you in the bar, say in an hour?" Kinne asked.

"Okay, in an hour," Clayton said rising. He paid the cashier and slowly climbed the carpeted stairway to his room.

"Just time to get packed so I can catch the early stage," Clayton said to himself.

The three miners, would-be horse breeders, were sitting at a table in a corner of the bar when Clayton entered.

Roy Kinne stood, sticking out his hand as. "Hey, we decided what the hell, we'll give it a try," he said, pumping Clayton's hand. "Why don't you go ahead and write that letter?"

"I already have," Clayton replied, reaching into his inner pocket. "I figured you were the kind of fellas that would know a good deal when you see it."

Handing Kinne the envelope containing the letter, Clayton added, "I'm heading back to Moccasin in the morning. I own the C-Bar-M up there and we are always looking for good saddle broncs. If this works out, come up and see us. Maybe we can relieve you of some stock."

"Sure, will do," Kinne replied, and everyone shook hands as the alert barkeep came rushing over with a bottle of his best.

He hadn't tended bar for over forty years without learning to read the signs.

The stagecoach labored up the Burke Stage Road leading to the rim overlooking Billings and the Yellowstone Valley. Clayton, again began feeling the depression that had been periodically hounding him since leaving Sheridan.

Of course, his head still pounding from last night's social hour didn't help any. He knew his feeling were something he'd have to battle for a long time. He had so planned and worked towards the day when he and Bonnie would be rancher and wife on the C-Bar-M.

Now the dream was shattered and, although he longed to be back home, the enthusiasm he once felt was no longer there. Clayton wondered if he really wanted to continue that kind of life. Maybe he should go back into law enforcement.

He knew he was a good lawman and being single was a definite asset to that profession.

Suddenly, the stagecoach came to a halt and the driver bellowed out, "Just a stop to let the hosses blow folks. We'll be on our way shortly."

Thinking he might feel better in the open air, Clayton called out, "How about me riding shotgun for you awhile, driver?"

"Sure, come on up. I can use the company," the tobacco-spitting old man said.

As he clambered to the seat beside the driver, Clayton looked around, awed by the view. The new snow created a spectacular scene before them.

To the south, the Pryor's glistened in new snow, to the southwest, the Beartooths, westward the Crazies, and to the northwest, the Little Belts and Big Snowies all sparkling in a new coat of white.

Suddenly, Clayton felt better. Amid all this beauty, how could anyone feel despondent? What the heck, he thought, I'm no worse off than before I met Bonnie. Just have to pick up where I left off.

The stage rolled across grasslands to the northwest. It stopped at Broadview Station for a change of teams and on over the low divide between the Bull Mountains and the Cayuse Hills, then down towards the Mussellshell.

At the Lavina Station, the road forked and the stage turned left towards Charley Cushman's Crossing and Station. The right fork heading north towards Lewistown was the main Burke Stage Road but the route through Shawmut Crossing, Merino, Judith Gap and Moccasin provided the shortest and most level route to Fort Benton. This stage road received more and more traffic as a result, which didn't hurt the economy of the small towns along the way.

An overnight stay at Cushman Crossing and teamed again with fresh horses, the stage rattled along the Mussellshell towards Shawmut Crossing and Merino.

A stop for lunch at Merino and the stage turned right on the Fort Benton stage road, heading towards Judith Gap and U-Bet, where they would again spend the night.

At U-Bet, Clayton was tempted to abandon the stage, saddle up Shoshone and ride on towards Moccasin and home, but he had ridden the faithful pinto so hard the last few weeks that he relented.

"You deserve better treatment than that, Shoshone," Clayton said to the pinto as he patted the patchwork neck.

The gentle grade to Buffalo went rapidly, then across the east fork of the Judith and the buildings of Moccasin came in view.

Marshal Garwood stood in the street as the stage pulled to a stop. Clayton handed down his saddle and gear from the boot and then climbed down to shake the big hand offered.

"Damn, I'm glad to see you back," the marshal said, wringing Clayton's hand and smiling from ear to ear. "I knowed when I got back from that silly goose chase up north that you'd run 'em down, sooner or later."

"You seem to know a lot of what went on," Clayton said.

"Yeah, I got a letter from Marshal Spangler in Sheridan yesterday telling me everything. Said you shot hell out of one of those robbers and then had to face up to a young, would-be hero to boot."

"That's about right, but there's more to it than that. Let's go to the hotel restaurant and talk over a cup of coffee."

As they walked up the street, Garwood asked, "That Bryce fella' was Bonnie's brother and really wasn't in on the robbery, huh?"

"He would have prevented it if he could have, but Bonnie, or Michelle, or Missy, take your pick, had already recruited those two low-lifes, Curt and Cal. Bryce didn't help in the robbery. He just rode along to look after his sister."

"He always intended to return the money, somehow, and he took me right to where they'd buried it after both those other bums were out of the way. He could of killed me easy, if he'd wanted to, but he didn't. Even took a chance I'd shoot him."

As the two savored their coffee, Clayton said, "Spencer, I'm asking you to drop the charges against Bryce Girouard and retract the wanted notices. He's no criminal."

"As far as I'm concerned I'd do that, but the bank has to drop all charges first," Garwood said. "They're gettin' all their money back so I don't see why they wouldn't"

"I've already talked to Stebbins, Post and Mund in Billings and they're neutral about it," Clayton explained. "Sheridan's just going to ship the money back up there and then they'll re-distribute it here and to Maiden."

Marshal Garwood nodded in understanding. "All right, I'll do what I can. I'll go over and talk to Sutherland in the morning. When you riding out for the ranch?"

"First thing in the morning,. I left a lot of work behind for Curly to take care of. I owe him and Juanita a lot and I'd better be making it up to them."

"From what I hear, the C-Bar-M ain't in too bad of shape," Garwood said with a twinkle in his eyes.

Clayton wondered what the marshal had meant as he walked back to the hotel. The Quessing boys must have come over and helped out with the hay, he mused. They're good neighbors.

The ride to the C-Bar-M seemed to take forever, even though Clayton rode on past the Q2 without stopping.

Entering the gate and turning up the lane, he could see Curly standing in front of the barn, waving.

Clayton rode past the ranch house, noticing something different. The once plain building now had blue and white curtains in the windows and the porch had some fall asters blooming in a row of flower pots.

Juanita sure has been busy since I left, Clayton thought as he reined the pinto up in front of Curly.

"Hi, you old fart, how are you?" Clayton said, as he swung down and grabbed Curly's hand.

"Well, as good as we can be, havin' to do all of the chores round here while you was galivantin' down south," Curly moaned.

"We'll catch up on the work in a hurry now," Clayton promised. "How much hay we got to get in?"

"Oh hell, the hay's all in the barn and stacked in the meadow. Hayin's all done," Curly said with a mischievous grin.

"Marvin must have come over and helped then," Clayton ventured.

"Nah, Rob came over and helped some, but Marvin, he done fell in luv and went and got married."

"Married? Who to?"

"He hitched with that Blackfoot gal, Kalee, and they're both prancin' on clouds," Curly said, as he spat a quid in the dust.

"Well, how did you get all this work done?" Clayton asked.

"I just hired me some help, that's how. Damn fine help too," a beaming Curly said. "Here's one of 'em now, Clayton," Curly said as a slender boy came from the barn to stand beside him.

Putting his arm around the boy, Curly said, "Tommy here is the best team driver in the country, and he's just a boy. He's a natural with hosses and he's learnin' real fast. He's gonna' be a top wrangler someday. You'll see."

Clayton reached out a hand to the boy who said, "Howdy, Mr. McMahon, how are you?"

"Well, I'm just fine now Tommy, but I thought you and your mother would be on your way back East by now."

Before the boy could respond, Curly cut in to say, "Hell, once they gotten here on the C-Bar-M they just couldn't leave us and they done paid their way, too. Tommy drove team, me and Juanita pitched hay, and Pauline loaded the wagon. We made a good team and look at how Pauline fixed your old shack too."

"Looks mighty nice all right, Curly, but where am I supposed to live now?" Clayton asked.

Curly looked at his boots as they scuffed in the dust. "Say, you gotta' tell us all about how you run them fellas down ... " Curly stopped abruptly to add, "Oh, here comes Juanita and Pauline. I reckon I better get back to feeding hosses." He hurried toward the barn.

Clayton looked toward the house and saw dark-skinned Juanita walking towards him, hand-in-hand with a tall, lithesome woman, her fair skin and golden hair in sharp contrast to Juanita.

Tommy stood next to Clayton and grabbed his hand as the two approached.

Curly, apparently forgetting his chores, peered from the barn as the ladies drew near.

"Clayton, we're so glad you're safely home," Juanita said with tears in her dark eyes. She wrapped her arms around the tall, lean figure.

Kissing Juanita gently on the head, Clayton looked across at Pauline.

She was not the gaunt and haggard Mrs. Nelson he recalled from that night in the creek draw. The cheeks were now full and golden tan in a smiling face. Her blue eyes sparkled and the long, flaxen hair was neatly brushed back and tied with a pale, blue bow.

Extending a graceful hand to Clayton, Pauline said, "Tommy and I owe you so much, Mr. McMahon. I don't know what we would have done without your help. Juanita and Curly have been just wonderful to us and they spoil us like we were their own."

Clayton smiled awkwardly, unable to find words so he just nodded and pushed back his hat with a shaky finger.

"You have such a nice house, Mr. McMahon, but it certainly needed a woman's touch. I hope you won't mind the things I've done to dress it up a bit," Pauline offered.

"No, I'm sure I won't mind a bit, Mrs. Nelson. I admit, it was kind of a bear's den," Clayton finally found words.

"Please call me Pauline," the tall blonde said, "and would you like to see how I've done the inside of the house? I salvaged my old Singer and a lot of material when we left Diamond City, so all it took was a little work."

"Oh ... sure," Clayton stammered as Tommy grabbed his hand and pulled him towards the house. "And you can call me Clay, if you want to."

Curly came out to stand beside Juanita as she watched the trio walk towards the ranch house. Tommy still clutched Clayton's hand as he and Pauline walked shoulder to shoulder.

"Oh Curly, aren't they a handsome couple? Just like the children I've always wanted and even a grandson, too. Oh dear, I hope everything works out all right."

Putting his arm around Juanita's waist, Curly pulled her close and said, "Now don't you worry none, Mrs. Wilphart, everything is gonna' work out fine. I can tell from here."

CHAPTER VII
TOUGH WAY TO MEET

He sat astride a weary mount, surveying the scene before him. The brawling young town of Laramie, Wyoming lay sprawled below on this cold and dreary fall day in 1882. The weak evening sun peeked from beneath a curtain of storm clouds to glisten on the wet rails of the Union Pacific as they narrowed to infinity in the east.

Bryce Girouard felt extremely tired after four days of hard riding since parting with Clayton McMahon near Sheridan. The fatigue he felt rasped away at other inner emotions like the nagging of an aching tooth. He had just buried his only and dearly loved sister, Michelle, then was forced to ride away from the first warm feelings of brotherhood he had ever experienced.

He was returning to the only life he had known before the futile trip to Montana. It had been a painful effort to prevent Michelle from further complicating her wild and impetuous young life, and even knowing that he had done all humanly possible did not rout the feelings of failure and loss over what had transpired in the recent past.

Bryce just wanted to get as far from that land of sorrow as possible. Where to? Back to the Mississippi and the paddle wheels with their casinos and his old life as a professional poker player. This was the only sanctuary he could envision.

He rode down the stage road into the young town sprawled astride the Laramie River, contemplating some rest, good food and a poker game or two before giving up his horses and saddles. Now he would sell them and buy a train ticket to Kansas City.

The sign "MEDICINE BOW LIVERY" drew Bryce from the mélange of humanity and livestock milling back and forth on the main drag of Laramie and into the dim light of a huge building.

A bald-headed old man limped forward with a, "Howdy mister, need to put your hosses up for a few days?"

"Yeah," Bryce replied, "Rub them down real good and feed them the best you got. I'll be here for a few days and then I'm heading east on the train. Curry them down and pretty them up real good so I can sell them. You might work the saddles and halters over with saddle soap too. I'll be selling it all."

"You bet, mister, I'll give you the best service this side of Crawford and I'd like to make an offer on your hosses and gear too. I can't keep up with sales and rentals nowadays. This town is explodin' since the railroad is through to San Francisco."

Bryce worked his way up the street towards what appeared to be the center of town. He stopped from time-to-time, amazed as he observed the hustle and bustle of humanity and beast about him.

New buildings were being erected; older buildings enlarged. Upper stories were under construction on others, and although it was near dusk on this raw fall day, the sounds of hammer and saw continued. Lamplight shone through the gaping window holes as work continued inside unfinished construction. It was a bloom of civilization such as Bryce had never seen before.

Across the street the sign, "WOODS HOTEL AND EMPORIUM," attracted his attention and he crossed the busy street to enter a rustic but neat lobby.

As he signed the register, a short, stocky man with a shock of erect white hair came to the desk and looked at him with "owl eyes" magnified by extremely thick glasses.

"We ain't got much to offer but if you're by yourself, we got a room with a single and a back door out to the privy. Will that do?"

Bryce nodded and the desk clerk turned to fumble through a box of keys, finally coming up with one which he handed across to Bryce.

"The wash room and barber shop are in the back, dinin' room to your left and the bar to your right. Plannin' to stay long?" the man asked.

"Maybe a couple of days," Bryce replied, "maybe longer if my luck is good."

"Oh, a gambler, huh? I thought you didn't look like a cattleman or a miner. Well, there's lots of that goin' on around here these days. Players start showin' up about 8 o'clock," the big-eyed man offered.

Bryce lazed in the comfort of a tub of steaming water, contemplating the weeks of worry, heartbreak and travel now behind him and suddenly confronted a life yet ahead of him with no particular meaning.

In the past, he had gone about his life in the gambling halls of the riverboats, always deeply engrossed in the rituals of betting, bluffing, calling, and usually winning. The process of judging other players, studying them until he knew their innermost thoughts and ways kept him totally involved and oblivious to the drive for dreams of greatness, love, success and happiness that other young minds held.

Tonight, the old rapture and thrill of gambling seemed gone, replaced with a feeling of lonely emptiness. For the first time since childhood on the bayou, when his Mama had left him and Missy to join their Papa, a surge of panic and a feeling of being trapped welled up within him. Those long-ago memories returned to haunt him.

He forced himself from the warm tub, dried off and donned fresh clothing, polishing the dust from his black boots and adjusting the tie and vest with care, more through habit than desire. He shouldered his travel bag and headed for the dining room.

A hot meal of roast beef, spuds and coffee improved his outlook considerably and after stowing the war bag in his room, Bryce entered the bar. Play was just starting and there were open chairs at every table. After surveying each one, Bryce sat down at a table that seemed to have the highest stakes.

At first, the old skills were there and Bryce immediately started to build his stack of chips. Soon, one of the other players, apparently a regular, began making muttering remarks about strangers butting into their game. This kind of atmosphere was not new to Bryce and he appeared not to hear but moved so that the little trick pistol in its elastic cradle sewed to the inside of his jacket was in easy reach. He also moved to the right side of his chair so that the pistol on his hip hung free and loose.

These slight adjustments did not go unnoticed by the dark-haired man doing the grumbling nor by at least two others of the five at the table. Bryce noted with satisfaction, that all talk ended but the black eyes of the man glittered in hatred as he raked Bryce with a look of malice. Obviously he was used to bullying his way around in Laramie and didn't appreciate being disregarded—even challenged.

As his stack of chips mounted, Bryce grew more and more disinterested in the game and soon he started losing more hands than he won, which brought an occasional leer of triumph from the dark-haired bully. Bryce knew it was time to get out of the game and when a shapely house girl set a shot of whiskey in front of him, he downed it in a gulp, handed the girl a five dollar chip and pulled the rest into his hat.

The others at the table were obviously distressed when Bryce moved towards the cashiers window. Just when they had a chance to recover their losses, the guy bails out. At least one of them was aware that he had been in a game with a truly professional gambler and a dangerous man to trifle with.

Bryce cashed in his chips and dropped the assortment of eagles and other coins into his jacket pocket. Through all this, the little hustler clung twittering to his arm and when she pulled him towards a table he numbly obliged.

Bryce occasionally indulged in the services afforded by ladies of the night, always being discreet, and then only after he had come to know them well enough to trust them. Many had pursued this dark-complexioned and handsome man only to be left behind in sorrow. Tonight, though, he experienced a new feeling of loneliness and readily sat down at a table as the girl pulled her chair over close and clung to his arm.

The floor waiter, well trained to take advantage of the girl's lure, immediately arrived with two glasses and a quart of what he proclaimed to be "the best in the house." It probably all came from the same keg, Bryce knew, but this had been poured into an ornate, cut-glass bottle and possibly wasn't watered down.

Judith Basin Homestead

The mouthy little whore leaned on Bryce's shoulder as he slowly downed shot after shot, the girl obligingly making refills. Talking only enough to be amiable, he began to feel a glow and an uncaring feeling he had never experienced before. Each time he looked at the girl, her painted face appeared more and more lovely.

As the warmth of her young and scantily clad body pressed against him, he put his arm around her slender waist and pulled her close. Knowing the time was right, the girl whispered, "Why don't we go to your room?" He followed her, unsteadily, up the stairs as she held him by the hand and after some concentration, remembered where his room was. They entered and she immediately began untying his tie, unbuttoning buttons, and doing other things she was very adept at. He fell back on the bed and pulled her soft and yielding body to him. He felt the final uncontrollable spasms of climax and then the world whirled away from him in an eddy of spiraling darkness.

Mid-morning came in a hell of pounding temples and a convulsing stomach. His thirst and dry mouth clamored for water, but knowing if he arose to pour a glass, he would surely retch, Bryce could only lie there, moaning occasionally. He rolled onto his side facing the center of the room, where, if he vomited, he would do so on the floor. He noticed he was alone. The dance hall girl he had been so infatuated with last night was gone. Undoubtedly, she was resting up for another night and another victim. He didn't even know her name.

After what seemed like hours fighting spells of nausea and a never-ceasing headache, he finally felt well enough to struggle to a sitting position on the bed. He was able to down a few swallows of tepid water from the ewer on the night stand and hours later, washed and dressed, he unsteadily descended the stairs and entered the dining room. The waiter took Bryce's condition and undoubtedly hellish breath in stride as he took the order of oatmeal, toast ,and coffee.

Bryce struggled through breakfast and two cups of coffee, feeling better physically if not emotionally. He felt shame, but most of all, an inner panic at the knowledge that he had lost his hold on an heretofore iron self-control. Why this sudden feeling of worthlessness?

He moved to pay his bill, reaching into the pocket that held last night's winnings only to find it empty. Of course, what more should a fool expect? He knew he deserved this kind of treatment and heaped mental abuse upon himself. Telling the clerk to charge the meal to his bill, Bryce retired to the privacy of his room to inspect his money belt for solvency. As he found these funds untouched, Bryce muttered, "To hell with this town," and started packing his belongings.

With the money he received from the livery owner for his horses and rigging jingling in his pocket, Bryce stood on the depot platform waiting for the train east. He gazed about at the other passengers.

His temples still pulsing with little bursts of pain, he noticed an incredibly slender and dainty young lady sitting on a huge traveling bag against the depot wall. One tiny hand held a small ladies purse and the other clutched an umbrella neatly folded and tied. She was dressed in one of the fancy, black traveling dresses of the day with upper sleeves smartly puffed and fringed. Lacy, well starched frills cradled a delicate face accentuated by a saucy, impertinent nose. Her soft, brown hair was rolled into a bun with a large pin protruding.

As Bryce unabashedly gazed at this wonder, she abruptly turned and catching his eye, her lips curved in a faint smile. She turned away, leaving Bryce to wonder had he really seen those silver-gray eyes with flecks of deepest blue or was it just reflections from a now cloudless sky?

He boarded the train and walked down the aisle of the passenger car in time to see a Negro porter cramming the huge traveling bag into an overhead boot above the young lady's seat. As she patiently waited, he could see she must not stand much over five feet tall and her waist was so tiny that it could surely be completely encircled by his hands.

Taking a seat across the aisle and one row back, Bryce watched as she literally had to jump to attain her seat. The shiny, black, high-button shoes fell two inches short of the floor as she settled back and carefully spread out the folds of her skirt.

With a squeal of spinning wheels, the train pulled out, slowly gaining speed. The clickity-clack of wheels on rail settled into a steady staccato rhythm and Bryce found drowsiness creeping over his abused body. He slowly drifted off into a sound sleep.

A harsh and arrogant voice somehow penetrated Bryce's foggy mind and he struggled to awaken. Peering from beneath his lowered hat brim, he could see a big, ruddy faced man now seated next to the tiny lady.

"Now, it ain't no need to get all smartin' up at me. I'm just lookin' out for your welfare. A little lady like you just shouldn't be travelin' alone and Mike here is just the guy to take care of you. I'll just stay right here beside you and make sure no one bothers you."

"I do not need any primate like you protecting me," the diminutive lady snapped back, "now please move. Your repulsive firearm is chafing my side."

"Well, now, that there gun is what's gonna' protect you little lady, you shouldn't be makin' bad about it like that," the big man replied, obviously enormously enjoying the discomfort he was causing her.

Bryce had packed his gun belt away, not foreseeing any need for it on a peaceful train ride. He still carried the small caliber gun inside his jacket but it was not the weapon to be used in a draw down. Nonetheless, the rude actions of the big man could not be ignored.

Bryce was a lithe five foot nine of well-coordinated, cat-like muscle, but in the close quarters of a Pullman car he would be at a distinct disadvantage if this situation escalated to a brawl. Also, he was still weak and shaky from the prior night's foolishness. Knowing he was tactically in a bad position if the bully failed to back down, Bryce arose to stand in the aisle behind the crowded seat.

"The young lady asked you to move, mister, why don't you be the gentlemen and oblige her?" Bryce quietly asked.

"Oh, what have we here, a hero in black to rescue the fair maiden?" the ruddy faced man roared as he sprang to his feet with amazing agility, a sneer on his face.

Bryce knew immediately he had fallen into a well-staged trap. This brute of a man was of a familiar type—a breed who reveled in humiliating any one smaller than he, pounding those who failed to back down to a pulp. If Bryce had been armed, he knew this man would back down rather than risk a gunfight, turning the situation into a big joke instead.

But Bryce was not wearing a gun and he was aware that the bully knew this before he became obnoxious. The man was not as interested in the young lady as he was in provoking a fight where he could unleash his primitive instinct to dominate.

Without another word the bully snapped out a monstrous left fist at Bryce. Slipping the punch over his left shoulder, Bryce countered with two lefts to the face and a hard right to the ribs. The last punch thrown with all his power did not even evoke a grunt from the brute.

As he backed quickly away, Bryce saw the sneer on the scarred face and knew the man would be immune to pain. Only a fist or kick to the groin would affect this animal but Bryce noted he always kept one leg to the side, protecting his crotch. An old and experienced brawler.

As he gazed at this behemoth he had so foolishly challenged, he heard a sharp, clear voice call out, "Stop it you savages, stop this idiocy now!"

The little lady now stood on the cushion of her seat, umbrella clutched in a tiny right fist, her bright gray eyes sparkling in indignation.

Ignoring the lady's commands, the big man moved forward, maneuvering to trap Bryce in the small aisle now crowded with onlookers.

As Bryce backed against the mass of passengers, the big man lunged forward. A left jab peeled hide from his cheek, followed by a crushing right to the mouth. He felt his head reel and his knees buckle as he sank to the floor, the rocking of the Pullman only accentuating the feeling of vertigo.

He heard the big man roar, "Now, you damn half-breed, you're going to learn what it's like to screw around with Big Mike."

Through a haze, he could see the man drawing back his right leg as if to drive the point of his boot to the ribs. Bryce rolled to the left, his hand snaking under his jacket and exploding forth holding the little trick revolver. It was aimed right at the bully's chest.

Bryce heard a sucking of breath from the crowd as the bully slowly, lowered his leg, stepped back and poised a hand over his holstered gun.

There was a moment of silence before Bryce heard a swish and a black umbrella cracked across the bully's gun hand. As the man grabbed his wrist and turned to face the enraged little lady, the next blow caught him square across the bridge of the nose. He fell to his knees, blood spurting between the fingers which now clasped his nose as the conductor and porter shouldered their way through the crowd.

"What the hell's going on here?" the conductor bellowed, as he pointed a big military revolver, first at the bleeding "Big Mike" and then at Bryce. "Put the gun away mister," he ordered and Bryce nodded weakly, wearily replacing the revolver in its elastic sheath. "I should throw you both off the train," the conductor raged, "what do you say to that?"

"Just let me move to the furtherest car from this god damn little hellion and I won't give you no more trouble," the bleeding 'Big Mike' snorted nasally. "Just get me to hell out of here."

Holding a bandanna to his nose, a now tame, "Big Mike" followed the conductor down the aisle towards the car coupling.

Everyone returned to their seats, leaving Bryce on one elbow fighting back waves of nausea. Closing his eyes in misery, Bryce was feeling his battered lips when a small, gentle hand grasped his and slowly pulled it away to place a soft and sweet smelling cloth to his mouth.

"I declare, you males are so Neanderthal. What did you expect to accomplish by trading blows with that brute? What did you expect to gain by hurting him?"

"You're the one who bloodied him up, Ma'am," Bryce hoarsely replied.

"Yes, I know, and I probably prevented a killing," the little lady on her knees answered. "Now what's your excuse for this idiotic display of male egoism?"

"I was only trying to protect your honor, Ma'am," Bryce uttered lamely.

"As you can see, I don't need your help. You could have gotten killed or maimed for life and stop calling me Ma'am."

Helping Bryce to his feet, she led him to her seat and pushed him to the corner near the window. Sinking to her knees next to him, she examined the scuffed cheek and muttered to herself, "We'll have to trim the loose skin away and then clean it up."

"What are you ma'am, a doctor or nurse or something like that?" Bryce mumbled.

"I am none of those—a ma'am, doctor, or nurse—young man. I am Sandra Viola Millin. My father, Samuel, is a doctor and I've helped him patch up many a savage such as you. You may call me Viola or Miss Millin if you wish. You are a half-breed, aren't you?" she added.

As Bryce rolled his eyes in awe at this oration, Viola continued. "Of course, I suppose I'm a half-breed of sorts as my Scottish mother did marry a half-pint Welshman to sire me. I guess one mixed-blood human is no different from the other."

The porter arrived with a well-stocked first aid kit which Viola rummaged through and found a pair of surgical scissors. As she trimmed the flaps of skin from his abraded cheek, Bryce could see her warming up to more lecture so he quickly interrupted.

"Jesus, Miss Millin, do you always talk this much, or only when you have a helpless victim cornered?"

"Communication and the ability to communicate is the quality that defines civilization from primitiveness, sir, but that's not proper either, I should be calling you by your given name."

She looked at Bryce and he noted that her eyes really were steel gray with blue flecks.

"I'm Bryce Girouard and I'm pleased to meet you Miss Millin. You must be an only child, though, because you sure don't know much about men."

"I know plenty about men and who needs to know anything about savages? I have two brothers and I'm familiar with the crude ways of the male. Well, Calvin, anyway is kind of the wild, outdoor type who loves to shock me with his banal utterances. Harlow though, he's more refined and mannerly," Viola continued as she trimmed and salved wounds.

She finished her first aid and sat down beside him. Bryce found himself very curious about this vociferous little woman.

"Where did you learn to use the English language as you do?" he asked.

"Oh, we just were born to it, I guess," Viola replied "It runs in the family. My cousin, Edna, and I used to practice our prose and vocabulary on each other and we were always trying to out do the other's vernacular. Edna is a good poet and I'm not too bad at it myself."

The train clicked and rolled laboriously toward the summit of the Laramie Range, Bryce watching the pines along a clear, boisterous stream slip by, fearing any comment might set Sandra Viola Millin off on another one of her eloquent speeches.

Undaunted though, Viola again offered more of her life history. "I'm a degreed elementary school teacher, you know, and as such must have good command of the English language with all its nuances. How else are we going to foster future statesmen and scholars?"

After a short pause, when Bryce turned to her with a painful grin, she continued. "I'm also a summer actress. That's what I was doing in Laramie. The Woman's League of Voters hired me to bring some culture and refinement to their raw and wild city. They've succeeded in getting the woman's vote in Wyoming, you know. We believe woman should have the right to vote. Don't you?"

Bryce was on the verge of replying in the negative when he suddenly pictured Mama and sister Missy. What would they have been proud to hear him say? "Well, yeah, I guess so, Miss Millin, but how can you put on a play by yourself? Were there other actors and actresses there?"

"Heavens no, I'm not a dramatic, stage actress, I'm an impressionist and an elocutionist. I perform by myself."

"What's an elocutionist?"

"An elocutionist is a speaker who tells stories in a dramatic way. A good elocutionist can keep a crowd spellbound," Viola proclaimed proudly.

"I'll guarantee that you're a speaker all right," Bryce stated dryly.

Paying no attention to Bryce's sarcasm, Viola continued. "We had a big crowd in Laramie and I was well received. They demanded two curtain calls and insisted I stay for a second appearance. This is beautiful country, but what raw uncivilized settlements. But I suppose they will become more refined in time."

After a short pause, Viola turned to Bryce and said, "How impertinent of me, here I go on and on and I know nothing of you except that you are a valorous, if indiscreet, young man."

Although he found it difficult to start, Bryce soon related it all, from two children on the bayou to the present. When he painfully told the part about Missy, her wild, lavish ways and untimely death, Viola interrupted only briefly to say, "How tragic, I shall have to write a poem about it someday."

Bryce wondered why he had poured out his life story so easily to this diminutive stranger, but it came to him that it was much like how he and Missy used to talk openly to each other.

As the train chugged over the pass at Tie Siding, they stopped long enough to disconnect the "helper" engine and were soon rolling downhill through Buford and towards Cheyenne.

At Cheyenne there was an hour delay for changes in passengers so Bryce invited Viola to have lunch with him in the depot dining room. They walked across the platform, where Big Mike, with a huge bandage on his nose, turned away as they passed. Bryce knew that by now the arrogant man realized he had come within a whisker of dying. Maybe the incident would lead him to temper his ways.

As they lunched, Viola asked, "Surely you don't intend to continue gambling the rest of your life?"

"It's all I know, Miss Millin, and about all I've ever done. I don't think I could earn a living any other way."

"Oh, poppycock! A bright, young man like you can do anything he wants to do if he'll just set his mind to it."

"Like what?"

"You have to have extensive skills to be the successful gambler you are. You have to be able to know, understand and judge people instinctively. Those qualities could take you far in any of a number of vocations. You just have to convince your bull head that you can do it, if you will forgive the adjective."

Viola looked across the table with impertinence in her sparkling eyes and said, "I wish I could have you as one of my students. I know that together we could turn you into a diplomat, banker, or some other outstanding citizen. You see, I also have great ability at judging character. Trust me."

Bryce brooded on the insights of this saucy little woman beside him as the Union Pacific coasted downhill to the Great Plains of America. Across the miles of buffalo grass and down the South Platte River they rode on in idle conversation.

Bryce was amazed when Viola asked him to teach her to play poker and soon she was betting, drawing and bluffing like an old timer. Behind that mien of artistic tinsel was a rare intelligence and deepness of thought not immediately apparent.

Too soon, the train pulled into Kansas City and the commercialism of a large urban area. They stood in the huge lobby of the new Union Pacific depot, neither seeming to find the words that go with parting.

How can this be, Bryce thought, from a woman who had chattered incessantly for four days? Finally, it was Viola who opened a conversation.

"I shall want to write to you from time-to-time so where should I send your mail? I am going to cram you with culture and sage advice until the day you decide to leave the riverboats and gambling."

"I'll collect my mail general delivery at Memphis. It's a mid-point and a sure stop."

"Well, I'm going to expect you to come and see me someday in Bogard, Missouri. I live with my parents there and teach elocution at the Chillicothe Normal School during the winter terms. I also perform sometimes on the weekends and would be honored to have you come to a performance."

They both stood in awkward silence until Viola, in her first sign of failing composure, blurted out, "Well, if you expect me to kiss you good bye you will have to get me something to stand on. I know you would be embarrassed to bend down to my stature."

Bryce moved his war bag between them and Viola nimbly stepped up to put her arms around his neck. At the feel of the gentle, yet firm kiss upon his battered lips, he trembled with emotion.

Viola jumped back to the marbled floor, picked up her purse and ever-present umbrella and turned away. After several steps, she wheeled to say, "Now, you write, you hear? And please come see me."

Bryce could only nod and wave a feeble hand as she turned and walked away, not looking back.

Bryce salved his lack of speech with the thought that it didn't matter. Sandra Viola Millin was going to get in the last word anyway.

Bryce Girouard

Hoodoo Pony

CHAPTER VIII
REALITY & MATURITY

Back aboard the Cairo Queen, Bryce renewed old acquaintances and turned to the poker tables with a vengeance. At first all went well but he soon found the games boring and he would cash in early and retire to the bar. Night after night he went to his room where he faced loneliness, finding sleep elusive.

More and more he found himself retiring from the games early only to drink up his winnings in an effort to bring sleep upon retiring.

At every stop in Memphis he would find several letters from Viola, which he would hungrily digest. At first he answered each one but found it more and more difficult to respond until it was rare that he took the time. What do you write about when your life is a monotonous parade of unchanging activities?

The intimacy they had shared on the train was now lost to Bryce. How could he tell her of the continuous cycle of gambling, drinking, sometimes seeking comfort and companionship in the arms of a lady of the night or the lonely nights he lay awake trying to make sense of a life dulled by alcohol.

The months slipped by and Bryce grew to detest the card games, the smoke, noise and glitter of the casinos. Sometimes after arising he would just lean on the rail and watch the Mississippi countryside slip by. The fresh cool air stirred senses he had not realized were deep inside. Then his mind would flash back to the crisp, cool air of Montana.

At times, he could smell the sage and rabbit brush in bloom, see the gold of rolling hills, purple asters and snow capped peaks. The sparkling clear streams he had forded without a glance now came back so vividly that he could hear the bubbling of the falls and see the glint of morning sun on the ripples.

The Cairo Queen docked in Memphis one muggy mid-May day and Bryce turned towards the post office where he knew there would be the usual three or four letters from Viola.

His head pounded from a night of unusually heavy drinking as he asked for his mail, but instead of the usual three or four, the postmaster handed Bryce only one.

It was an unusually thick envelope with the familiar scrolled handwriting of Viola. Seating himself on the bench outside the post office, Bryce carefully opened the letter with his pen knife.

> *Dear Bryce,*
>
> *Even though I have not heard from you in over a month, I am writing you this one last time. I could tell as time went by that the closeness we shared on our train ride was leaving you.*
>
> *Your letters became more and more brief and more and more seldom as time passed and I could foresee the day when they would cease altogether. Knowing you must have found a new life without me in it, I am writing this last time to let you know I do care about you and how you are. However, if you do not reply, I will understand.*
>
> *I have thought of you though, and I have written a poem that I believe addresses all of our lives in this strange world. I hope you will understand its meaning and gain some useful message to aid you in years to come.*
>
> *I will remember, always,*
>
> *Love,*
> *Sandra Viola Millin*

Bryce sat in silence, staring at the inlaid brick sidewalk, trying to think. Oh why, wouldn't his pounding temples let his brain function! There had to be some answers. There had to be some sure, patented solution to all this. Damn last night's whiskey; damn the casinos he was trapped in; damn the whole world; and damn that silly poem. What good are poems? Nothing but silly drivel from immature, idealistic minds dwelling in fantasy land.

Bryce stood and started walking. He had to get away from all the humans, all the noise and smells of the city. How the hell could a man think with all the distractions?

He arrived at the levee on the river bank and turned up-stream until he was surrounded by cottonwoods, river and fresh air. The only sounds were the lowing of cattle and the faint clank, clank of their bells.

Shortly the levee ended at the base of a bluff. Bryce said in despair. "I can't go back. I just can't stand to go back."

He followed a deer trail up the bank, laboriously climbing the bluff. The exertion made his head pound viciously and he had to stop from time-to-time before reaching the crest.

On top of the bluff, sucking great draughts of air into aching lungs, Bryce looked at a serene and spectacular view.

Below him the broad Mississippi, now swelled with distant snow melt, drifted by. On the distant bank, wooded bluffs walked step-by-step upwards towards a green bench land, while behind him the mountain ranges of Tennessee reached upward in a haze. To his left, the burgeoning city of Memphis lay nestled beneath a haze of ever-present city pollutants.

Finding a grassy hummock, Bryce sat down and his pounding pulse subsided. Surprisingly, he found the pounding in his head receded as his breathing returned to normal. He actually felt quite well and could feel his mental faculties begin to come alive.

As he gazed down at the sparkling river, those persistent flash backs of his time in Montana began to recur. He could picture the main street of little Moccasin. Smell the sage, horses and hay and hear the sounds that traveled forever in the clear air. He relished the dark eyes of the shy, Indian children, especially the little one who had given him a poignant smile when he winked at her.

He again felt the kinship of Clayton McMahon as they were drawn together by the death of Missy and Clayton's invitation to join him at the C-Bar-M. Clayton had warned him that he couldn't gamble all his life, just as Viola had said.

Bryce removed the letter he had angrily crammed into his pocket, straightening the pages of message and verse. He held the poem in shaking hands and began to read:

THE FLEETING OF LIFE

For we are the same as our Fathers have been,
We see the same sights our Fathers have seen.
We drink the same stream, we view the same sun,
And run the same course our Fathers did run.

The thoughts we are thinking our Fathers would think,
From the death we are shrinking our Fathers would shrink;
To the life we are clinging, they also would cling,
But it speeds for us all, like a bird on the wing.

They loved, but the story we cannot unfold,
They scorned, but the heart of the haughty is cold.
They grieved, but no wail from their slumbers will come,
They joyed, but the tongue of their gladness is dumb.

They died, aye they died; and we things that are now,
Who walk on the turf that lays over their brow,
Who wake in their dwelling, a transient abode,
Meet the things that they met on their pilgrimage road.

Yea! Hope and despondence, pleasure and pain,
We single together in sunshine and rain,
And the smiles and the tears, the song and the dirge,
Still follow each other like surge after surge.

Tis the wink of an eye; tis the draught of a breath,
From the blossom of health to the paleness of death.
From the gilded salon, to the bier and the shroud,
Oh, why should the spirit of mortal be proud.
   Sandra Viola Millin   *May 6, 1883*[1]*

---

1   * Written by Sarah Viola Millay (McPherson) about 1900. The date has been altered to accommodate time of story.

Bryce sat in silence, his mind whirling in confusion. Suddenly, it all became clear. He must make some changes in his life. As his mother, before him, had done when she fled to the bayou country rather than be imprisoned on a reservation, he, now also, must leave this place, this life, and start anew.

He remembered that wild country fronting on the Rocky Mountains and the seemingly insignificant things that he had not noticed at the time. Yellow-eyed Brewers blackbirds picking insects around buffalo chips, the harsh caw of Clarks nutcrackers and the constant chattering of long-tailed magpies. Images of these, other birds, the deer, elk, antelope, wild mustangs and native people began to claw their way to the surface of his consciousness.

Yes, he would leave tomorrow for the C-Bar-M and a new life, whatever it might be, in a new land. First, letters to Viola and Clayton, then by river boat to Bismarck and Northern Pacific to Billings. Soon he would be home.

Bryce returned to the Cairo Queen, packed his belongings, and after saying good bye to Captain Rouse, disembarked. Loaded down with two big traveling bags and a small personal kit, he flagged a dray and headed for the center of the city where he checked in at the Southern Star hotel. Bryce felt more at ease than he had for months as he relaxed on the well-cushioned bed.

He suddenly awoke to the whistle of a departing paddle wheel. Bryce glanced at his watch. He had napped for over two hours and it was now past four o'clock in the afternoon.

He drained an extended bladder and washed up. Bryce discovered he was ravenously hungry and remembering he had not had any food since the previous day, headed downstairs to the dining room.

The meal of steak, spuds and salad tasted amazingly good and he had not enjoyed such a meal for many months. Bryce leaned back in his chair and savored the coffee as he cogitated on the things he must do before leaving.

The letter to Clayton McMahon in Montana would be easy. Straightforward and brief, but what to write, how to say it, and what to relay to Viola about his plans for the future left him in a quandary.

He got some hotel stationery from the desk clerk, returned to his table and began writing.

> *Dear Clayton,*
> *The statement you made when we parted company last fall about not being a gambler all my life has come home to roost.*
> *I no longer feel the challenge and excitement in a card game that I used to, in fact it has become boring. I guess the loss of Missy and my experiences in the West have changed my views and goals. It has been a long and lonely winter, Clay, and I now know I must seek a new life.*
> *Trusting that your generous invitation to the C-Bar-M still stands and that I am no longer wanted by the law, I will be leaving as soon as possible for Montana.*
> *I guess Montana became more a part of me than I realized and I am looking forward to returning.*
> *If all goes well, I will see you soon.*
> *Sincerely,*
> *Your brother-in-law, Bryce (Girouard)*

Re-reading the letter and finding it to his satisfaction, Bryce carefully folded it, placed it in the envelope and sealed it. He found himself struggling mentally with his next task and fought back the cold knot developing in the pit of his stomach. He so wanted just to say, I love you and miss you. Will you marry me? But she deserved better than that. Maybe a better man. Possibly, she had already turned her thoughts to someone else.

If so, he certainly deserved it. Bryce made three attempts to write the letter, only to crumple them up still at a loss for what to write.

He held his head in his hands and gazed at the red-and-white gingham tablecloth. Suddenly, he knew what he must do—go see her in Missouri before starting West. He must see her again, feel her hands on his cheek, feel again the tenderness of her kiss. He had to look again into those sparkling eyes and pour out his feelings, regrets, and penitence.

The final decision made the chore of answering her letter much simpler.

Dear Viola,

It is with shame and misery that I am finally responding to the many letters you have so faithfully written.

These winter months since we parted have been lonely and difficult for me. I've tried to convince myself that I am strong in myself and do not need anyone else near me.

I know now that I have been wrong. Everybody needs someone and has the responsibility to reach for that human contact that is so necessary in the pursuit of a whole life.

I have given up the gamblers life and now want very much to see you again. I will leave immediately for Missouri in the hopes that the invitation you extended is open.

The poem you sent is beautiful and had much to do with this decision.

I've missed you very much.

Love,
Bryce

Bryce boarded the packet, *Southern Star*, that evening and as the thumping, hissing engine propelled the fast little sternwheeler up the Mississippi towards St. Louis, he slept his first good night in months.

The broad Mississippi, now in full flood stage, tested the might of the Pierce steam engine and the skill of the helmsman as logs and other debris swirled down the swift and muddy currents.

Bryce stood at the rail the next morning, feeling an ease creep over him as the new greenery of the shore line passed by. He had boarded the *Southern Star* because she was reputed to be the fastest packet on the river, but against the swift current, it would take two full days to reach St. Louis, a one day trip on more placid waters.

His heart ached for the moment when he would again see Viola and he burned in remembrance of that tender kiss they had shared upon parting. Yet a wildness he could not explain kept nagging at him to go west by north until he reached that strange and beautiful country of the Judith Basin in Montana Territory.

As his mind sifted the many variables of the road ahead, he could not explain nor understand the powerful yearnings tugging at him; feelings he had never felt before seemed to beckon at a new person, dwelling within his body. He only knew he could not turn back and must follow his new life through to some meaningful conclusion.

The *Southern Star* moored at the teeming hub of St. Louis the afternoon of the following day and Bryce disembarked. He immediately headed to the ticket office of the "Great Mandan Shipping Company" where he booked passage on the *Bismarck Chief* for the next morning. He hailed a passing surrey to aid in the search for overnight lodging.

St. Louis was bursting at the seams with hotels and boarding houses, almost always full it seemed, but the surrey drivers knew which places had rooms and what other services were available.

The congenial and talkative old black man skillfully maneuvered the surrey through the hordes of humans, drays, riders and stray livestock as he shared his vast knowledge.

"What you all want, mister? The Gypsy Doll has good food, drinks, gamblin' and the best lookin' gals on the 'Sippi. They's usually full up but Ah knows the manager real well and Ah can always get a room for a gentleman like you."

Knowing these drivers got a tip from the hotel manager for every good customer they brought in, Bryce asked, "How much side money do you make if I book at the Gypsy Doll?"

"Why mister, Ah don't get nuthin'. Ah just like to see folks find good lodging. I'm just a kinda' hospitable, southern fella' that way," the black driver admonished in wide-eyed innocence.

"Yeah, I know," Bryce said, "but would five in gold get me a nice quiet room somewhere so I can get some sleep?"

"Oh! yassah, yassah, mister, I'll bet Mrs. Gurney has got a room at her boardin' house and she's the best cook in Louey."

Bryce handed the driver five coins and settled back as the surrey dodged and veered its way through the turmoil of St. Louis, the driver whistling gaily. At Mrs. Gurney's Board and Room, Bryce reminded the black driver to pick him up at nine o'clock the next morning and climbed the stairs to a huge verandah.

The room was indeed clean and quiet and the breakfast next morning that Mrs.Gurney provided had to have been formulated in heaven. Bryce speculated on what a little coin in the palm could do for a person's amenities as he waited for the surrey.

The *Bismarck Chief* was a huge side wheeler, broad of beam and shallow in draft. She was designed specifically to navigate the fast-flowing and ever-changing currents of the Missouri. As Bryce boarded, he noted the ship was loaded to full freeboard with commodities of all sorts.

Flour in broadcloth sacks, yardage in bales of twenty-four bolts each, machinery and hardware were neatly stacked, allowing only a narrow passage along the rails. The two huge Corliss twin lungers pounded in syncopation as they turned the massive paddlewheels against silty Missouri waters. The fertile bottom lands, now mostly flooded, slipped by as the *Bismarck Chief* relentlessly churned its way towards a distant Fort Benton.

Much cargo was unloaded at the many stops along the way and the coal firing the boilers was soon replaced by cord wood found neatly stacked at every port. The chore of providing cord wood for the ever-increasing river traffic kept Norse woodsmen employed along the Mississippi. Many became quite wealthy as they hired crews to do the cutting, skidding and piling of four-foot faggots.

Bryce collared the steward and questioned him about where he should disembark to find the shortest route to Bogard. The man said he had never heard of the place and he guessed Bryce would have to go to Kansas City and take a stage from there.

He probed his memory for the name of the other town Viola had mentioned and remembered the letter tucked away in his luggage. Bryce dug it out. Yes, there it was— Chillicothe.

The steward had never heard of Chillicothe either and Bryce was wondering what to do next when a portly man with a large mustache turned from the rail and said, "Chillicothe? That's a small town in northern Missouri near the Kansas border. There's a girl's normal school there. I had a niece went to school there once. She's teaching school in Nashville now."

"Do you know the shortest route to there from the river?" Bryce asked.

"Well, I never been there but it seems to me she left the river at a little town this side of Kansas City," the man ventured as he stroked his mustache in concentration. "I know she had to ride a stage quite a ways to get there though."

Bryce decided that he would just have to make inquiries at each stop until he got to the town the man mentioned. His excitement mounted as he neared a reunion with vociferous little Sandra Viola Millin.

The *Bismarck Chief* throbbed its way up the busy Missouri, stopping at every small town, or so it seemed to an impatient Bryce Girouard. At each stop he asked about a stage route to Bogard or Chillicothe.

Finally, at a fuel stop where the woodcutters loaded a huge pile of boiler fuel, Bryce approached a well-dressed man leaning against a piling and made the usual query.

"Bogard? Yeah, it's a little town northwest of here. There's a stage that leaves from Waverly, goes to Bogard, then to Chillicothe and then west to St. Joseph. Waverly is the second stop up the river from here."

Bryce's heart pounded in anticipation as he thanked the man and re-boarded. Soon now he would see Viola again. Was that fright or love that gnawed at his stomach? His head was spinning with doubts and questions. Was she still waiting? Did he dare face her? He only knew he had to see her, regardless of the outcome.

The Overland Stage rolled through the gentle Missouri countryside. Farm lands and newly cleared homesteads alternated with stretches of magnificent hardwood forest.

A pretty young blonde seated across from Bryce did her very best to attract his attention. Smiling as she caught his eye, sighing very audible sighs and constantly re-arranging her skirts did not evoke the attention she was accustomed to receiving—not from this dark and thoughtful young man.

Finally, throwing all proper etiquette aside, she asked, "Are you going far?"

Glancing up, Bryce realized that she was addressing him. "Only as far as Bogard," he replied.

"Bogard, why heavenly days, that's my home town. I'm returning from a shopping trip in St. Louis. What a coincidence. We'll both be getting off there. I must show you around our town. My father is president of the Bogard Trust and Realty Bank. You must meet him."

The young lady's face lit up as Bryce showed interest and for the first time looked directly at her with eyes dark as pools.

Aha, I have him now, the pretty blonde thought. Just give me time and I can capture them all. She basked in her wonderland of self-adoration.

Bryce asked, "Do you know the Millins?"

"Oh yes, the Millins. You must mean Doc Millin. He delivered me as a baby. He's delivered almost every baby in town the last twenty-five years. His son, Calvin, had an awful crush on me once, but he's just too wild and uncivilized for me so I spurned his attentions. It like to broke his heart, but a girl has to be careful, you know."

Bryce interrupted the drivel to ask, "Can you tell me where they live?"

"Oh, they live about a mile north of town, right on the stage road. Just tell the driver where you want off and he will stop for you. Are you a relative of the Millins? Fine, fine family, even though a little rural."

"Thanks and I hope to be a relative someday," Bryce replied, "I'm Viola Millin's fiancé."

The smiling blue eyes suddenly turned cold as the blonde swung her head to look out at the countryside. How could this handsome young man be so attracted to a skinny little intellectual like Viola Millin? The spinsterly little school teacher with all the big words and many characters.

"Well, I certainly never figured that skinny little Millin girl would ever attract a man, but I suppose these intellectuals know how to work a man's desires once they set their minds to it," the blonde announced with finality, becoming more upset as time passed without any response from Bryce.

The stage stopped briefly in the small town of Bogard where the blonde and several huge trunks departed. Bryce noticed with vague interest the fancy surrey driven by a uniformed driver as it rolled over to the boardwalk in front of the blonde egoist and her luggage.

Leaning out of a window, Bryce asked the stage driver to stop at Doc Millins and receiving a nod of understanding, he settled back in his seat.

His stomach was again cold and knotted as the stage screeched to a halt and the driver bellowed, "This is the Doc's place."

How could a cool gambler such as he, who never felt this way even when confronted with possible gun play, now ache with such doubt and apprehension? Catching his war bag and slinging it over his shoulder, Bryce picked up the small overnight case and turned to the huge house before him.

A white picket fence, lined with a profusion of spring flowers, circled the huge, white-trimmed gray house. White railings encased a large verandah and stairs leading up to the front door. Above, ornate carved wood decorated high gables.

As Bryce neared the gate, a young man of slight build and sandy hair came around the corner of the house, hollering, "Just a sec and I'll get the gate." He sprinted to flip the latch.

Bryce felt himself being sized up as the young man held the gate open for him.

"You must be that Bryce guy Viola's been writing to. Huh?"

Sensing the testiness in the young man, Bryce replied calmly, "Yes, I'm Bryce and you must be her brother Calvin that she's spoken to me about. She shows great affection for you and her family."

Before Calvin could reply, the oaken front door banged open and a tiny whirlwind of percale dress, long curls and flushed face raced down the steps towards Bryce.

"Oh Bryce, I knew you'd come! I've been waiting since your letter. I knew you'd come. I knew you'd come." Viola cried as she jumped up to throw her arms around Bryce's neck. She pulled her cheek up to his with such unrelenting grip that he was forced to drop his bags and clasp her by the waist to ease the strangle hold.

Viola turned her head to look at Calvin and said, "See Cal, I told you so. I told you he would come to me someday. You just don't know Bryce like I do."

Bryce lowered Viola to the ground. She clutched his hand and pulled him towards the house, unmindful of the hostility Bryce recognized in a sullen Calvin.

"Come in and meet my mother and grandparents."

Mother Roxanne was a trim, neat-appearing lady, her silver-gray hair tied with a blue ribbon so that it hung down her back. Her ankle-length dress with tight bodice and lacy sleeves was fronted by a flour-tinged apron.

She welcomed Bryce with a smile and a hug and he felt the closeness between mother and daughter as he was proudly presented. The uneasiness he felt after meeting Calvin melted away in the warmth of this lady.

"I'm so pleased to meet you, Bryce. Viola has chattered constantly about you since she returned from Wyoming and now I understand why. She shows excellent taste in her choice of a man friend."

Bryce should have blushed, but did not. It all seemed to come natural in the midst of this frank and unabashedly honest family. He immediately saw the precise and articulate poise of Viola in her mother.

Over a cup of coffee, Viola plied Bryce with questions about his activities since they had parted. Not able to divulge all, he nonetheless did quite honestly describe the loneliness, drinking and disillusionment with a gambler's life. He noted the sudden shadow that passed over Viola's face as she looked away when Bryce mentioned his intention to return to Montana to find a new life.

It was apparent that Viola had shared her deepest feelings with her mother as Roxanne looked at her daughter in sudden concern and compassion.

Bryce understood there was more to this reunion than just a meeting of old friends. He felt a pang of regret at the pain his reckless ramblings had wrought. He also knew they had to be alone soon so he could bare his true feelings.

Viola jumped up in feigned cheerfulness to say, "We have plenty of time to gossip later. Let me show you to your room. You must be tired after that long stage ride."

She preceded him up the wide, hardwood staircase and led him down the second floor hall to a sunny room in the east dormer.

"This used to be brother Harlow's room before he and Eva married, so it's male friendly. Make yourself at home," Viola said in more formal tones.

"There's a bathroom down at the other end of the hall where you can freshen up. When you feel up to it, please come down so I can introduce you to Grandma and Grandpa. You'll love them, I know," she said as she stood small and forlorn at the head of the staircase.

Emotions, including panic, rushed through Bryce as he tried to make sense of all the mental confusion. Hell, he was just a backward bayou boy again, ill prepared to cope with the intricacies of love, romance and possible marriage. He'd never been in love before. He'd never even had a childhood infatuation. Forced into maturity so suddenly when he and Missy found themselves alone, he had missed out on a stage of youth normally experienced by others.

Washed, shaved and changed to clean clothing, Bryce reluctantly descended the stairs.

Viola and her mother were still sitting at the dining room table when Bryce re-entered the room. They both flashed him a ready smile but he did not miss the redness around Viola's eyes, nor the hanky, hastily wadded up and shoved under the edge of a cut glass fruit bowl in the center of the table.

Viola quickly arose and clasping Bryce's hand in hers said, "Come and meet Grandpa David and Grandma Joy. You'll love them. They have their own little house out near the horse meadow. Grandpa is a Presbyterian minister. He used to ride the circuit throughout Missouri, but he's retired now and only preaches as a guest or substitute. He has married hundreds of young folks in this country and baptized many babies."

As she rattled on, Viola gripped Bryce's hand tightly as if he might break free and run. Mother Roxanne followed them out the back door and across a flower bordered backyard, which Bryce recognized as a show of emotional support for Viola.

The grandparents lived in a neat little English-style cottage, white with red trim. Planter boxes of multi-colored petunias and geraniums hung under each window and the flagstone walk was neatly bordered by sweet william and other colorful plants.

They were typical elderly Scots. Trim and lean, straight of posture, well groomed and although the clothing was worn, it was neat and clean.

Grandmother Ross's white hair was neatly rolled into a bun on the back of her head over those same blue-gray eyes that sparkled in Viola.

Grandfather Ross's was as white haired but thinning to little wisps on top. As if to compensate, he sported a huge white mustache, stained brown where it hung over the upper lip.

Bryce thought, I'll bet he spits Spark Plug out and sucks coffee back in through it. Such a tinge just doesn't come naturally.

The grandparents were just as warm and friendly as Roxanne, and Bryce enjoyed the visit immensely. Everything went famously until the Reverend Ross made a comment.

"I've married one of my grandsons and I'd sure like to say I also married my granddaughter. I'm an expert at those things you know. Done a few in my time."

Viola made light of the situation by giving her grandfather a big hug and asking they be excused so she could show Bryce around the small farm.

Typical of Missouri farms, the place was not big, but fertile soil and ample moisture provided lush, green pasture and hay fields. A small stream meandered across the pasture and into a concrete milk house where the cold water kept milk, cream and buttermilk fresh.

A business-like Viola led Bryce around the grounds. She did not hesitate to gather in her skirts to bare shapely little legs as they vaulted the small stream. "And these are father's pride and joy," Viola proudly announced as she displayed two magnificent bay horses. Long of leg and bright of eye, they readily came to the white rail fence.

"They're called Tennessee Walkers and they trot in single step fashion. Dad uses them to pull his medical buggy. They can go at their own pace all day without tiring and they draft very smoothly, not jerky like a trotter."

As Bryce stroked the smooth and shiny necks, Viola said, "Father took the stage to Kansas City for a seminar and won't be back until tomorrow night. Why don't we hitch up Cicero here and drive into town tomorrow? Mother needs some groceries and I can show you around that way."

Bryce readily agreed for it gave him a chance to be alone with Viola.

He awakened after a restless night to sun streaming through the open window. Robins chirped and mocking birds echoed back in their own melodious fashion.

During a bountiful breakfast, where Viola and her mother chattered away continuously, Bryce felt the hostility in Calvin as he detached himself from the conversation. When through eating, he quietly excused himself and left the group as Roxanne's concerned eyes followed her son out the door.

Although he was at the barn doing chores as Viola and Bryce hitched Cicero to the buggy, Calvin stayed detached and aloof. Viola appeared not to be concerned, but she couldn't hide the occasional quick glance of rebuke she directed at him.

The short ride into town went smoothly as the single stepper moved with amazing speed and grace. Viola prattled on ceaselessly and although this was the one-on-one, situation Bryce had hoped for, he just couldn't find the words to start, even though he wanted to tell this charming creature that he loved her and how much he wanted her. He cursed his backwoods heritage and inexperience with the opposite sex as they entered the only street of Bogard.

They shopped for groceries and a few hardware supplies at Gaines Mercantile, where Viola proudly introduced Bryce to Charlie Gaines, then strolled down the boardwalk. Viola pointed out shops and places of interest.

She spoke to everyone they met but offered no more introductions and they were soon at the end of the business district where she directed Bryce across the street for the return trip.

They had just completed the tour of Bogard and were standing in front of the Bogard Trust and Realty Bank when a syrupy, sweet voice called out, "Why, hello, Bryce. How are you today? I want you to know how much I enjoyed our trip together from Waverly. We had such an interesting conversation. Oh, hello, Viola. And how are you today?"

Turning in unison, Bryce and Viola faced the simpering blonde before them. She was dressed in spring finery of pink and carried a matching parasol.

Viola remained notoriously quiet as Bryce touched his hat brim and stammered "How do you do ma'am, nice to see you again."

As the smirking blonde stood coyly smiling at Bryce, Viola finally replied, "Hello, Coreen and how are you? Have you picked any pockets today to buoy up your father's investments?"

The blonde's rouged cheeks paled in anger as Bryce, suddenly gathering his wits, reached for Viola's elbow. With a "Nice to see you again Miss Coreen" he propelled the rigid little body off the boardwalk and across the street towards the waiting horse and buggy.

Bryce placed a hand under each arm and literally tossed her onto the black leather seat. He crossed to the other side and clambered to the seat beside Viola and picked up the reins.

"So you and Coreen Jones had a pleasant trip from Waverly, did you?" hissed a furious Viola. "Apparently she completely captivated you with her mewing and cooing. No wonder you aren't interested in our relationship any more. You're just another unconscionable lady's man. Well, you don't fool me now."

"Good God, Viola, she started the conversation. All I did was ask her for directions to your house when I found out she was from Bogard. I didn't even tell her my name. She must have read it from my luggage."

"Oh sure, she really forced herself on you didn't she? And you were just an innocent pawn in the grasp of a designing woman. Honest to God, Bryce, how stupid do you think I am?"

She was really getting wound up and Bryce, not knowing how to respond, just sat in the seat looking down at the harness.

As she sucked in her breath for further diatribe, gunshots rang out from across the street. A drunken young man astride a startled horse whooped and blasted into the air in front of Bogard's only saloon.

The startled horse began bucking across the street as the drunken rowdy continued his rampage. Completely out of control now, the terrified mount slammed into Doc Millins's prize Tennessee Walker and then crow hopped on down the street.

Bryce yelled after the drunk, "Hey, you crazy son-of-a-bitch, what the hell do you think you're doing?"

The drunken bronco buster had his hands full with a spooked horse and continued down the street hanging onto an extremely mobile saddle horn unaware of the words Bryce had thrown after him.

"My, what an outburst of gutter language," Viola remarked as Bryce calmed the prancing horse and slapped the reins to start him down the street.

"I suppose if I had said, 'Desist you dastardly cad, you are indeed a scoundrel,' that he would have immediately come back to apologize," Bryce responded sarcastically.

"I don't see him coming back to apologize after the tirade you just directed at him."

"No, but if we were face-to-face, he'd have understood my language," Bryce said. "I was only speaking down to his level."

"That may be so, Bryce, but you were speaking below your level. That's where my concern lies. Hank Jackson is an illiterate savage. Everyone in town knows that, but you are capable of a more genteel nature if you would just try," Viola hotly declared.

Bryce just looked skyward and muttered, "Oh, Dear Lord."

"Don't look to the Lord for assistance. I'm sure He would agree with me and would undoubtedly render harsher judgment than I."

Knowing there was no way he could out-debate this tiny, mobile dictionary, Bryce just grimaced at Viola and said, "Yes, dearie."

"Dearie? Well! That's a term of affection usually reserved for betrothed or soon-to-be betrothed lovers. I suppose I could honor the pronoun if it were accompanied by a proposal of marriage from you," Viola rattled on.

Good Lord, Bryce thought, the more I open my mouth, the more she pours it on me. One minute I'm a scoundrel and the next minute she's proposing. Is she really serious?

After a rare moment of silence, Bryce gathered his wits and turning to Viola said, "Any man would be proud to have a beautiful and talented lady like you as a wife, Viola, but I don't know how long he could endure the unrelenting pressure to change him from what he is. It seems that if a man was willing to accept you with your sometimes strange ways and your constant prattle that it should work both ways."

Bryce felt a sudden pang of regret for his words as he looked at the once saucy head, now bowed in silence and the tiny hands mercilessly twisting at a lace hankie.

Before he could say a word of atonement, Viola reached over and took his hand, squeezing it tightly with her own trembling hand.

"You are right, Bryce, I have been terribly uppity and callous of your feelings. I'm so sorry and I realize you are right. No marriage will work if either cannot accept and love the other for what they are and not what they fantasize them to be."

They rattled on down the country road in silence, hands still entwined, the bay now settled down to a steady pace.

Suddenly Viola said, "Bryce, please stop. Can we pull up in the shade of that big tree? Please?"

He reined the bay in under a magnificent pin oak and Viola turned to rise on bended knees beside him. Putting her arms around his neck, she placed a tear drenched cheek against his and held him close, the small body shaking uncontrollably.

"I lost you once and now I've driven you away again. I'm a small person, I guess. All but my mouth, it just keeps rattling away and I don't seem to be able to control it, even when I know I'm wrong. I was so blind that I couldn't see how kind and sensitive you are and how my words could hurt," she sobbed.

Bryce pulled her to him and placed her head on his chest, gently kissing her soft and sweet-smelling ringlets.

"I'm the one who was too blind to know the truth when we first parted. I was too insecure to turn loose of my old life style. I had to learn it the hard way and it was an extremely difficult education. I know I've hurt you these last months apart and I know now that I love you dearly. I don't want to spend the rest of my life without you, Viola, and I am asking you to be my wife," Bryce found himself softly saying.

She did not answer but pushed herself against his chest, the sobbing increasing.

"Please, don't feel bad. If you cannot accept marriage to a bum like me, I'll understand."

"I'm crying be ... be ... because I'm ha ... happy dear. We ... we females are si ... si ... silly that way I g ... guess," Viola blubbered.

Bryce pushed her head up and gazed into a tear-streaked but smiling face. He tugged the twisted hankie from a trembling hand and began to gently wipe away the tears.

Viola gazed up at him. "You big softy, give me that hankie, those aren't all my tears on your face,"

As she began to dab at his face, Bryce had to admit that he had shed tears—something he had not done since a child.

After both cheeks were reasonably dry, Viola leaned back, arms still around Bryce's neck and studied his face.

"Oh, how I love you and need you," she said.

He drew her to him and kissed her softly. She returned the kiss and another before placing her head on his shoulder.

At a mocking, "Whoo, whoo, Viola's got a beau, Viola's got a beau," they turned toward the road, where two young boys sat astride huge draft horses. Big smiles stretched across their freckled faces.

"Mark and Lanny, you be good now and just mind your own business," Viola called, laughing. "They're the Martin boys, the little brats," she added as the boys rode hooting down the road and out of sight.

She continued clinging to Bryce and he could clearly feel firm young breasts against his chest. His arms around her waist revealed a sinewy and vibrant body, warm and alive.

Strange feelings of passion, hot, yet tender, coursed through him as his hands caressed soft rounded buttocks.

Holding him close, Viola breathed, "Oh, Bryce, we've such an adventure in store for us. I've always dreamed of a love like you, children, a home and old age together. We must be patient though, my dear. The good things in life elude those who are reckless."

As she gently pushed herself away, Bryce savored a warmth in his heart for this little lady who had awakened his first feelings of true love. He felt grateful for this new emotion and knew he could wait. Would be proud to wait.

Bryce held the spirited horse in check to lengthen the ride back, Viola clinging to his arm, her head on his shoulder.

"I know I dismayed you and your mother when I rambled on about the beauty of Montana and how I longed to return there," Bryce said. "I did not mean it to sound as though I was excluding you from my life. I guess I just got ahead of myself. When I said those things, I had visions of you by my side."

"What you are saying is that you still intend to go back to Montana but you want to go back as Viola Millin's husband. Why certainly.

When I marry, that means I will follow my husband to his destiny, wherever that may be."

Bryce squeezed the little hand on his sleeve.

"I've never had dreams of staying all my life in drab little Bogard,. I've always dreamed of teaching where my skills would be most needed. Someplace where what I can offer will have an impact on the future of our nation. Montana sounds like the perfect place for me to be. Of course, I'll leave here for Montana with you. We must hurry and tell my family. Oh, I'm so excited, and they'll be so happy for me."

"What about Calvin?"

"Yes. Calvin! Well, he told me last night that he wasn't going to have his sister marrying any half-breed and I assured him that it didn't look like there would be a marriage. Now, I'll need to have a talk with him, but don't you worry, I can handle Calvin. He's really a nice boy, but you can't blame him for looking out for his only sister."

As Bryce and Viola entered the kitchen arm in arm, Roxanne looked up from the bread dough she was kneading and her face lit up with a warm smile as she and Viola's eyes met.

The inscrutable ability to communicate that epitomized this family left Bryce in awe. Roxanne knew in that brief exchange of looks that things had gone well for her daughter and there was a wedding in the offing. Without a word she approached and with floury hands, embraced the two.

Wedding plans evolved amid the female chattering of three generations as Granddad Ross beamed with pride. He was going to see his wish become reality. He would survive to perform the marriage of his only granddaughter.

The plans were interrupted by sound's from the living room and a voice calling out, "Roxy, I'm home."

"Daddy!" Viola squealed, bolting from the room. She returned, arm-in-arm, with a man only slightly taller than herself.

Dr. S. P. Millin was a stocky man with curly, graying hair and rosy cheeks. He smiled broadly as he extended a hand to Bryce. "Well, I finally get to meet the young man my romantic daughter has been incessantly chattering about," he said with the same openness that seemed to pervade the family.

"So, she finally snared you did she? Are you ready to put up with the never-ending prattle that I've endured all these years?"

Bryce only grinned as Viola squeezed her father's arm, a pink glow on her face. She clearly enjoyed the laughter of the other family members.

That evening, as Viola and her mother still discussed marriage, Calvin again silently disappeared.

Rising from the supper table, Dr. Millin said, "Let's leave these ladies to their big plans, Bryce, and get to know each other better."

They walked to the corrals where Bryce and his future father-in-law leaned on the rails to stroke the glossy coats of the Tennessee Walkers.

"We're all so glad for Viola and also for you, as you undoubtedly care deeply about each other. We do want your marriage to be a happy lifetime experience," Dr. Millin said.

"Thanks for accepting me into the family. I do love Viola very much and will never do anything to hurt her. We've already hurt each other, but we now understand one another better for it. We believe we're ready for marriage," Bryce said.

"Yes, you both seem to have attained the maturity necessary for a successful marriage but there are some things newly weds need to know. Simple things, but things that can seriously impact a marriage if not treated properly."

As Bryce puzzled over where this was leading, Dr. Millin continued, "Do you know what the hymen is, Bryce?"

"No, I guess not."

"Well, you've probably heard of it as a maidenhead or when some uncouth youth bragged about getting into some virgin as breaking her cherry," the Doctor rambled on easily.

Good God, Bryce thought, doesn't this family shrink from any subject?

The silence on Bryce's part seemed to alert Dr. Millin to the embarrassment. "I don't mean to shock you, Bryce, but remember, I'm a doctor and I discuss these things with patients all the time. Her mother and I have discussed this with Viola and she is prepared for your first night together, but it will take the knowledge of both of you to make things turn out right."

Feeling more at ease, Bryce said, "So what should I know?"

"The hymen is a membrane that obstructs the female vagina in virgins. Some have them and some don't. Some are tough and painful to break and in such cases patience and gentle stretching is the proper way to proceed. It may take several days or a week to allow for normal relations but brutal and hurried penetration can so traumatize a bride that she may never recover emotionally. Such a trauma can seriously damage or even destroy a marriage."

"Is this always the case?" Bryce asked.

"Oh no," the Doctor continued, "some virgins have very little hymen. Others have none at all. They may have broken it in an accident or during physical activity. We did not intrude on Viola's privacy so we don't know how she is, but she is aware of possible conditions and is now ready to cope with it."

"What about prostitutes?" a confused Bryce asked. "Are they some of those who never had a hymen?"

"Oh no, Bryce. Many of those unfortunate girls have been brutally introduced to sex at a young age through rape and incest. The life-long trauma that I spoke of earlier is evident in these tragic cases. They are so emotionally damaged that they cannot function as a wife, mother and homemaker."

After a pause, Dr. Millin added, "Our supposed civilized society can be very savage and primitive at times. We brutalize our children and then call them whores and urchins."

Bryce studied the scene before him with unseeing eyes, deep in thought. The embarrassment had faded to be replaced with respect—respect for the loving, intelligent and candid family he was marrying into. He recalled the little saloon girl in Laramie and others who had given away their bodies to him. Bryce had always felt a tenderness towards these unfortunate outcasts of civilization and he now understood more about the backgrounds of those often times terribly young girls.

He vowed then and there that no child of his would be exposed to the horrors of physical, sexual or emotional abuse.

As the good doctor and Bryce continued their silent meditation, Viola's voice called from the back door where she stood side-by-side with Calvin. "Father, we have some questions only you can answer. Will you come in please?"

As Bryce and Dr. Millin turned towards the house, Calvin walked out to meet them. When they came abreast of one another, he extended a hand to Bryce and said, "I guess I've been kinda' standoffish Bryce, and Viola says I must get to know my future brother-in-law. I do love her dearly and want the best for her, but I had no right to pre-judge you. She told me how you got badly beaten defending her honor and the sorrow you've endured in the tragic death of your little sister. I know how fortunate I am to still have my sister and just can't envision losing her. It would devastate me."

The two strolled toward the meadow in silence, Bryce struggling to overcome the emotions stirring inside.

"To lose Viola would devastate anyone who has ever known her," Bryce said in a trembling voice, "I love her dearly and will never do anything to hurt her. As you probably know, we will be traveling to Montana to start our new lives together, but we are not leaving you folks behind. We must keep in touch through the mails. And with the new rail systems being built, frequent visits will be very possible."

"Well, you might very well find me following you out west, Bryce. I really don't have any roots here and I'm a lousy farmer," Calvin said. "Harlow and Eva are the farm folks of the family and will carry on here when Mom, Dad and Grandfather can no longer handle things. I just haven't decided where I belong. Maybe I'll find it further west."

We'll get in touch as soon as we're settled and you will always be welcome. Our first child will need an uncle nearby to tell the tall tales every child loves to hear," Bryce said and the two shared a hearty laugh.

Viola Millin

C-Bar-M Ranch

CHAPTER IX
SURPRISES

The wedding took place on an absolutely magnificent spring day in the little Presbyterian Church in Bogard.

Reverend Ross beamed with pride as he performed the ceremony that united his only granddaughter to the dark and handsome man of only recent acquaintance. Brother Harlow and his beautiful wife, Eva, served as best man and maid of honor and their little daughter, Frances, tagged behind as flower girl.

Bryce had only known Harlow and Eva for two days but they readily accepted him into the family with warmth and understanding. Harlow took the time to ease Bryce's apprehensions prior to the ceremony by telling of his own fright and how he mixed up the wording of the vows. Eva laughed as she carried on the story and imitated Harlow's jumbled wording.

After a bountiful reception at the Millin farm, the newlyweds boarded the stage for St. Joseph amid torrents of tears, hugs and best wishes.

Viola's luggage included the huge trunk that contained her stage costumes. She was emphatic that culture be introduced to the raw wilds of central Montana. Bryce had also observed the text books she slipped into her luggage and grinned helplessly at the stage driver who groaned in disbelief at the volume and weight.

The stage rumbled towards St. Joseph as the young lovers, unmindful of the humor displayed by the other passengers, clung tightly to each other.

That first night in the New Yale Hotel was one of awkward exploration, discovery and understanding. Morning found two entranced and sleepy honeymooners aboard the *Piegan Princess* steaming up the wide Missouri River.

Each night in their lavish stateroom brought Viola and Bryce closer together as they continued to build upon and relish their new relationship. Bryce was completely captivated by his bubbly little wife and the constant love and attention she lavished on him. She was quick to tease and flirt with him one minute—loving him the next. The lonely, pointless years as a professional gambler faded into obscurity as he experienced a sense of rebirth.

On the fourth day, the *Piegan Princess* docked in Bismarck, Dakota Territory, and the Girouards checked in at the Grand Western Hotel, a huge and beautiful building constructed by the Northern Pacific Railroad Company to serve the masses of humanity now streaming westward.

The Grand Western bulged at the seams as salesmen, whiskey drummers, cattle buyers, miners, thieves—they and many others jammed together in Bismarck, waiting for seats on the overloaded rail passenger service.

The desk clerk of the Grand Western forlornly informed Bryce that the only room he had left was the bridal suite and it was quite expensive. His face broke into a smile when informed they were, indeed, newlyweds and would be pleased to have the suite. Bryce scooped Viola in his arms and carried her, giggling, up the wide stairway to the second floor suite. As he proceeded down the hall, Viola whispered in his ear, "Honey, we can't afford the bridal suite."

Bryce just laughed and said, "Now that you're my wife I guess I should tell you of our money belt. I've been saving my poker winnings for some time, converting them to bank notes and storing them in the belt. I don't know how much is in there, but I'll wager there's enough. If we run low, I'll just sit in on some poker game and replenish our roll."

"Oh no you won't! I'm not taking any chances on a relapse. I hear gamblers are just like alcoholics and I'm not gambling on losing you to lady luck." Viola stood defiantly before him on the plush carpet of the bridal suite.

Bryce responded with a twinkle in his eye, "A well-loved man isn't apt to stray away to lady luck. What do you say to that, Mrs. Girouard?"

"That sounds like blackmail to me but I suppose, if the lady was wildly in love with the man and just couldn't wait to feel his hands caressing her bare body, it would be a mutually pleasurable agreement," Viola whispered in his ear.

He swept her up and carried her to the ornate bed, gently laying her down, teasing, "I love you, you intellectual little hussy."

The three days of waiting for passage on the Northern Pacific were wonderful and happy times for the newlyweds as they loved, finding the closeness and intimacy that is unique in those truly bonded to each other for life. They lay in each other's arms and openly bared their hearts and souls—each childhood fear, nightmare, each long, lonely night waiting for the relief daylight would bring; those times during puberty when their bodies cried out for something they did not understand and the doubts that they were loved by anyone. The three days and nights welded the young union of passion into a firm, lifelong commitment to each other.

The fourth day found them traveling westward across endless miles of waving buffalo grass. Towns became fewer and fewer. Farms graduated to ranches and ranches became farther and farther apart. Viola bubbled with excitement as herds of antelope loped beside the chugging steam locomotive, only to race away and leave the train far behind whenever they wished.

"It's unbelievable. I didn't know anything could run that fast," she exclaimed.

Herds of elk began appearing and Bryce kept a sharp eye open for the possibility of seeing a herd of buffalo, although he realized that they had just about disappeared from the west.

Across the rolling grasslands of the Dakotas and the Makoshika badlands—where renegade redmen still hid out, stubbornly resisting the white man's efforts to herd them onto reservations—the Northern Pacific barreled down newly-laid tracks to the wide Yellowstone Valley, then southwest toward the distant snow capped peaks, lush basins, cold rushing streams, multi colored rim rocks and spires of the Rockies.

As they passed Pompey's Pillar, the conductor explained how Captain Clark had camped there and scratched his name in the ancient stone. Viola had an insatiable thirst for knowledge and constantly plied Bryce with questions he could not answer. He explained his brief and rapid trip through this country had not allowed for absorption of local history. He did explain though, how the area had etched smells, sounds, sights and impressions forever in his consciousness and how they had come back to haunt him at some of his most lonely times since leaving.

Too soon for Viola, the ride west ended in the young cattle and rail town of Billings. Bryce marveled at the growth since his furious ride west less than two years prior. A brand new "Custer Hotel" welcomed them with promises of the "Softest Beds and the Best Food" this side of Chicago. The Girouards settled in and shortly were testing the veracity of this boast.

As Bryce held his wife's warm and yielding body close to him in peaceful relaxation, he remarked, softly, "Well, the bed is pretty much as they said it would be, but we've yet to test their food, honey. Love needs sustenance too, you know."

"Just like a man, to love a lady and then clamor for food, your two most important staffs of life," Viola quipped, as she held him close. "Please, can we stay like this a bit longer till a well-loved wife catches her breath?"

Bryce responded by nibbling at a small ear and tenderly kissing soft eyelids.

Bathed and changed, they later descended to the dining room as Viola explained how the days became longer when you chased the sun westward. Bryce had to agree that something was stretching his growling stomach beyond usual meal times.

They settled into their chairs, facing a red and white gingham table cloth and Bryce scanned the hotel dining room.

A huge walnut counter under a ceiling-high mirror decorated the entire south wall. Checkered table cloths and napkins were neatly stacked upon the shiny surface with clear water glasses and china cups also neatly stacked to each side.

As he studied the neatness, Bryce noticed a slender, dark-skinned girl with dark hair and eyes standing on tip-toe to reach the napkins. Counting out four, she silently hurried to a recently vacated table, folded the napkins into a point around silverware and hurried back to the bar where she again strained on tip-toe to reach for glasses.

Forgotten memories from long ago stirred in his mind as he mulled over how much this little girl reminded him of Michelle. Not only in looks but also in actions, this little girl brought on a rush of feeling and pain as he recalled Missy playing on the verandah and dock at their home on the bayou. A love he thought was scarred and callused beyond recall was once again a hemorrhaging wound.

The little girl, no older than ten or eleven, walked by, casting a shy glance at Bryce and Viola. When Bryce caught her eye, he could not suppress the tender smile that automatically came to his face. The busy little set-up girl quickly looked away, a quick flush of embarrassment tinting her cheeks.

Viola was busy studying the menu when the girl again passed by their table, an act that Bryce noticed took her out of direct line to the table she was setting up. She again shyly and solemnly glanced at Bryce.

He suddenly remembered the shy little Indian girl at St. Xavier and how his wink had evoked that winsome smile he could not forget. The smile and wink he now offered this girl did not disappoint as she smiled in return before scurrying away, the pink again rising on her cheeks.

Viola, looking over her menu said, "Why you old flirt, I saw that. On your honeymoon and you just can't resist playing up to the ladies. What a Casanova I married."

Finding his own cheeks reddening, he looked away, stammering, "Well, a guy just don't know when he'll need a lady friend, and ... and." By now he felt he was in deep doo doo so he lamely continued, "She looked so kind of lonely out there and working so hard, I just thought a little wink wouldn't hurt none."

"I know, darling," Viola said as she reached for his hand and with uncanny insight said, "She reminds you of Michelle, doesn't she?"

He nodded dumbly and Viola continued, "You're nothing but an old softy and a warm, caring person and I love you for it. She is a darling little lady, isn't she?"

Interrupted by the waiter, Bryce and Viola ordered and as they turned to fresh cups of coffee, a woman's harsh voice echoed throughout the dining room.

"Wendy, get a leg in it. We got the dinner crowd coming and you're way behind in your work. If you want to eat tonight you better get a move on."

They both looked towards the kitchen where a big, raw-boned woman stood with arms akimbo. She glared in disdain at the little girl who now scampered around with head down and shoulders bowed in obvious fear and submission.

Looking at Viola, Bryce saw gray eyes flashing with blue flecks as they followed the brute of a woman into the kitchen. The last time he saw such a look was on a train just east of Laramie.

What had ensued that day caused him to say, "Easy, honey. It won't do the little girl any good to tie into that female Simon Legree."

Viola continued to stare at the swinging doors behind the departing woman and said, "No, you're right, but I sure as hell can help that poor child out. I've been setting tables since I was her age and younger."

Shocked by the first profanity he had heard from this articulate lady he had married, Bryce numbly watched as Viola got to her feet and approached the frightened girl. He stared as she put her arm around small shoulders and heard her say, "You clear the tables and replace the linen and I will set the silverware and glasses, Wendy. We'll have you all caught up in just a little bit."

He watched in awe as the dining room hummed with activity. Like a well-oiled machine, the two wee ladies worked in unison as table after table became neatly dressed. Viola occasionally spoke softly to Wendy and Bryce could see the head and shoulders stand more erect with each contact.

He marveled at the seemingly unlimited talents of his wife when she approached the table, her arm around Wendy's waist.

"Bryce, may I introduce Gwendolyn Nickel. Wendy, this is my unconscionable flirt of a husband, Bryce Girouard."

The girl extended a small hand which Bryce held as he again saw that shy smile.

They were so poised when the kitchen doors swung open with a bang and the familiar harsh voice yelled, "Hey, what's going on here? Wendy, you get back to work before I tan you. You think I'm boardin' you for free?"

The bulky woman, with a complexion like ten-day old whey, glared balefully at the group through the eyes of a brush-beat Basset. She moved towards the trio, her huge hands swinging by hips mounted above calves and ankles larger than her knees, a forbidding sight as she approached, her enormous feet plopping like cow dung with each step.

Bryce continued to clasp the girl's hand and Viola never relaxed her arm around Wendy's waist as she slowly turned icy eyes to the woman.

"And who might you be, madam? Are you the girl's mother? I am Viola Millin Girouard and this is my husband, Bryce. We were just introducing ourselves to this fine young lady."

"Well, she ain't got time to socialize. She's got work to do and no, I ain't her mother. I'm just stuck with boardin' her 'cause she ain't got no family," the crude woman growled as she neared their table.

Looking up with contempt in her face, Viola stated, "If you had taken time to look around before you started persecuting this young lady, you would have seen that Wendy is all caught up. We'll see to it that everything gets done as needed. Right now, Wendy is a guest at our table and if we ever expect to get served it would behoove you to get back to your culinary tasks so that your customers may expect to eat before bedtime."

An elderly couple at an adjacent table had been listening and watching intently as the situation developed. They now started clapping in unconcealed approval at the turn of events. Soon others joined in as they watched this fiery little lady standing eye-to-eye with the much larger Amazon of a woman.

The big woman stammered in disbelief and then abruptly turned and headed for the sanctuary of her kitchen.

The waiter approached their table as Bryce seated Viola and Wendy. He smiled broadly as he said, "Miss Wendy, may I take your order, please?"

The abusive one never re-appeared and soon orders were pouring from the kitchen where she undoubtedly was drowning her frustrations in work.

As the three slowly ate their meal, Viola and Wendy would jump up to clear and reset a vacated table and then return to continue eating.

As they dined, Viola gently drew forth a tragic story from Wendy. She related how she, her mother, dad and grandmother were moving west with a wagon train headed for Fort Ellis and the Gallatin River Valley. Their wagon had broken an axle and the wagon master had gone on with a promise to send out a farrier from Billings. He assured them that they would have a new axle and be on their way in a few days.

When Wendy seemed no longer able to continue, Viola pulled her to her breast and held her close as the small frame shook with wave after wave of sobs.

As the crying stilled, the elderly couple approached from their table and introduced themselves as John and Bessie Trowbridge. Bryce pulled up chairs and they sat down, offering to fill in with what they knew about the incident and how Wendy ended up in bondage to a mean old dining room manager.

When the repair wagon arrived, they found three mutilated bodies and a hysterical little girl hiding in the willows.

A renegade band of Blackfeet had done their hideous work well but were wise enough to know that killing or kidnapping a helpless child would not endear them to their own people, who had just signed a treaty agreeing to allow free passage along the Yellowstone. The murder of three adults would be enough to bring the wrath of the Unites States Cavalry down on the entire tribe.

The farriers buried Wendy's family and returned to Billings where they turned Wendy over to the town marshal, Barney Carver, who just happened to be the enormous woman's brother.

"He said he was gonna' find some relative if he could and until then, he turned her over to old lady Carver here," John related. "I don't think he's working too hard at it though, 'cause it's been three months now and she's still here slaving away for his sister."

"What happens if he doesn't find any relatives?" Bryce asked.

"Well, he said he'd put her up for adoption, if anybody wanted her."

As Bryce thanked the Trowbridges and they arose to go, the hotel doors burst open to admit a short, squat man with a gun on each hip and a star on his chest. He looked around the dining room, quickly focusing on the Girouards and Trowbridges, and strode importantly towards their table.

Even though they were ready to leave, the Trowbridges glanced at the approaching figure and quietly re-seated themselves.

"What's going on here and what right do you people have to interfere with the law? I could throw you in jail for this you know."

Turning her still icy gaze to the pompous little marshal, Viola, coolly replied, "Yes, why don't you do, that you arrogant little fake of a lawman? I have an excellent attorney cousin who would love to come and embarrass you in my defense."

Bryce felt a wave of apprehension at his wife's outburst, but noticed the Trowbridges watching with calm interest.

"Now, you listen here, lady, I'm the law around here and you can't talk to me that away!" Marshal Carver roared. "I have legal custody over that girl and can do whatever I think is right for her. You got no right to stick your nose in this."

"As citizens, we have every right to ask that this girl be treated right. Apparently, you know nothing of child abuse and child slavery laws. My cousin would be glad to explain these laws to you before a U.S. Magistrate," Viola sharply replied. "We just fought a war to release the Negro from slavery and you think you have the right to place this child in bondage to that kitchen witch of a sister of yours?"

The marshal stepped back, surprise showing in his eyes. Bryce guessed that he knew little about the law and probably couldn't even read a law book. The bluster turned to uncertainty and fear as the dumpy town marshal whined, "Well, heck. Madge don't mean no harm. She's just grouchy like that 'cuz she ain't got no man."

"Maybe she doesn't have a man because she's always mean and bitchy," Viola said with a triumphant smirk. "A sweet smile and disposition can turn anyone into an attractive person."

"Well, maybe lady, but she's always been shitty that way. Even when she was a girl," the marshal whined on, "But what do you expect me to do with Wendy, here? I can't find no relatives and nobody wants her. What the hell else was there for me to do?"

"I expect you to give the girl to my husband and me for adoption, that's what I expect you to do, sir," Viola stated firmly, without even looking at Bryce for agreement.

The Trowbridges glanced at Bryce, who only shrugged with a wide grin on his face.

John interjected, "That sounds like the thing to do, Barney. The Girouards can give Wendy a good home and you'll be off the hook. Bessie and I will sign the papers as witnesses."

Marshal Carver studied the group, his lethargic brain trying to analyze the fast-developing events before him. He knew he would have to weather the wrath of his vitriolic sister, but he wanted less to test his legal standing in court.

Finally, he loudly stated, showing he was back in authority, "You come down to the office in a couple of hours and I'll have the adoption papers ready for you to sign. I'll also have the town clerk there to notarize them." He turned away and stomped importantly out the door as malevolent eyes followed him from the kitchen.

Viola turned defiantly back to the others and found three smiling faces. The lips tight in determination slowly relaxed in a sheepish smile as she realized, although impetuous, she had done a good thing. Starting to reseat herself, she instead walked to Bryce and clasped her arms around his neck, kissing him tenderly on the cheek. Little Wendy watched from Bryce's side in wonder.

Viola again took her seat and Wendy moved to her side, putting her arm around Viola's neck to squeeze herself tight to her new mother.

Smiling across the table at Viola, Bryce said, "Now, dear, we best be planning how we're going to fit our new daughter into our honeymoon. Which one of us is going to sleep on the divan?"

Viola flushed a deep red as John Trowbridge roared and Bessie jabbed him in the ribs in mock disapproval.

She said, "Why don't you all come out to our ranch till this is all settled? Those papers are going to have to go to Helena for recording and that will take several days. We've got rooms for everyone and we'd love to have you. Besides, we'd like to get to know you better. Montana needs more fine folks like you and we selfishly demand the right to be the first to welcome you."

> *Dear Clayton,*
> *A note to let you know I am in Billings but will be delayed for a few days. I now have several surprises for you when I arrive at the C-Bar-M. I am looking forward to seeing you again.*
> *Your brother-in-law,*
Bryce

The four days at the Trowbridge ranch were a wonderful time for the newlyweds and instant parents.

Viola and Bryce seized the time to get acquainted with their new daughter and to explore this new land. Wendy attached herself to Viola in shy silence as they borrowed their host's horse and buggy to explore the ranch and themselves. Bryce proudly pointed out the various mountain ranges, wildlife, flowers and rolling grasslands now turning a rich green. Viola waxed poetic in all this new beauty.

Too soon, the recorded papers arrived and the Girouards bid an emotional good bye to their hosts and new-found friends. As the stage coach labored up the bluffs toward the rim of the Yellowstone Valley, Bryce felt a warm satisfaction at belonging, of being loved and needed, that he had never experienced before. Most humans were reluctant to make changes in their lives, fearful at leaving their old ways for new. If they could only know the wonderful feeling and freedom available for those with the courage to reach. He pulled his beautiful wife and daughter close.

The stage road was much improved over the trail Bryce remembered from a year ago, the traffic also much heavier. Herds of long horned cattle grazed everywhere on the lush new grass and Wendy and Viola excitedly pointed out each herd of antelope and elk they saw. Mule deer looked down from rocky rims and little white tailed deer peered out of the cottonwoods along fertile stream courses.

Wendy clung tightly to Bryce and he could feel her small body shake when they passed groups of Indians. Although they were no longer on reservation lands, there was considerable movement among the various tribes as they still migrated to and from hunting and forage grounds. Viola gently explained that the hate-filled group of young warriors which attacked her family were not typical of all Indians and Wendy should not hate nor fear all Natives.

Bryce wondered about the monumental task before them. Would they ever be able to wipe out the terror and trauma buried deep within this young mind?

The stage rumbled across the Broadview Plains, here and there tilled and sprouting spring wheat, then into the gentle breaks of the Bull Mountains. At the crest of Lavina Ridge, a world new and wondrous to Viola and Wendy came into view.

The sharp, jumbled peaks of the Crazy Mountains appeared to the west, their deep gorges now softened by last winter's deep snows. To the north, the softly rolling bulk of the Snowy Mountains arose in gentle contrast. Bryce smiled to see the look of awe on the faces of his ladies as they turned to view the southwest.

The massive ramparts of the Beartooth and Absaroka Ranges soared before them.

Wendy said softly, "Jiminy! Look at all them mountains!"

"*Those* mountains, honey," Bryce beat Viola to the punch as he corrected his daughter and called their attention to the southeast where the reddish rim rocks of the Pryors framed more snow-capped peaks glistening in the distance.

"That's the northern end of the Big Horns," Bryce explained. He pointed out the approximate location of the St. Xavier Indian Mission where he had laid his beloved Missy to rest, which inadvertently formed a brotherly relationship with Clayton McMahon.

"Darling, now I am beginning to understand your fascination with this beautiful land and your urge to return. What a wonderful place to start a new life," Viola exclaimed as she held Wendy close. "What wonderful challenges and opportunities we have before us. I'm so excited!"

The team well rested, the stage driver herded everyone aboard to begin the long, gradual descent into the Mussellshell Valley and Cushman Landing.

After a night over at Charley Cushman's less-than-plush accommodations, the stage continued up the Mussellshell. They traveled through the wee community of Ryegate and onward past Deadman's Basin, where Bryce pointed out the place of crossing, when in flight, after Michelle had master-minded the bank robbery in Moccasin. After a lunch break at Shawmut Crossing, the stage bounced onward up the Mussellshell to Merino.

They obtaining lodging, freshened up and an exuberant Viola insisted on touring the bustling community.

"This is so exciting. We just have to learn everything we possibly can about our new home. Isn't that right, Wendy?"

Wendy was all smiles, jumping up and down impatiently, tugging at Bryce's coat tails until he finished tying his string tie and turned to the door.

The community of Merino boomed with growth just as every major crossroads town in the west. It was here that the Billings to Fort Benton road intersected with the Carrol Spur to Bozeman and the Yellowstone Trail to Big Timber. Northern Pacific had just completed a siding at Big Timber and goods of all sorts were pouring north into the Mussellshell and Judith Basin countries.

A friendly store owner explained how completion of the railroad up the Yellowstone had already dried up the shipping business of the Carrol Freight Company and the warehousing at Carrol's Landing on the Missouri.

"And we're going to have our own railroad soon," he proudly proclaimed, relating how the Milwaukee and St Paul Railway Company was surveying for a railroad up the Mussellshell, over the Big Belts and to the territorial capitol of Helena.

The town teemed with many different bits of humanity, the Girouards being the most unusual in their eastern garb. Miners, loggers, ranchers and farmers filled the streets, with an occasional inscrutable Indian among them. At every such meeting, Wendy clung tightly to Bryce's hand.

Viola remarked at the guns on the hips of many and the rifles showing on every saddle. Bryce explained how the guns were necessary for hunting game, protection from rattlesnakes, grizzly bears and unscrupulous gangs who roamed the West taking advantage of the helpless.

"I suppose they are still shooting Indians out here also," Viola remarked sarcastically.

Bryce tried to explain, without bias, that yes, there were still roving bands of quite wild Indians in the unsettled lands that would quickly pounce on an unarmed person and steal their belongings. They would also kill, if necessary, to gain such spoils. "I know you find this hard to understand," Bryce continued, "but believe me, whenever this family travels alone out here, we will be armed. Someday this may change when we have adequate law enforcement but more likely, not until the West becomes as civilized as you found Missouri. Remember that less than a generation ago most people carried guns there too."

"No," he replied to Viola's question, "they probably don't need to wear their guns in town, but they become a part of a man's habit and he feels undressed without them."

He paused in thought before continuing, "They wear their guns most of the time, just as you carry that umbrella on sunny days. A pretty potent weapon in itself. I can attest to that."

Bryce grinned down at the impertinent face now staring grimly straight ahead, knowing the indignation would soon turn to loving conciliation. Wendy studied the two, attempting to ferret out the many moods and unspoken dialogue of her new parents.

The third day of wearying stage travel found the family crossing Judith Gap where Bryce again pointed out the place of crossing with Missy and the bank loot. Lunch at U-Bet, a stop to deliver mail at Buffalo, and finally, late in the evening, Moccasin.

Bryce felt a chill run through his body as he surveyed the tiny town. Little had changed since his sudden exit over a year ago. The native stone bank building looked the same and he could still see Michelle as she bounced down the stone steps, black hair blowing in the wind and dark eyes shining. Would these visions haunt him forever? Could he make a home here if they did not fade from memory?

Two small arms girdled his waist, returning him to the present and he looked into understanding eyes.

Viola said gently, "Perhaps we should find lodging, dear, before it gets too late. A good nights sleep and we'll all feel better."

He looked down at Wendy as her small, brown arm squeezed his leg. Her tanned cheek pressed tightly to his side and two dark eyes looked up adoringly. Again, a chill passed through him and he tingled with a new-found knowledge.

He had not lost Michelle! Some mystic power had returned Missy to him. She was standing at his side now, dusky skin, dark eyes and raven black hair. Little sister Missy was still here as he remembered her many years ago, returned to him in Wendy! He shook uncontrollably as he clutched his family close to him.

Feeling the shaking in his body, Viola wiped away tears that rolled down now ashen cheeks to splash at their feet.

"It's all over now, darling. You've faced up to the past and you've beaten it. You didn't run. You didn't hide in the bottle. Wendy and I are so proud of you and we're here to be with you from now on."

Ignoring the curious looks of passersby, the little family stood until emotions died away.

Mrs. Calahan stared at Bryce in disbelief, "Well, glory be, if it isn't—you, Bryce," she stammered. "So many times I've wanted to apologize for my behavior last summer and now, here you are. Clayton said you might return someday but I just didn't believe it. I understand things now and realize I was wrong to think you and Bonnie were misbehaving."

"You didn't have any way of knowing, Mamie, You were led to your misunderstandings by our cover-up, just like everybody else in town. You have no need to feel guilty," Bryce said. "My family and I would appreciate a place to stay tonight though, if you can accommodate us."

Mamie Calahan welcomed all the Girouards with open arms and said, although dinner was formally over, she had plenty of chicken and noodles to heat up with cornbread still in the warming oven.

"Please come down as soon as you freshen up," she pleaded. "We have so much to talk about."

It was a meal that only Mamie could create and as the family dined, she plied them with questions. Her eyes lit up as soon as she heard that Viola was an elementary school teacher.

"Well, what do you know," she marveled. "Here I just get appointed to the school board and I have a certified teacher right here in my own home. We only have one teacher for all eight grades right now and just haven't found anyone willing to move out here to Moccasin to help. Please say you'll take the job, Miss Viola. We so badly need someone to teach grades one through four."

They left Moccasin for the C-Bar-M the next morning after promising Mamie Calahan to seriously consider the job offer.

Following Mamie's directions, Bryce reined the team past a high gate where an engraved sign proudly identified the Q2 ranch. They continued on, arriving at a junction where a sun-bleached sign post indicated Utica to the left and C-Bar-M to the right. Taking the right hand fork, Bryce released the reins and allowed the team their heads as they sprightly trotted towards the distant cone of Big Baldy.

Bryce reined the team back to a walk as they passed through the gate sporting a neat C-Bar-M sign. They passed the large ranch house neatly trimmed in red and bedecked with bright petunia beds and he turned the buggy towards a lone figure staring at them from the barn door.

"By damn, if it ain't Bryce!" Curly exclaimed. "Hey, Clay, get your butt out here an see who showed up," he hollered in the direction of a small tool shed.

Bryce smiled down at the grizzled old face as Curly gazed at the trio. "By God, he ain't alone neither, Clay."

"Well, I was wondering when you were going to show up, Bryce. Every letter you kept stalling. Thought you might have changed your mind," Clayton McMahon shouted as he sprinted toward the group.

Leaping down, Bryce met Clay with a warm handshake and a slap on the back, before turning toward the buggy.

"I want you to meet the two surprises I wrote about. Meet my wife, Viola and our daughter, Wendy. Girls, this is Clay McMahon and this here is Curly. Owners of the C-Bar-M."

"Welcome to the C-Bar-M, Viola," Clay said, as his powerful hands lifted Viola from the seat by her waist and, with toes dangling, hugged her against his chest. "We're sure glad to have you here. By God, Bryce, you sure know how to pick 'em. What two beautiful ladies you have."

Curly beamed as Viola and Wendy each gave him a hug. He turned to the dark-complexioned lady approaching and said, "Come over here and meet these nice folks, Nita."

As the little group chattered and visited, Clay stood at Bryce's side with a sly smile on his face until Juanita said, "Yes sir, this is some surprise isn't it! Who'd have thought Bryce would show up here with a ready made family? That doesn't happen too often does it?"

"Nope, not too often but then you never know, do you?" Clay said as he turned to the ranch house, an arm around Bryce and Viola's shoulders. "Let's go down to the house so we can relax and visit."

They walked towards the ranch house, Curly and Juanita following, Wendy between them.

As they rounded the corner of the house and Clay led them toward the front porch, the front door opened and a tall slender woman, her arm around a freckle faced lad, stepped out.

Bryce and Viola gaped at this sudden turn of events. The apron worn by the beautiful blonde before them swelled with obvious advanced pregnancy and her smooth cheeks glowed with that blush peculiar to ladies in such condition.

The young lad at her side smiled shyly at these strangers, as his mother said, "Well, honey are you going to introduce us?"

"I just kinda' wanted our surprise to linger a while, Pauline," Clayton said gleefully. "Bryce has been tantalizing me with his promises of a surprise. He didn't have any way of knowing we had our own surprise. Folks, meet my wife, Pauline and son Tommy. Honey, this is Bryce, Viola and Wendy. The Girouards."

Amid hugs, giggles and rounds of laughter, the three families quickly felt at ease. Pauline and Viola hit it off immediately and both showed their excitement over the baby due in August.

Clay chided Bryce, "I'm one jump ahead of you all the way. I married first, my son is a year older than your daughter and my wife is pregnant. You just aren't ever going to catch up."

"Oh, I don't know," Bryce said, looking slyly at his wife. "Viola and I just may decide to have twins. Maybe even triplets. Right, honey?"

Laughter echoed through the large room as the banter continued and they all discussed the rare chance that two individual families could experience such similar circumstances.

When the ladies had retired to the kitchen to prepare lunch, Clayton seized the opportunity to ask Bryce if he would consider joining he and Curly in the ranching business.

Bryce admitted that he had little experience at ranching but would be willing to learn. He also told them about the offer Mamie Calahan had made to Viola about teaching in Moccasin, in which case they would have to reside in town.

Clayton responded quickly that they had some plans afoot that might work out well if Bryce did live in town, at least for a while.

"There's another man I want involved in this and he's supposed to be here in a few days. He's Roy Kinne, a horse breeder I've had dealings with. Let's all get together in a meeting when he gets here and I'll go over it all then."

On the long ride back to town, Viola sat silently in deep thought until she suddenly said, "Honey, how are we going to arrange for Tommy to attend school? Maybe he could stay with us on weekdays and we can all return to the ranch on weekends."

"So you've already decided to take the teaching job. Is that right?"

"I hope you agree, honey. My heart is set on teaching and this country needs teachers so badly. Please try to understand."

Bryce reached around Wendy to put his hand on Viola's shoulder. "Of course I understand. You made your goals clear to me before we married and I'll do all I can to help you, but where did Tommy go to school this past winter?"

"He didn't. There was no way to get him to Moccasin and back each day. Sixteen miles is a long way, especially in winter weather."

"Then he just lost a year in his education?"

"No, not really. Pauline and Clayton tutored him at home and probably did a good job, but they didn't have any text books or study material at all. Don't you think we could work it out, Bryce?"

"I'm sure we can, but let's wait until after the meeting Clay has planned and I'll know more then about our future."

Mamie welcomed the family back, brimming with exuberance and chatter.

"Oh, Miss Viola," she said, "I've talked to the other members of the school board and they are so excited that you are here. We really want you to take our teaching job. I hope you two have talked it over and can give me a good answer. Please?"

Viola looked at Bryce quickly and seeing the smile on his face turned to Mamie. "We'll work it out somehow, but there will need to be a lot of planning. There are so many children scattered around these ranches that have no way to town each day. That will require some thought."

"Oh, thank you, Miss Viola. I'm so pleased," Mamie responded, then nervously fidgeted with her apron before continuing, "I also told them that you are an actress and they want so much to see you perform. Do you suppose ... well, heck, I already told them you would put on a show for the PTA next meeting. Did I do wrong, Miss Viola? I just kinda' got carried away."

Putting her arm around Mamie's ample waist, Viola pursed her lips before breaking into laughter. "Of course, I'll do it. We'll give Moccasin the best routine I have. You just give me the date so we can plan it."

"Oh boy, oh boy! Mother's going to teach and she's going to act. Can we go to the show? Please Dad, can we?" Wendy chirped.

Bryce nodded, beaming at her first use of the title, "Dad."

The next few days Bryce and Wendy were left pretty much to themselves as Viola met with the school board time and again, talking text books, curriculum and a multitude of other school-related business.

They wandered about the town and met many fine folks. All were friendly and ignored the fact that Bryce was once involved in the robbery of their bank. They visited Marshal Garwood and Deputy Griffing, banker Roy Sutherland and Wilma Byrd. Bryce expressed his regret for the part he had played in the scheme but found no malice. He knew this was a tribute to Clayton McMahon and the respect the town folks held for him.

On the evening of the day Viola was to perform for the townspeople, Curly and Juanita drove up to Mamie Callahan's boarding house with a team and wagon. Wendy bolted down the steps to greet her adopted grandparents with hugs.

"Mother is going to perform at the school tonight," she proudly stated, "Dad and I are going to be there. Will you come too, please?"

Hugging the little girl, Juanita looked up at Curly and said, "I do believe we can. We planned to stay all night anyway and take you folks back to the ranch with us. We could do that couldn't we, Curly?"

Curly, clearly uncomfortable about possible exposure to eastern culture, nonetheless, nodded assent. How could he disappoint this excited little girl?

Curly and Juanita brought word of Roy Kinne's arrival at the C-Bar-M and Clay's plans for a meeting the next evening. Curly described the surprise when Kinne recognized Curly as an old friend from Texas where they had been bronc busters for the same outfit.

"I knowed when Clay described him that he had to be the same guy I wrangled with down in the thicket," Curly laughed, "Boy, did his eyeballs bug out when he saw me a standin' there.."

The two-room school house had been converted to an opera house by rolling back movable partitions and turning all chairs towards a small stage set up at one end.

There was a curtained off back stage area in the right corner and the necessary props, such as chairs, stools, and podium were already in place.

Viola helped seat her four most ardent admirers in the middle of the room and near the front. "You will have the best view and the most impact on the crowd. Now at the end of each act, I want you to clap real loud. A whistle or two won't hurt either to get them applauding," she said with a wink at Bryce, "You can't catch fish without bait, you know."

Viola retired back stage to prepare for the first act as people poured in and seated themselves.

"It looks like the whole town is turning out, Wendy," Juanita remarked as Mamie Calahan took the stage to make the introduction.

Proudly addressing the standing-room-only crowd, Mamie elaborated on Viola's education, talent as a noted impressionist and even read newspaper articles lauding her. She topped off her eloquent introduction by announcing that Sandra Viola Millin-Girouard would be elementary school teacher for the coming school year in Moccasin. Mamie exited the stage amid thunderous applause.

As the applause died to expectant silence, suddenly an old, bent-over lady appeared from behind the curtain. Her cane tapped loudly in the stillness as she shuffled across the stage to seat herself in an old rocking chair.

Bryce was amazed at the transformation. Other than in diminutive stature, this little old lady looked and acted nothing like his beloved Viola.

Adjusting her shawl about her shoulders, the old lady peered at the crowd over lowered spectacles. After many motions and actions typical of an elderly female, she began to speak. In a quavering but clearly audible voice, she began to grumble about the problems of being an old lady, problems in understanding the youth of the day and her "By God" solutions. The crowd roared at the humor in her mental ramblings and clapped at the sage advise and anecdotes.   The old lady went tapping off stage to end act one amid thunderous applause and Bryce knew then, that his sly little wife had put another one over on him when she suggested they get the crowd involved.

The next act featured spoiled little Sally Bly. A self-centered brat who screamed and threw tantrums when not getting her own way, was followed by classical singer, Florence Meadowlark, in flowing gown and fan. The operatic passages mixed throughout the performance were delivered in a clear, perfectly pitched voice that Bryce had no idea his wife possessed. Would her talents never end?

From the mournful and eerie, Little Orphant Annie, which held the crowd spellbound, to Rosy Plumb, the harlot, each act, in complete contrast to the other, brought down the house. Bryce felt pride swell within him at the completion of the show when the crowd gave a standing ovation, calling for an encore.

One more short skit, again, a different character, and the show ended with Wendy squeezing Bryce's arm tightly. "She's wonderful, isn't she, Dad? My mother is about the best actress there is, isn't she?"

Bryce nodded, holding Wendy close, observing the people about him. Most were on their feet applauding and whistling, Curly and Juanita among the loudest. "Yes, honey, your mother is some kind of lady. Some kind of lady," he shouted above the crowd.

The following afternoon found the four en route to the C-Bar-M as Curly rambled on about the many far-reaching plans Clayton had in store for the ranch. "He's a thinkin' years ahead all the time. Hell, I have trouble plannin' for tomorrow, but he just keeps a comin' up with new idears."

They found Clayton leaning against the corral rails in deep conversation with an older, lean and graying man sporting a huge, drooping mustache.

Bryce locked eyes with the older man as he distantly heard Clayton say, "This is Roy Kinne, Bryce. An old side kick of Curly's and the horse breeder I was telling you about."

The two stared at each other, ignoring Clayton's introduction, until Roy blurted out, "God a mighty, You're the guy what shot hell out of that redhead we buried. This guy's the fastest draw around, Curly, believe me. Clayton, you knew we'd met and you never said a word."

Wendy knotted her brow in consternation as she looked up at her foster father. Juanita smiled, indicating she had heard it all, while Viola looked off in the distance as if she wasn't concerned.

"This guy was one of the bank robbers you was a chasin' Clay. How come you're friends now?" the confused wrangler asked.

After a brief explanation over Curly's roars of laughter, the two shook hands sheepishly and Roy remarked, "That three hundred you paid us to bury the guy got us started in the hoss breedin' business. I just want to let you know, we put it to good use."

"That's the mark of a wise man and I am glad to see you again," Bryce answered warmly. "Looks like we may be working together again, but in a much more civilized way this time."

The ladies retired to the main ranch house as the men set to unloading supplies. Tommy came sliding to a halt astride a big blocky chestnut and leaped to the ground to do his share with a "Howdy fellas" attempt at man talk.

The wagon unloaded, the men relaxed in the shade of the barn.

"Them same two fellas' that was with me last fall are my partners in this hoss breedin business, Roy said. "We quit mining and started homesteading. We had 480 acres to start out but we're buying out a couple of other dudes and we'll have over 800 acres to work with now."

"Where you gettin' your breeding stock, Roy?"

"Well, we managed to buy a few big hosses like the one Tommy was ridin' but we found good ones was scarce until we met Clay, here."

"How could this broken-down old law man be of any help to a horse breeder?" Bryce quipped.

"He set us up with the Injuns down on the Crow Reservation to capture the wild broncs a runnin' all over the place for a fifty-fifty split."

"Did you get some good ones?"

"Yeah, we got away with sixty-two pretty good hosses before the Fed's found out what we was a doin' and kicked our asses off the Reservation. Just like Clay said, the Injuns wanted only the fast hosses. They're crazy to gamble on hoss races and they let us keep all of the ones that would make good cattle mounts."

"Well, they wasn't all good stock was they, Roy?" Curly asked.

"Oh no, that was part of the deal. We was supposed to teach those Injuns how to improve their herds. We gelded a lot of stud colts that wasn't much good and knocked a bunch of the pure culls in the head. Only a few of those Injuns was interested in workin' with us though. Most of the older ones scorn the physical labor needed to get things done."

"Did you get any help form Curly Coyote and Longtail?" Clay asked.

"Yeah, those two boys took to roundin' up them broncs, cullin' and breakin' 'em real good. Some of the other bucks took to ridiculing them and calling them 'horse women' but Curly Coyote just told them that, someday he would have many hosses, the prettiest wives and the fattest papooses. He told those other bucks that they'd be a fightin' with the camp dogs for his scraps. I don't doubt it'll come true too. Some of those Injuns just ain't gonna' adapt."

After a long silence Roy continued, "Anyhow, Bryce. we got a pretty good bunch of quick, agile hosses and I think some of 'em will turn out to be good ranch stock. We'll be through breakin 'em by mid-summer and we'll run some up here for you fellas' to try out. I think we could come up with a better cuttin' hoss if we could breed for it though. Trouble is, findin' the right stock to mix in for what we want."

The conversation came to a halt at Juanita's call, "Dinner is ready. You cowboys get washed up and come on down."

CHAPTER X
THE TEST

As the men retired with their coffee to the spacious living room, the cozy sounds of dishes clinking, silverware rattling and the chatter of three busy homemakers emanated from the kitchen.

The men sat in silence other than an occasional groan of overindulgence in the sumptuous meal.

Tommy burst through the front door calling, "Hey Wendy, where are you? I gotta' shut in the colts and chickens for the night. Want to help?"

Wendy appeared from a bedroom, jumping up and down. "Yes, yes! Oh boy! Oh boy! Can I pet the colts?"

The men smiled as the two bolted out the door towards the barnyard.

Bryce was amazed at the change in Wendy since their arrival in Moccasin. The sad, beaten look was now gone and her eyes sparkled with enthusiasm for each new day. She was even sassy and assertive at times, a change that both Viola and Bryce accepted with understanding and love. He knew their adopted daughter loved him dearly as a father but he had to admit that most of the credit for Wendy's adaptation had to go to the remarkable little woman he had married.

He watched in amazement as Viola read to Wendy, accenting the text with dramatic vocal and facial expressions that wrapped Wendy in enchantment. Viola would seat Wendy beside her as she taught her the difficult elocution and vocal orations that accompanied the text. He realized that she was inspiring the girl to hunger for education and to readily learn everything placed before her—nothing like the usual boring and dry education offered in most public schools.

As the four men sat, each deep in his own thoughts, Viola and Pauline entered from the kitchen to take seats in two of the many bent willow chairs Clayton had placed around the room.

Curly cleared his throat and turned to Roy to say, "It's been a long time since we was workin' together down in the thicket, Roy. I don't miss it none, though. Say, do you remember old Saddle Ass?"

"Hell yes, how can you ever forget old Saddle Ass," Roy answered.

Juanita burst from the kitchen and with hands on hips said, "Curly!" in an exasperated voice.

Curly just ignored Juanita as he continued, "Yeah, old Saddle Ass was quite a guy; good worker and one tough jose."

Juanita again interjected, "Curly, you don't have to tell that disgusting story every time we have guests. There are two refined ladies present now and you're not sitting around the campfire on a trail drive tonight."

As Juanita stood facing Curly, her black eyes snapping, Clayton turned to Bryce and winked. Bryce knew then that Clayton had witnessed this baiting of the trap before. He waited and watched the personalities about him and their different expressions.

Curly just shrugged hopelessly as he pulled out a pouch of Peerless. Digging out a pinch between thumb and index finger, he examined it carefully, as if it might possibly contain bugs and slowly tucked it between cheek and gum. He groped around behind his chair for the spit can he faithfully carried with him whenever inside.

An awkward silence fell over the group as Juanita glared at Curly. Pauline sat in innocent, wide-eyed curiosity, while Viola studied Curly with a wry smile on her face. Bryce could see his wife was not fooled one bit and would patiently wait as the plot developed.

Finally, Pauline could stand it no longer and said, "Well, at least you could explain how this unfortunate man got such a colorful nickname."

Juanita covered her face with her hands as Curly's eyes lit up and he said, "He wasn't always called that, Miss Pauline. His real name was Fritz and that's what we always called him, until the accident."

"What accident?"

Roy broke in to continue the story, "Fritz, Curly and I was breakin' broncs for a trail drive we was about to go on. Fritz was a real good bronc buster and we were taking turns ridin 'em down so we could put 'em in the remuda."

Curly continued the story, "Fritz was on a real big, wild one we later called Back Breaker, when this hoss shook Fritz loose and tossed 'em in the sky. Fritz sailed up and cum down right on ole Back Breakers rump, just as it wuz goin up. He then flew up and come down right on his back, across the top corral rail."

"He just hung there like a wet gunny sack for a while and then slid down onto the corral dirt," Roy added. "We all thought he was dead, layin' there, all twisted up and blood coming out of his mouth, but pretty soon he started moanin' and floppin' his arms like a wrung chicken so we started hollerin' for the hoss doctor."

"When the doc got there he looked him over and said that if the blood was comin' from his guts that he was a goner, but when we looked in his mouth we seen that he had just bit his tongue and that was all, so the doc started lookin' him over real good."

"Then all of a sudden, Fritz started talkin', kinda' weak like, that he couldn't feel nuthin' in his feet," Curly, eyes sparkling continued, "The doc done pulled off his boots and told Fritz to wiggle his toes, but he couldn't do nuthin'. He kept a sayin' his legs was gone. Broked clear off he said."

Pauline sat, her blue eyes wide with horror, completely entranced. Not so Viola, who relaxed in her chair, the quizzical smile still on her face, nor Juanita who still hid her face in her hands, thoroughly embarrassed.

Roy did not let things slow down, as he carried on. "The doc said Fritz had a broken back and the only way we could save him was to stretch him out on somethin' flat like a door and tie him down so he couldn't move 'til he healed."

"The only thing like that around there was the front door to the ranch house so we knocked out the pins and carried it down to the corral. We folded up a hoss blanket on the door for some padding and then we stretched poor old Fritz out like a branded calf and laid him on the door."

"The doc said we couldn't let 'em move, so we done augured some holes on each side of his ankles chest and ears and tied him down real good with bandanners," Curly said. "That door was one of them fancy ones from back east and it had two panels in the top half and two rows of three panels in the bottom half. Ole Fritz's ass fit right in one of them panels perfect and he said he felt right good when we got done except he still couldn't feel no legs."

By now Juanita had removed her hands from her face and sat staring daggers at the two old wranglers.

"Yeah," Roy said, "We carried him into the bunk house and laid him across two benches and then went back to work a roundin' up stock and breakin' horses. The doc said that was no good and we had to get somebody to care for him all the time, so we got a couple of Mexican fellas' that was roustaboutin' for us. One could understand English and so doc told him, water, soup and liquids, that's all."

"Those vaqueros done a good job too," Curly continued, "When old Fritz had to piss, they carried him out and leaned him up, face inward, against the corral and he just let 'er fly. His hands was free so he could shake it out and put it away and all that. He just couldn't walk to the can."

"Hey, Roy, do you remember what happened when Fritz got hungry?"

"Yeah, as I recall, after about a week he got hungrier than hell and started bellerin' for solid food. Well, these two Mex's figured that chili beans was a sort of soup so they whipped up a big batch, stood Fritz up against the wall and gave him a bowl. Jesus, Fritz just went nuts over that chili, so he ended up downin' three bowls."

Curly broke into uncontrolled laughter as he gasped, "Tell 'em what happened next, Roy."

"Well, it seems about midnight, Fritz woke up hollerin' that he had a bellyache and needed to shit real bad. This put them Mex's into a panic and they just set about fixin' Fritz up so he could crap."

"They grabbed an old hammer and started beatin' the panel out of the door that was right under Fritz's ass, which tenderized it up some. When they got that done, there was the goddam hoss blanket so this one, he pulls out his castratin' knife and starts hackin'."

As Roy gasped for breath, Curly took over, "He got the blanket cut out all right but he sliced up Fritz's cheeks some doin' it. All the time Fritz was a hollerin', hurry! hurry! Them two Mex's then lit out for the corral carryin' Fritz between 'em when pore ole Fritz couldn't hold it no more and they left a brown streak all the way to the corral."

"They laid Fritz against a hitch rail and got up wind of him while he continued to blow shit and gas all over the ranch. The Mex's got busy buryin' the brown streak until Fritz got through blastin' off," Roy said, "And then they didn't know what to do with him. They was scared to take him back into the bunk house for fear he'd let fly again and they'd all have to move out, so they just left him out there in the dark and cold until mornin'."

By now, Pauline had her apron up over scarlet cheeks, only her shocked, blue eyes showing above the inverted hem. Juanita had turned her chair around in disgust and would not even look at the story tellers nor the two other crude males who were laughing as tears streamed down their cheeks.

"Next mornin', we didn't know what was wrong with Fritz," Curly continued, not wanting to lose the drama of the story, "But you could smell him a mile from the ranch." He looked at Viola uneasily as she still sat back, relaxed and smiling, but couldn't drop the story line now, so he raised his eyes to the ceiling and continued.

"Fritz was a beggin', 'Please do something, I'm burnin' up. My ass is on fire,' but them Mex's didn't want no more to do with him. They said they would quit the job before they would clean him up. Then we explained to them two heathins that they was to blame fur feedin' him all that hot chili beans and we didn't appreciate it none."

"As I recall," Roy interjected, "We told them we'd take their boots away and they could walk back to the border if they didn't continue to take care of Fritz and by golly, that did it. They said, 'Si, si, senors, but please have mercy on us,' so we all kicked in a buck apiece and they got busy cleanin' him up."

"Yardage was scarce in Texas them days so they took their bandannas and washed him with one and wiped him with the other 'til they had him clean and then dosed him up with saddle salve," Roy finished.

Shawmut Town

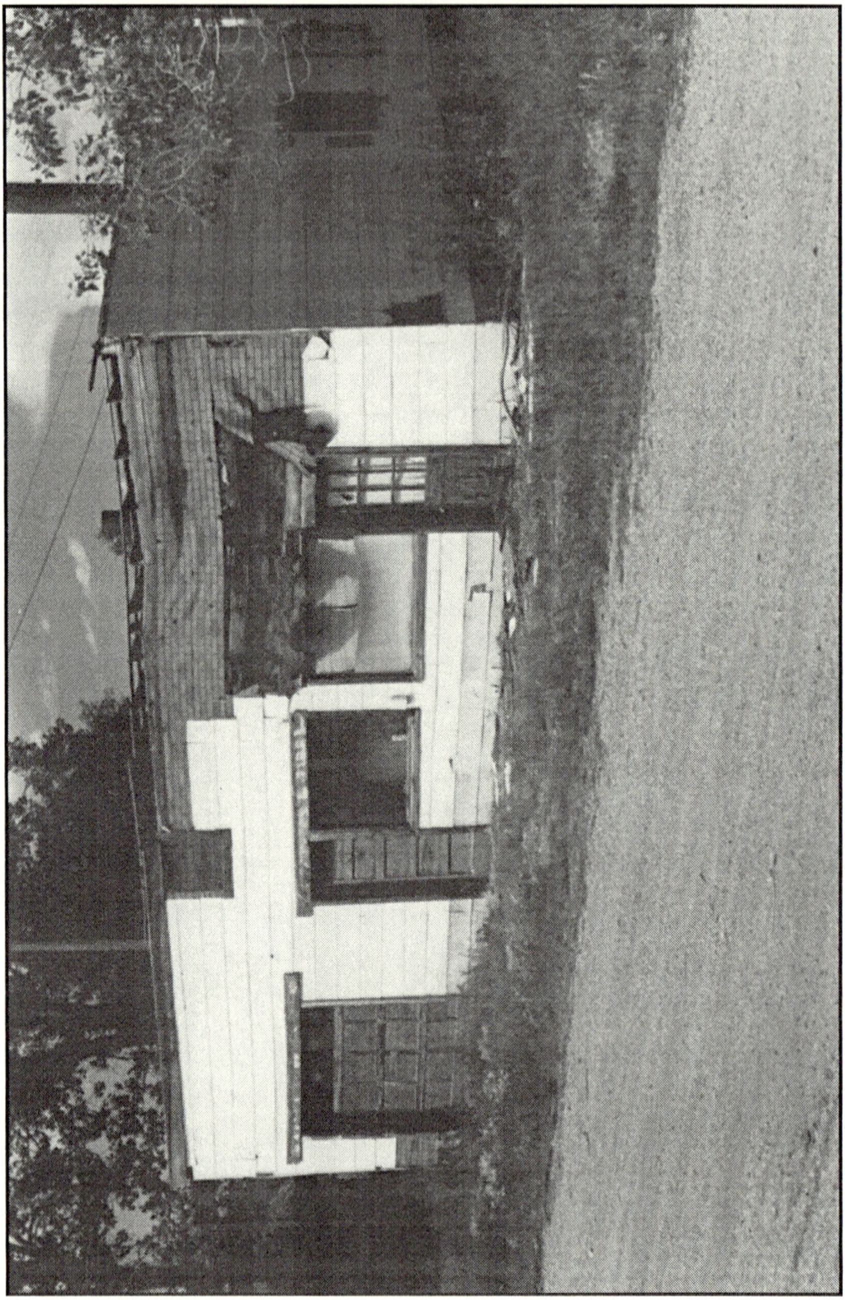

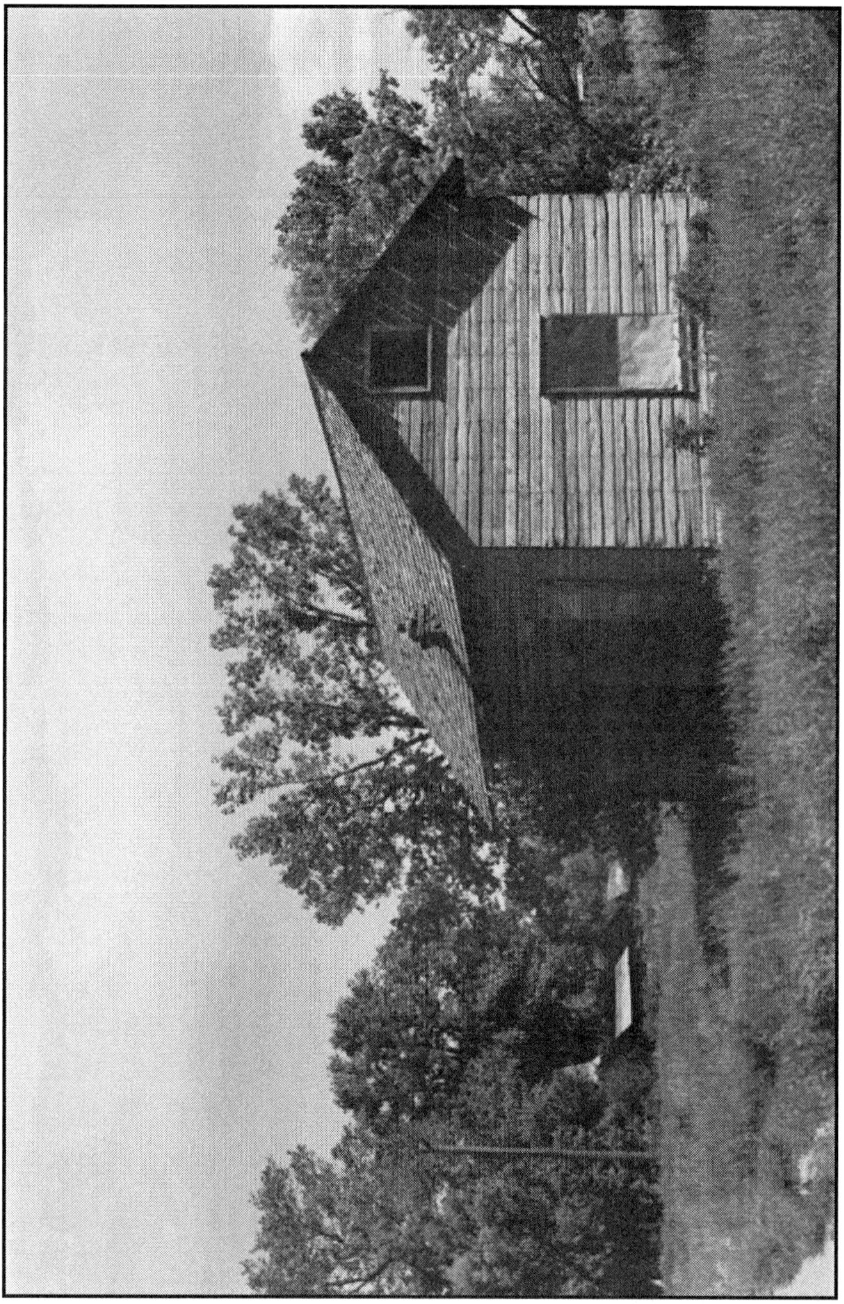

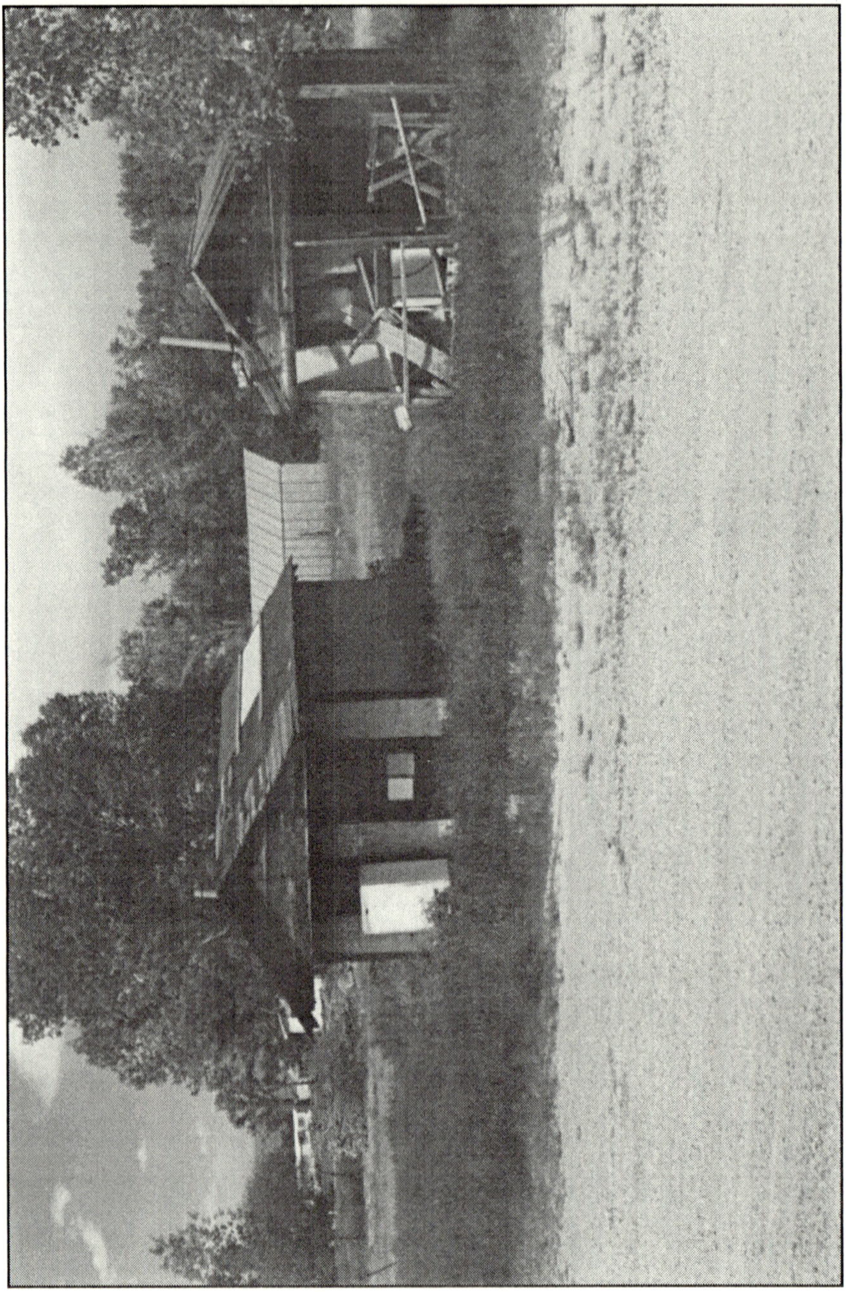

Two Trails to Judith

There was a lull as Roy, Bryce and Clayton continued to laugh and wheeze their enjoyment and Curly looked about for the effect on the ladies.

Pauline still sat in shocked horror at this display of crude and brutal western humor. Juanita had now turned back facing the group, her eyes still shooting daggers at the men and a look of exasperation on her face.

Only Viola seemed unperturbed, and still smiling she said, "Well, I don't see anything strange or funny about one human caring for another. My father was a doctor, you know, and we had one room reserved in our house to accommodate those who were sick or injured and unable to help themselves. Mother and I washed and wiped many an anus, both male and female. There's nothing unusual or hilarious about that. It's something we nurses do all the time and get little enough credit for it."

The crude laughter subsided to an occasional clearing of the throat and activities shifted to fumbling for a spit can, rolling a quirly or reaching for a cup of now cold, coffee.

Juanita's face lit up with a smile and Pauline's apron came down to reveal a knowing smile. She realized now that she had been the victim of a carefully orchestrated test of acceptance for western frankness and simplicity.

Understanding that the ladies now had the floor, Pauline took advantage of the silence to say, "It's obvious that none of you cowboys has ever changed a baby or washed out a dirty diaper like we ladies must do. If you had, you would not be so quick to indulge in this ribald humor about some poor unfortunate human such as Fritz."

The silence grew more intense until Viola broke the spell by saying, "Curly, you and Roy have wasted much time detailing the crude aspects of poor Fritz's accident and we still don't know how he came by his nickname."

As Bryce observed the people about him, it brought back his days as a professional gambler when he would play light as he analyzed the character of each player before committing himself fully to the game. He then knew who to call, who to bluff, who played conservatively and would not bluff. His ability to judge people was the quality that made him a successful gambler.

Dexter C. McPherson

Now, as he studied each one, he saw hurt in the eyes of a crest-fallen Curly who had just been put down by an extremely intelligent little woman with complete command of the English language.

Roy Kinne was well aware that he had been chastised for his part in the lurid tale, but not having any kinship with the ladies, showed aloofness with only a hint of shame.

Clay McMahon looked at Pauline with a glow of love and pride for his beautiful, tall wife who had shown maturity and understanding for it all.

Juanita now had a look for Curly that said clearly, I tried to stop you but you ignored me. Now you suffer. However, I know you will be wiser next time. When their eyes met, there was no doubt that they could communicate at a glance. Only a man and woman in love many years had such magic.

Pauline was now aglow and smiling. She had endured the test. She was indoctrinated into Western culture. She would now be accepted as one of them.

Viola still maintained her dignity and command of the situation. A slight smile still lingered on her lips as she studied the three other men before her and Bryce realized, with a chill, that she was analyzing each one of them, just as he had. He thought, My God, she can be cool and cold if need be, and he felt a deep pity for poor old Curly.

Roy responded to Viola's challenge by saying, "Well, needless to say, Fritz did heal up in time, and got the use of his legs back but he could never walk upright after that. He was sway backed and walked with his buttocks sticking out behind and in little short steps. We started calling him Saddle Ass after one of the hands remarked that he could be saddled and rode like a two legged hoss. Fritz didn't like it at first but kinda' got used to it, I guess."

"We only called him that later when talking about him and then called him Fritz to his face. I left Texas right after that and never knew what happened to Fritz. Do you know anything about him, Curly?"

In quiet and subdued words, Curly slowly responded, "Fritz couldn't break broncs no more, so we just kept him around to do camp chores. He got real good at it and even learned to cook pretty good. When me and Juanita started ram roddin' trail drives, we took him along and he was real good help for Juanita. He rustled firewood, packed water, even helped Juanita cook and serve."

"Do you know where he is now?"

"Not for sure. He fell for a fat little gal what run a small restaurant in Abilene and wouldn't go north with us no more. Last I heard, they was married and doin' great."

As the talk died down, Clayton broke in to say, "Pauline and I invited you all here tonight because I want to talk over some new ideas and projects for the ranch. I value all of you and your knowledge, experience and intelligence, so I've got some proposals to make."

Turning to Pauline, Clayton asked, "How's the coffee supply, honey, got us a refill?"

All three ladies arose as one, and Viola, passing at the back of Curly's chair, placed an arm around his neck and kissed him lightly on the cheek. Bryce heard her softly say, "Thanks for a most interesting and unusual story."

Curly's face glowed with a flush of gratitude and relief.

Bryce knew that of all the people he had met, his little wife was the one he could not characterize. How can one small person show so many sides of personality? But he knew he loved her more deeply each day.

CHAPTER XI
BIRTH OF A DYNASTY AND A CHILD

With coffee cups full, Wendy and Tommy playing checkers on the floor, and the ladies all re-seated, Clayton began explaining the reason for the assemblage.

"As you all know, the C-Bar-M has grown considerably in just a little over a year. So has the Q2, and we are considered fair sized ranches now, but we're only small peanuts compared to what is happening just east of here.

"Big industrialists from back East, and even from Europe, are starting to invest money in ranching and are buying up any ranches that will sell. I hear they lock out the other ranchers from water and free range until they starve out and have to sell out for practically nothing. It hasn't happened here yet, but it will and we want to be in a position to survive when it comes. We will need title to adequate water, summer range, hay fields and access to the free Government range. I've talked this over with the Querrings and we've come up with some ideas. What we need now is a plan and a form of agreement, like maybe incorporation to make it work.

"I'm going to tell you all the ideas we are mulling over," Clayton said, "We don't need to make any final decisions tonight. I just want each of you to consider everything and we'll get together again in about a week to put it together. Each of you, and that includes the ladies, have varied backgrounds and skills. Please, give your honest opinions and I know we'll come up with a plan that will let us survive and grow."

Bryce was impressed by the leadership qualities Clayton displayed and he eagerly awaited continuation of this meeting and the impending challenges.

"There are many ranchers here who believe all they have to do is buy cattle and turn them loose on the range and sell the surplus in the fall," Clayton continued. "They may make out all right for a few years, but I'm convinced that these outfits are doomed to failure. Many have failed already and we've bought out some of them. The Q2 has bought out some others."

"What makes you believe that kind of ranching will fail in the long run, Clay?" Roy asked.

"Well for one thing, we're raising the wrong breed of cattle for this Judith Basin country. These longhorns aren't adapted to the winters we have here. One bad winter and we could lose most or all of our herd."

"What do you propose doin' about it?" Curly ventured.

"We need to start breeding for more sturdy and hardy stock. If we can pick up some bulls of a hardier breed, castrate all the longhorn bulls and cull out all the misfits, lean cows and such, in a few years we'd be ready for that bad winter that hits here about every ten to twenty years."

"Why are you so sure we're going to have those bad winters?" Bryce asked.

"Marvin Querring's wife is a full-blood Blackfoot and Kalee insists they had such a winter about nine years ago and many Blackfeet died of starvation. All the buffalo migrated to the southeast and the few that stayed starved or froze to death. Now if a buffalo can't survive a winter like that, our longhorns don't stand a chance."

"Where we gonna' get bulls like that?" Roy asked.

Before Clay could respond, Viola quietly said, "Aberdeen Angus."

"Aberdeen what!" Curly asked.

"Aberdeen Angus cattle," Viola explained. "They have been bred for centuries to withstand the vicious winters of northern Scotland. They are small, stocky cattle, but heavy of weight. They're coal black and they put on loads of fat in the fall which tides them through bad spells. They also rustle for food good. They'll burrow under the snow like a buffalo when other cattle will just bunch up and die of starvation.

They say the black color keeps them warmer by absorbing more heat from the winter sun."

"That sounds like the breed we're looking for," Clay said. "Curly and I have already started cross breeding with a big roan Durham bull we picked up from a broke rancher last winter. Trouble is we're working him to death during breeding season, even though we're only breeding him to select cows. We've got somewhere around 660 cows now. We need more bulls, like those Angus. Do you know where such bulls can be bought, Viola?"

"The best bulls are still in Scotland and very expensive, what with shipping and all, but there are quite a few in Northern Wisconsin, Michigan and New England," Viola replied.

"I recall seeing some in Ohio, too," Pauline interjected.

"Good," Clay said, "But in addition to hardier stock, I'm convinced we should be reserving our lands close to the ranch as hay fields and winter range. If we can put up about a thousand tons of hay in stacks and build some long loafing sheds for the young stock, I believe we can come through the worst of winters with minimal losses."

"Will we have the man power to do all of this haying and stuff?" Bryce asked.

"As you all know, we've got the Steve Lytle family on the ranch now. Steve's a good farmer and knows haying from A to Z. I also hired a young fellow named Richard Ochs the other day. He sits a horse good and throws a good rope. I think he'll be a top hand with cattle and we can't over look Tommy. He's a natural with horses and Curly's got him doing men's work now. All in all, I think we're a good, tight outfit and ready to grow if we do it right."

Tommy looked up from the checker game, a big grin stretching the freckles broad across his face as Curly and Pauline beamed with pride at Clay's compliment.

"Mebbe' we oughta' explain why Roy's here, Clay," Curly interrupted.

"Yeah," Clay said, "Any cattleman knows it takes a good horse to work cattle, especially at round up time. Well, we've got pitiful few really good cuttin' horses. Roy here, is an experienced horse breeder and he's breaking some pretty sturdy riding stock he and his partners got in the deal with the Crow Injuns, but now that the Bureau of Indian

Affairs have stuck their nose in and stopped anymore deals, we're down to breeding our own horses. Roy here, is interested in doing that for us as part of our corporation."

"What kind of horses are you talking about?" Bryce asked.

"A good cattle horse has to be quick of hoof and agile. He also has to be an intelligent animal you can train and work with. There are lots of strong, agile horses around but many are knotheads and you just can't teach 'em anything. If we believe we can breed a better steer, there's no reason we can't breed a horse to suit our needs."

"Where do we find that kind of breeding stock?"

"We had some ugly hosses down in Texas called grullas," Curly explained. "They're descendants of Spanish war hosses. Real strong, quick and real smart. They're usually a mousy gray or a kinda' dirty buckskin and the purest breeds has a dark stripe down their back with dark stripes across their withers. I know I could make one trip down there and haze back some real good ones."

Roy cut in to say, "The Nez Perce Indians down in Oregon have developed a kind of mountain hoss called the Appaloosa. They're spotted hosses. Mostly on their rumps but sometimes all over. Beautiful animals, but the best thing about 'em is their strength and agility. They're also real smart and quick to learn. If we can pick up some of Curly's grullas, some appaloosas and maybe breed in some Morgan, I'll bet we can come up with a new breed of hoss just right for workin' cattle. We could sell breedin' stock for top dollar too, if we're successful."

"Sounds mighty ambitious but exciting," Bryce said. "When should we get back together on this?"

"How about having a potluck next Sunday afternoon?" Juanita asked. "We could all meet here after the Girouards attend church and drive out here to the ranch."

As everybody cheered the prospect, including a now drowsy Wendy and Tommy, Clay added one more thing.

"Curly and I believe that you can't keep good help if you don't treat them as one of the family so we're going to offer a plot of deeded ground to the Lytles and then help them build their own house on it. Steve, Mildred and Little Lorena have been living in the bunk house, you know, but now that we've hired Ochs and maybe more crew in the future, they need a place of their own. Bryce, we hope you and your family will eventually do the same."

A clapping of hands by all sealed the deal and after pleasant good nights, everyone retired.

The days rolled quickly into summer and the Girouards found themselves spending more and more time at the C-Bar-M. They shared a divided bunkhouse with the Lytles as bachelor, Richard Ochs, cheerfully moved to the barn. Meanwhile, the Lytles' new home rapidly took shape.

Other facets of the Judith Basin Cattle Company began to also take shape when Curly and Roy left for Abilene in June on their horse-buying trip. Bank president Roy Sutherland readily approved the loans necessary for expansion and Bryce quickly purchased two small ranches nearby that were giving up the cattle business.

Sutherland agreed to keep them informed of any ranchers in financial trouble and receptive to selling out. He also predicted that the coming winter would be the deciding factor for many small ranchers in the area.

All hands worked long, tiring hours building loafing sheds, drift fences and corrals in preparation for the coming winter and Bryce was elated when he read Calvin Millin's letter, the last line of which read:

> *"I have decided that it is time for me to leave Missouri and find my own life. I will be leaving tomorrow for Montana and the C-Bar-M. I hope that there will be a place for me in the corporation and that I may have something to contribute."*
> *"I will see you in about a week."*
> *Love, Calvin*

Viola bubbled over with anticipation at the prospect of again seeing her dear brother and the men were all pleased at the prospect of gaining another, much needed, ranch hand.

Bryce and Viola selected a spot in the bend of a small creek that meandered through the area as the site of their new home. They would be near the Lytles, yet close enough to the home ranch so they could be involved in the day-to-day operations.

Wendy waxed poetic about the new home site as she sang: "I love our home by a little rill, Where flowers bloom on every hill. Soon a child will come to bless, Someone to care for and caress. One to sometime take our place, And our lives of love to trace. To where flowers bloom upon the hill, Gracing this home beside a rill."

Bryce, impressed by this display of poetic artistry, asked Viola if she had taught Wendy the poem.

"Certainly not," he was informed, "All I have done is open her mind and natural talents to the vast world about her. The words are her own."

"What's this stuff about a child to bless? Did you tell her something I would like to know?" Bryce asked, as he pulled Viola against him.

Watching the winsome girl singing her way through lupine, bitter root, daisies and sweet clover, Viola replied, "No, not a thing, but it's kind of weird because I'm not sure, but maybe ... well, another month and we'll know for sure. But how could Wendy know? Maybe she's just hoping ... ." the sentence was never finished as Bryce's lips found hers.

With the arrival of Calvin, everything picked up in tempo. Richard now had company in the barn and the Lytles moved into their new home, leaving the Girouards to themselves in the bunkhouse. Sheds and corrals were completed and drift fences across the winter range progressed.

Everyone was in a pleasant mood when Marvin and Kalee Querring drove their Pierce surrey into the C-Bar-M barnyard one bright and sunny day.

Kalee quickly and shyly joined the ladies as Tommy unhitched the Morgan and Marvin gathered the men around.

"Clay, you know how we've been discussing the probability of rustling problems? It looks like that may have started. Rob and I bought out the Rockin-K over in the Mussellshell and we had the Rockin-K stock all bunched up to drive over here this week. Somebody ran 'em off night before last and shot up Jimmy Day a doin' it."

"How's Jimmy?"

"Doc Mac says he's going to be okay but we sure lost some pretty good stock. There was some of them new Hereford bulls in the bunch."

"Do you think the Stringer Jack bunch from up on the Missouri has spread out into the Mussellshell?"

"No, I don't think so. Jimmy said he didn't recognize anybody, but he did notice that they didn't know much about herding cattle. They sat their horses like a bunch of dudes and besides, Stringer Jack ain't known to readily gun down nobody, which is why he's gotten by so easy to now. Jimmy said this bunch just threw down on him and started blazin' away as soon as he rode up. He said if they was good shots he'd be fulla' holes. He thinks it was just a lucky shot that got him. Hell, they plugged his horse twice before Jimmy went down and he just laid there like dead until they run the herd off."

Clay thought a moment and then agreed, "No, it sure don't sound like John Stringer and his bunch, although, if the boys at Gransville Stuart's place and the other ranchers around there don't run him down and break up his gang, Stringer's gonna' be down here sooner or later."

"What do you propose we do, Marvin?" Bryce asked. "If they're strangers just moved in, they've got to be hanging around one of the towns over there. The local people should be able to point them out. One of us could kind of snoop around over there and maybe get a line on them. I'd be glad to go over and nose around some, if it would help."

"Naw, that ain't gonna' work. You wouldn't know who to talk to. It hast to be one of us knows the people over in the Mussellshell," Curly said.

"Curly's right," Roy added. "I wonder if the Severance Ranch is losin' any cattle? They've got a big spread and old Jake Severance knows everything that's goin' on in the valley."

"Why don't I ride over that way for a few days and see what I can find?" Marvin said. "It was our cattle that got rustled and our hand that got shot up."

Everyone agreed with the plan, but Clay cautioned Marvin against taking any action on his own. "We don't want this bunch to get out of hand like Stringer's gang. If you find out something, Marvin, come back and we'll get together with the other ranchers to run them down."

Things settled down to an uneasy routine after the news of the rustling.

Calvin asked Bryce, "Good God, do they always just go around shooting each other out here till they get what they want?"

Bryce assured him that this was only a brutal few but that he should keep a rifle with him at all times when away from headquarters anyway.

Calvin had never owned a handgun but he was a good hunter and a good shot, so reluctantly agreed.

Seeking to ease the tension, Pauline suggested that they all have dinner that evening at the main house where get togethers always brought out the best of humor in all. After dinner, the conversation nonetheless drifted back to the shooting and rustling.

Standing at Viola's side, Pauline said, "Will Montana ever become a state and be governed by a law of the people? How long will this lawlessness continue?"

"Not until we woman have a vote in how Montana is governed," Viola blurted out.

"Well, I'll be damned," Curly said, "that little wife of your'n sure has a mind of her own, Bryce."

Bryce just smiled and nodded his head. Juanita moved up beside Viola and, as if by instinct, Wendy left the checker game to join them.

"I don't see why, if Wyoming can give the vote to women, that Montana couldn't do the same," Juanita joined in.

"Well, I guess we men have just gotten the word," Clay remarked.

Turning to pat Pauline's extended tummy and then her own, Viola stated emphatically, "And that goes for all six of us."

Curly slapped his leg and broke out in laughter. Shortly all were laughing heartily and tensions eased.

Everyone anxiously awaited the arrival of the McMahon's new child. Viola privately reminded Bryce that she was an experienced midwife and must be near when Pauline went into labor. Clay became nervous as an alley cat as the time grew shorter but kept busy making plans for a trip back east after the baby was born.

Both Clayton and Pauline longed to see the families they had left years ago and planned to mix business with pleasure. While in the area, Clay would be shopping for Aberdeen Angus bulls, which he would ship back by rail. If things went right, he hoped to pick up at least six, reasonably pure blood Angus.

The time came early in the morning, when Clayton pounded on the bunkhouse door. "Viola, Pauline's having pains. She says the baby is on its way. Hurry up! Please."

"Now don't get in a tizzy, Clay," Viola called, "These things don't happen that fast. You just get a fire going and put at least a gallon of water on to heat. I'll be right there."

Bryce jumped out of bed and started pulling on his pants when Viola calmly asked, "And just where are you going?"

"I'm going to help. You'll need help."

"One distraught father is more male help than I'll need. You just go wake Juanita, then get back here and stay in bed till breakfast. You and Wendy will have to shift for yourselves today and please stay out of the way until we call you."

Viola slipped into a dress, picked up a stack of white broadcloth and with a "Well! Go get Juanita," left Bryce fumbling to get his suspenders on the proper shoulders.

When Viola entered, she found Clayton on his knees holding Pauline's hand as she sat smiling, in a rocker.

"Do you have the water on yet, Clay?" she asked. "If not, get it started and then I will need your help in modifying the bed." She turned to Pauline and asked, "Have you timed them, honey?"

"No," Pauline responded, "But they're not too frequent. They just started about an hour ago."

Juanita showed up and the ladies were calmly timing contractions when Clay again bolted into the room. "Waters on Viola. What did you want to do with the bed?"

"Just bring me that ramp I had Bryce build last week and I'll show you how I want you to prop up the head of the bed."

"Why prop up the bed?" Juanita asked.

"So that Pauline will be more erect during delivery," Viola explained. "Instead of pulling on the poor baby to prevent retraction between pushes, we'll let gravity do that. There's less chance of injuring the baby that way and it's more natural for the mother."

Pauline listened, between contractions, as Viola continued, "Native peoples have been delivering their babies this way for centuries. The mother merely squats over a mat of moss or other soft matter. All they need is something to hang onto and pull against during pushes. American Indians usually have other squaws who take turns giving support."

Pauline, now beginning to sweat under more intense labor, gasped, "If you think it is easier that way, it's fine with me."

"My father has used the system for years," Viola replied, "He adopted it after attending several Indian births. Come on Juanita, let's get Pauline positioned and then we'll wash her up real good with warm water. Cleanliness is very important to prevent post natal infection in both mother and child. The warm compresses also relax the muscles to help dilation."

Clayton paced the living room like a caged animal, stopping in agony at each moan and soft cry of pain he could hear through the closed door.

After what seemed an eternity, all sounds ceased and Clayton stood still, listening to the silence. Fright welled up in his throat. Why so silent? What has happened? Unable to stand it any longer, he rapped on the door and called, "Viola, Juanita, what's wrong, is something wrong?"

A very cheerful voice responded, "Not a thing is wrong with Pauline or your beautiful new daughter, Clay. Just a minute, until the placenta is ejected and we clean up, then you can see your family."

Rushing out to the front porch, where a nervous Tommy rocked back and forth, Clayton sat down beside the boy and pulled him to his side. "Your baby sister is here and everything is fine, Tommy. Rebecca is born," he said.

The beautiful girl child at Pauline's breast entranced Clayton and Tommy. Round of head and cheek, little Rebecca looked toward their voices with soft, blue eyes as she drew in her mother's milk.

Stroking the soft, little head of white hair, Clayton remarked, "She has to be a good girl, Pauline. I never heard her cry like most newborns."

"That's because she wasn't spanked upon birth like most doctors do," Pauline said. "Viola and Juanita just gently cleaned the mucous from her mouth and nose and then laid her in my arms. The umbilical cord was still attached, Clay. She even smiled, I know she did."

Juanita laughed loudly at the remark as she left the room, shaking her head. "They're such a beautiful family. And don't I have a beautiful granddaughter? Rebecca was my mother's name, you know. She would have been so proud."

She and Viola embraced, delighted at the part they had played in the miracle of birth.

CHAPTER XII
THE CLEANSING

A group of grim men clustered about Marshal Garwood, looking apprehensively towards the C-Bar-M headquarters.

"We can't tell him now, Marshal, not now. Not just after the birth of his daughter," Bryce said and Calvin nodded agreement. "Let's just work this thing out ourselves with Bob and the other ranchers. Clayton can stay here and take care of things while we hunt those bastards down."

Curly and Roy, just returned from a tough trail drive from Texas, stood dusty and beat nearby. "If we can just catch a few of them sons-o-bitches and swing 'em from a limb, the others would just turn tail and run. We done that down in Texas once and that sure as hell broke up their gang," Curly remarked.

"They shot him in the back right in Merino?" Roy asked.

"Yep, Marvin had been askin' around about these strangers in town and they must of got wind of it. The guy that brought the news was from the Severance ranch and he said Marvin was workin' with 'em and Marshal Kline and they know who some of the gang is. They don't know who the gang's working for though." Marshal Garwood paused and then continued, "They seem to steal only from small outlying ranches that are having a tough time of it. Funny thing is, as soon as they steal a herd and the ranch goes belly up, there's an outfit from back east has already made a measly offer to buy 'em out. After losing their herd, what choice do they have? They've all sold out to this bunch."

"Who are they?" Calvin asked.

"We don't know any of the people but the deeds are all made out to the Amalgamated Cattle Syndicate of Chicago. Probably a group of eastern or maybe even European investors."

"If they're hiring gunmen from the east to do their rustling and killing for them, that accounts for why they seem to be such poor cowboys and shots," Bryce mused. "Where do we go from here, Marshal?"

"As you know, we have damn few sheriffs hired out here and we marshals don't have much authority out of town. There's only two U.S. marshals in the territory—one in Missoula and the other in Helena—so they ain't much help."

"What do you suggest?" Bryce asked.

"We vigilante 'em, that's what we do!" Curly bellowed out. "Just like in Texas. We form us a vigilante posse and we run their asses down and hang 'em."

"Curly's right," the Marshal said. "Me and all the marshals around here will jail and hold any you bring in alive. That we can do for you, but running 'em down, you'll have to do that yourselves. Rob Querring wants a meeting tomorrow in my office at two in the afternoon to put this together. How many from here?"

Bryce, Calvin, Ochs, Lytle, Curly and Roy all lifted their hands.

"Let's see, that makes six from the C-Bar-M then," Marshal Garwood remarked, as he started to write the names down.

"No," a commanding voice said, "That makes five from the C-Bar-M. Curly and Roy are staying and I'm going." They all turned to see Clayton as he stepped from behind a wagon.

"But, Clay, you can't run off and leave your new youngun that way. Roy and I can hold up our end. We've done this afore," Curly protested.

"Yes, I know," Clayton said in a more tender voice. "You two can contribute as much as anybody, but you are the only two I want to entrust the ranch and our families to while we're gone."

Bryce looked at Curly and nodded in agreement and the two old wranglers fell moodily silent.

"I'm going because of Rebecca, and her future, as well as to avenge Marvin's killing. I've the most experience at this sort of thing and we've got to succeed or we're all going to get run out. If we go about this intelligently and well planned, we can put a stop to it without too much danger. If we just go hurrahing after them with guns blazing, some of us are bound to get hurt or killed."

It was with difficulty that the married men said good bye to their families at the C-Bar-M. Bryce, in particular, struggled with how to explain it to Viola as he dug out the long-unused gun belt.

With tears in her eyes, Viola only held him close and said, "I more clearly understand the West now and I know these good things could not happen for us if we were not willing to fight for them. Just like my forefathers did, the good people in this world sometimes are forced to turn to violence in order to survive."

It was a subdued assemblage in Marshal Garwood's office that day. In addition to the five from the C-Bar-M, a bitter Rob Querring and Jimmy Day, representing the Q2, and the hand from the Severance ranch were there to make a group of eight.

Marshal Garwood started the meeting off with an admirable depiction of Clayton's background as a lawman and how he urged them all to accept him as leader of the group and trust in his decisions.

No one dissented and Clayton began to lay out a plan.

"Our study of this bunch and how they operate leads me to believe they are working for this Amalgamated Cattle Syndicate," Clayton began. "They seem to just hang around Merino until some small rancher is all set up by the Syndicate and then they go in and run their cattle off, forcing them to sell. Up to now, they haven't hit any of the bigger ranches but as soon as they get big enough, they will, believe me. They only ran off the Rockin-K stock when Jimmy, here, got shot because the Rockin-K sold out to the Querrings before the Syndicate could get to them. Probably pissed them off and they wanted to get even."

"Now, we could try to identify the next little ranch they are apt to hit, stake it out and when they come to run the herd off, probably at night, confront them. We'd end up in a gun battle under poor conditions and some of us are bound to get hurt."

Realizing more and more the leadership qualities in this intelligent man, Bryce said, "That makes sense, Clay, but what other course of action do you suggest?"

"We know that Marvin had identified quite a number of these rustlers before he was killed and Marshal Kline knows who they are. I suggest we slip into Merino individually and let Kline point them out to us, one-by-one. Then we catch each one alone and off guard, disarm them, spirit them out of town to the Severance Ranch or one of the other ranches where they can keep them locked up until they're fairly well decimated."

"If we do this right, they aren't going to know what happens to their sidekicks and are going to get spooky. Then those left are going to join up and stick together to cover each other's ass. They'll be easy to recognize then and we'll be able to see what we're up against."

"They may just pack up and pull out, too. Then what?" Rob Querring asked.

"Every town marshal around here has been alerted and if they show up, they'll let us know. Then we move to that town and start over again. They'll stick out like sore thumbs in any of these small towns, so if they are easterners I'll just bet they'll move to one of the larger places like Billings or Big Timber. If we do this right, though, we may not spook them before we get them all.

"One more thing," Clayton added, "Other than Bryce and myself, I don't want anybody trying to take one of these guys alone. We don't want any face offs or shoot outs. Work in pairs and catch each one alone, out of town, or in the dark. We don't owe these bastards any courtesies and we don't have to act honorably. Rob, I'll want you to be a liaison between us, the law, and the ranchers."

"Now just a damn minute, Clay. It was my brother that was killed and I got a right to help run them that did it down," Rob Querring bristled.

"That's why it won't work for you to do any stalking . You're too emotionally involved. One little slip that will identify us and we'll have the face-to-face confrontation we need to avoid."

Bryce placed his hand on the rigid shoulder and said, "Trust him, Rob, he's right. We're going to get the guy that shot Marvin. Let the plan work."

"That's about all till we get to Merino," Clayton said. "Now if we were a posse, eight would just be too many. Four to six is best, but for what we got planned, we've just got enough."

Once in Merino and lodged in separate quarters, the group set about putting Clay's plan into action. Bryce found himself deeply interested in the workings and realized it was not unlike the old intrigue of a poker game.

Marshal Kline identified eleven strangers as part of the group and one-by-one they began to disappear—some as they staggered to their rooms after a night in the saloon—until there were three locked up at the Severance Ranch, one in Hick Jensen's jail in Buffalo, one in Spencer Garwood's jail in Moccasin and another in a root cellar at the Winnecook ranch.

The remaining five suddenly disappeared from the streets and it was obvious they had grouped up or left town.

The six now under lock and key were grilled relentlessly and true to suspicions were found to be from the Chicago area. "Drugstore Cowboys," Jimmy Day scornfully called them.

According to the daily reports Marshal Kline received, none of those incarcerated had involved anyone else or any financial group, but he remained confident that in time they would break down and tell all. "Then we get a deposition from each that we can use in court and we go after the Syndicate," he said.

Two days after the rustlers failed to show their faces in town, Kline got a message from an informant that one of the five had slipped out of town and was riding hell bent for leather to the east on the stage road.

"Billings, he has to be heading for Billings," Clayton said. "Any way we can beat him there and find out who he's gonna' contact?"

Bryce spoke up. "Let me take out after him, Clay. You remember that cross country trip we led you on last fall?" As Clay nodded with a sheepish grin, Bryce continued, "I can cut off like we did then, skirt Molt to the south and then cut more to the east and be there in a hard day's ride."

Bryce arrived late that afternoon in Billings and wearily searched out Barney Carver. The tubby little marshal was surprised to see Bryce but welcomed him as an old friend and one whom he had helped out in the past, even if he was coerced into doing it.

Knowing things would go better if he stroked the fur, Bryce humbly apologized to Marshal Carver for asking another favor of him.

Could he help out? "You bet, I got a finger on everything in this town. I'll know the minute this guy hits town and who he gets together with. Why don't you go down and have Madge fix you a meal? She'll be glad to see you and find out how Wendy's a doin'."

Yeah, I'll bet that old bitch will be glad to see me, Bryce thought, but he knew the Marshal could find him easy that way, so what the hell.

The waiter's eyes lit up as soon as he saw Bryce and hurried over to his table. "Hello there, Mr. Girouard, nice to see you again. How's Wendy?"

Bryce explained how she was thriving and then asked if Madge had any arsenic in the kitchen. When the waiter gleefully replied, "No!" Bryce said "Well, then bring me the baked ham dinner and don't tell Madge I'm here, please. How's the old gal doing, anyway?"

"Not worth a damn, Mr. Girouard. She's been meaner hell ever since that little woman of yours chopped her down to size. I'm leaving here Monday. I got a job managing the dining room at the General Custer."

"Well, I'll know where to eat next time I'm in town," Bryce said as the waiter left with his order.

Bryce had just finished his meal when Marshal Carver came swaggering in. "Just like I told you, Mr. Girouard, we picked up his trail as soon as he hit town. He went straight to this shyster lawyer's office down on Grant Street. He's there yet, I guess."

"Who's this lawyer?"

"His name is Murphy and he just came to town early this spring from back east somewheres and set up a business. His signs say he's a land and title specialist. Whatever that is."

Bryce had just positioned himself outside Murphy's office when a tall skinny man came out, untied the salt-stained bay and led him down the street towards the livery stable.

Bryce studied the man as he paralleled his course on the wooden walkway. He was lean and hatchet faced with eyes set too close together. A forty-five hung low on each hip, each holster tied down with a thong. Bryce recognized the man as one of the many outlaw types ranging the west. Ready to do anything but work for a dollar, they would hire themselves out for any illegal activity, including murder. He was not fresh from the east and no novice at rustling cattle or drawing down on another man.

Watching the man leave the livery, Bryce eyed him as he crossed to the General Custer Hotel and entered.

The old courier was rubbing down the bay when Bryce entered on the pretense of checking up on his mount.

"That bay has sure been ridden hard today," he remarked.

"Yeah, kinda' like yours was too, mister. Only you didn't let your buckskin stand around and chill out like this. Hell of a way to treat a good hoss."

Bryce peered to read the brand in the dim light when the old man said, "It's Broken Star brand. Last time I seen that was down in Arizona. Near Wickenburg, I think."

Early next morning, Bryce was mounted and in the cottonwoods along the Mussellshell. Sooner than expected, the bay showed, going at a trot.

Bryce spurred Hoodoo out into the stage road and turned towards Merino as the bay gained steadily. When the hatchet faced man drew abreast he spurred the buckskin up to ride side-by-side.

The beady-eyed gunslinger looked over at Bryce and yelled, "What the hell do you want."

"Nothing but company stranger. I just thought you might enjoy the same," Bryce yelled back.

The grim face never changed as the rustler stared straight ahead and maintained the pace.

Pulling up at a small stream, he let the reins fall so that the bay could drink and stared hard at Bryce. "I don't need no company and I don't recall invitin' you to ride along."

"I can understand that, beings you're probably running from the law and would just as soon not be seen around here. I'd guess you're one of the men rustling all those cattle around here."

The skinny man jerked his mount around to face Bryce so that both pistols showed plainly. Dropping the reins his hands moved to hover over the butts.

"I wouldn't do that if I were you, mister," Bryce said, already in position, his six shooter riding free just below his belt. Hoodoo stood stock still.

"Why, you goddamned dude," the taut lips muttered as two hands streaked for gun butts.

Two shots rang out in rapid staccato and the lean face contorted in pain as his two pistols went flying in opposite directions. The terrified bay went plunging across the creek and up the other bank.

A long gangly body hit the water with a splat and muddy water turned dirty red as the man writhed in pain.

Bryce sat astride his still motionless buckskin and looked down at the gory scene. The right arm flopped about from the elbow down and the left hand the man tried to use to get erect kept folding into a useless blob.

"One time too many, mister, just one time too many," Bryce softly said as he dismounted. "Damn fool, you God-damned fool!"

Struggling to drag the gaunt body out of the stream and to a level spot beside the stage road, Bryce stretched the sobbing and moaning gunman out on the ground. He quickly pulled the man's bandanna off and cinched it tightly above the shattered elbow and then firmly wrapped the mangled left hand with his own.

"Why didn't you just kill me?" the man sobbed, "Why, Why?"

"Because you don't get off that easy, buddy. You've got some talking to do. You're going to explain a lot of things."

"Anything. I'll tell you everything. Just get me to a doctor before I bleed to death. Please," the man pleaded.

The man revealed his name as Clem Jackson and that he had been hired by lawyer Luke Murphy to lead a group of toughs sent out from Chicago by the Syndicate. They had been ordered to break the small ranchers down, forcing them to sell by any method it took, including murder.

"Is that why you gunned down Marvin Querring from the back?"

"I didn't do that, mister, believe me. It was Wilson did that."

"Who's Wilson?"

"You got him jailed somewhere. You guys got him right off the bat."

So the killer was one of the six they had locked up. That was all Bryce needed to know. Now to get this bloody mess of a man to Merino before he died of shock or blood loss.

Bryce was pondering his dilemma when he heard the welcome sounds of the morning stage. With the wounded man sprawled on the floor between horrified passengers and the bay tied on behind, the driver careened towards Merino at full gallop.

Bryce pushed Hoodoo to his limit as he slowly out-distanced the stage, riding through Shawmut Crossing and on to Merino, sliding to a stop at Marshal Kline's office.

When Bryce entered, Marshal Kline leaped to his feet. "Good God, man! What happened to you? You're all covered with blood."

Bryce related the story and asked, "Do you know which one of the six we got is this Wilson?"

"Yep, he's in Hick Jensen's lock up in Buffalo. The hands at the Severance and Winnecook scared the shit out of those gutless, eastern toughs and they all signed confessions. They've all blamed the Querring shooting on this Pete Wilson. We got all we need to bring him before the Territorial Judge on a murder charge. Clay thinks we've got enough proof to break that damn Syndicate too."

"How do we go about that?" Bryce asked.

"Clay says the first thing to do is bust the news to all the western newspapers. When they print that, the big eastern publishers will pick it up and blow it sky high. They'll investigate every board member and major stockholder. They'll strip 'em bare."

Clayton McMahon burst through the door to embrace Bryce's blood-soaked shoulders. "By God, Bryce, thank God you're back. I just helped carry that poor bastard you shot up into the doc. You outdrew a double gun and got each arm before he could even level up. Jesus, Bryce, what a chance you took. Why didn't you just take him in the head or chest. What if you missed?"

"But, I didn't miss. And here I thought you wanted to interrogate this guy but all I get is an ass chewing," Bryce complained.

The Marshal roared his enjoyment at the remark and Clay's sheepish grin.

Marshal Jensen delivered a whining Pete Wilson to Merino to stand trial and the other gang members were jailed wherever cells were available in nearby towns to await their turn in court.

Marshal Kline had taken one look at the hatchet face of Clem Jackson and went back to fumble through old wanted posters. "Here it is," he yelled. "I knew I'd seen that face somewhere. Ten thousand dollars, Bryce. Wanted for stage robbery and murder in Santa Fe, only that ain't his real name. He's really Hank Coleman and is a well-known gunman and holdup man down there."

"Do you suppose the reward is still good? We could use it to help restock some of the small ranchers, or buy them out if they want to give it up," Bryce said.

"Oh, most of them cattle is holed up on the upper Sweet Grass in the Crazies. They didn't want the cattle. They were just out to break the ranchers," Kline said. "I guess Injuns killed a few of 'em but they said they just run 'em up to good grass and only left one guy up there to keep 'em from strayin' down. Take a lot of work, but you guys should be able to round up most of 'em."

"Before we close this thing down, we've got to get hold of all those little ranchers that the Syndicate bought out and inform them of their rights and where their cattle are," Clayton said. "They can ride up the Sweet Grass and take care of that yahoo who's guarding the cattle. But that's government graze and they just as well leave the cattle up there until bad weather runs 'em down and then have a roundup."

As usual, Clayton's brain was clicking, calculating and weighing all the odds. He doesn't miss a bet, Bryce thought to himself.

"I'll get letters off to Santa Fe and Billings," Marshal Kline said. "I'll have Marshal Carver pick up this lawyer, Murphy, and impound all the records. You guys can all go back home and I'll keep you posted on what happens. You sure done a slick job. Montana's going to be a state someday and we'll need good representation and I've got some recommendations to make then."

CHAPTER XIII
CLASH OF CULTURES

It was a cool and breezy day in mid October, when the widowed Kalee Querring rode onto the C-Bar-M astride a big Q2 roan loaded down with two buckskin bags.

Pauline met Kalee as she dismounted and attempting to embrace the grieving widow, felt the small body stiffen in resistance.

Knowing the Indian culture did not entertain close emotions, choosing to be more passive, Pauline relaxed her arms holding only to the small, dark hand. "Kalee, how nice of you to come to see us. We're so honored to have you here." Observing the huge bags loaded with personal belongings, she continued, "Can you stay with us a while?"

Unleashing the bags, Kalee replied, "I'm gonna' live at the C-Bar-M, to hell with the Q2."

"Why, Kalee, what's the matter? You have a house of your own at the Q2 and I know Bob and Dorothy love you. Surely you can stay there forever if you wish."

"They don't want Kalee. They make me live alone. Blackfeet women don't live alone. To hell with the Q2."

Not understanding, but wise enough not to push the issue, Pauline cheerfully said, "Why certainly, you can stay as long as you like, Kalee. We'll find a place for you to stay."

"Kalee a damn good worker. I'll work hard for you, Mrs. McMahon. I can cook and care for baby and I can wash clothes. Wilma teach me to sew and I can make pretty clothes for you." The dark eyes were dull in an expressionless face.

"We can all use your help. Come on in and let's visit a bit. We'll have to find you a place to sleep but we'll work something out."

As they entered the house, Kalee muttered, "Damn Q2 don't want Kalee to sleep no place. Just all alone."

Not understanding the anger in Kalee, nor the meaning of her statements, Pauline went about making a pot of tea as Kalee held Rebecca and gazed down at the little face. Suddenly she said, "Rebecca sure is white. Like sky clouds."

After tea in silence, Pauline said, "Let's go visit the rest of the ladies and find you a place to stay."

Pauline, Kalee and Rebecca went visiting. First to Juanita's little house, to the bunkhouse and Viola, then the entire group walked on to Mildred Lytle's new home.

Kalee remained impassively quiet as the ladies talked and Pauline explained her decision to move to the C-Bar-M. Mildred Lytle, quick to grasp the situation, suggested that Kalee stay with them. They had an extra bedroom they had built into their new home in anticipation of other children.

Kalee only said, "Okay, I'll work real hard."

Mildred and the quiet Indian girl left to inspect the spare room as the three other ladies slipped away.

Conversing over a cup of tea at Juanita's, Pauline detailed the strange behavior Kalee had displayed and they pondered the reason she was so upset with the Q2.

"These Indians have strange ways that we can't always understand," Juanita said. "They react to trauma, such as the loss of a loved one, in different ways than we do, and they're so inscrutable that it's difficult to draw their feelings out."

Later that afternoon, Pauline heard the sounds of an approaching buggy and stepped out on the porch as Rob and Doreen Querring pulled up at the hitch rail.

"Is Kalee here?" Doreen asked and continued, when Pauline nodded affirmatively, "We're so worried about her and we need to talk about it. She seemed to revert back to Indian ways after she lost Marvin and has done some strange things."

The Querrings explained how Kalee chanted and wailed night and day for the entire moon of traditional Indian mourning. "She just kneeled on that blanket and went through these rituals. She wouldn't even acknowledge our presence when we tried to console her," Doreen said. "I don't know how much she ate, but she lost a lot of weight and that's not good either because she's pregnant you know."

"The real problems began after the mourning period," Rob explained. "She came to the house and announced that she was moving in. That it was my responsibility to take her in as a second wife and take care of her. According to Blackfeet culture, I would own her and could keep her as a wife, beat her if I felt like it, trade her for horses, or sell her into slavery, whatever I wished to do."

"When we tried to explain to her that white people didn't do that, but we still loved her and would care for her and the baby as long as she wanted to stay, she cussed us out and left," Doreen said.

"I guess, in her mind, she felt rejected and worthless if she didn't have a man of her own, being pregnant and all," Rob reasoned, "She took after our hand, Jimmy Day, like a hungry mountain lion. Cooking for him and waiting on him hand and foot. She wouldn't let him eat with the rest of us and hung around him whenever he was at the ranch. Then one night she entered the bunk house and tried to crawl into the bunk with him. Jimmy said she didn't have nothing on and was very insistent that he had accepted her as his wife and now he had to seal the bond.

"Jimmy said he kinda' panicked and wasn't too kind in kicking her out. She's been sulking and cussing us since, until she pulled out today. She doesn't seem to believe we love her and want to have her and our future kin child near us."

With more understanding, all the folks at the C-Bar-M tried to make Kalee welcome and true to her word, she slaved away at any and every chore asked of her. Mildred Lytle's house sparkled and little two-year-old Lorena proudly displayed the traditional Indian garb Kalee would doll her up in at times.

But, as time went on, in her own inscrutable way, Kalee began paying more and more attention to the single men at the ranch and constantly shadowed Calvin and Richard Ochs as they performed their duties about the ranch, insisting on doing the heaviest work for them. Slipping into their quarters, when gone, she would steal their clothing to wash and mend, then return them neatly folded, often with a treat of cookies or other snacks.

As her slender body began to show the swelling of her child, Kalee became more and more morose, responding only to Viola on those non-school days when she was at the ranch. Viola, had somehow opened a narrow door of communication with Kalee, trying to draw her out and to better understand her feelings.

On a clear, crisp October day, Bryce and Viola arrived at their temporary quarters to find Kalee sitting in the darkest corner. Refusing to respond in Bryce's presence, Viola sent him out and then pulled up a chair facing Kalee.

Reaching out for the stiff and unfriendly hand, Viola asked, "What is it Kalee? What's wrong? Why are you sitting alone in the dark?"

"To hell with you and your brother," Kalee blurted out. "You don't want Kalee. Your damn men folks too good to marry Blackfoot squaw. To hell with them all."

After some thought, Viola hazarded a guess. "You would like Calvin to take you as his wife. Is that it Kalee?"

"To hell with Calvin, he don't want Blackfoot squaw with big belly. I'm going to go back to my people where they ain't so damn fancy."

"Kalee, it isn't that Calvin doesn't like you, because I know he does, but we white people are different than the Indians. We marry for love, like you and Marvin did. You remember that love don't you, Kalee?"

"To hell with white man's love. What good does that do Indian squaw now? Nobody wants me."

"Did you know Bryce is half Cherokee Indian and this child in my womb is one fourth Cherokee? The unborn child in your womb is one half white man and one half Blackfoot and you can be proud of that. Also, did you know that Juanita is one half French and one half Mexican/ Indian? This is not uncommon. I'm half Scottish and half Welsh," Viola patiently explained.

"Me, I'm Blackfoot. I'm going back to my people," the bitter Indian girl adamantly said.

"Pauline lost her husband, just as you did and because she was patient and strong, she eventually found a new man and father for

Tommy. You can do the same if you just stay here with us and have the baby. Someday, the right man will come along and you will again be loved and cared for by a husband. We all love and care about you. Why don't you give our 'white man's' way a try?" Viola pleaded.

For the first time, Kalee looked directly at Viola and squeezed her hand, but Viola could read nothing of her thoughts in the fathomless eyes and expressionless face.

A tapping on the bunk house door at next day's light rolled the Girouard family out. Steve and Mildred Lytle stood at the door, little Lorena between them.

"Kalee's gone, Viola," Mildred stated. "She must have sneaked out last night. We didn't hear anything, but she's gone."

Sharing breakfast, the two families speculated about Kalee's actions and worried about what lay ahead for her.

"She tried to get in bed with Calvin night before last," Viola remarked, "Just like she did with Jimmy Day over at the Q2."

"According to Blackfeet culture, if either had accepted her and had relations with her," Bryce explained, "they would be stuck with her as a kind of common-law wife and would be expected to marry her formally."

"Apparently, she's completely crushed and demoralized at three rejections," Mildred reasoned. "That poor girl and the child won't stand a chance as a half breed among the pure blood Blackfeet."

The days passed quickly as the C-Bar-M continued to move ahead with plans for the future. Bryce purchased two more ranches and their non-descript herds. Both were among those who had sold out to the Amalgamated Cattle Syndicate, but had recovered their cattle and deeds.

The Syndicate was in bankruptcy and the members of the rustler gang were all convicted. Pete Wilson died by hanging for the murder of Marvin Querring, and Hank Coleman, alias Clem Jackson, was sent back to Santa Fe to stand trial for stage robbery and murder. Jackson was patched as best as Doc Mac could do, but ended up with only a stub of a right arm and a distorted claw for a left hand. The reward was still valid and Marshal Kline expected to receive the voucher any day.

Loafing sheds were completed and the hay piled in huge stacks in readiness for the long winter. Drift fences were all completed to keep herds from straying during winter storms, and the roundup was over.

All mature longhorn bulls had been marketed and all longhorn bull calves castrated as the first step in herd improvement. The Angus bulls had done their jobs well and all the selected brood cows were carrying young. Everyone at the C-Bar-M felt deep satisfaction over the results of the summer's labor.

The nights had turned sharply colder and sunny clear days alternated with snow flurries when Kalee returned.

Clayton found her one cold morning huddled against a wagon wheel, wrapped in a tattered and dirty buffalo robe, hair matted and her face a mass of scars and still-bleeding welts. He carried the small body, nothing but skin and bones, to the sanctuary of the ranch house. Leaving her in Pauline's care, Clayton rushed to get Juanita and Mildred.

When the two ladies arrived, they found Pauline, horrified and incensed at the sight of the brutalized body before her. Stripping Kalee of the dirty rags exposed a body covered with bruises and cuts, some old, some new. Long jagged cuts ran from the breasts to crotch and a series of slashes crisscrossed her breasts and buttocks. The bulge of pregnancy, so obvious upon leaving, was now gone.

"Who would do such a thing, who, who?" Pauline cried. "Who could be so brutal?" She wept as she clutched the emaciated little figure to her.

"Her own people," Juanita said.

"What?" Mildred asked.

"Let's get her in a tub of warm water and I'll tell you what I have learned. Curly was friends with a white man who had several Indian wives. I once found it hard to believe what Curly related to me, but no longer. No longer!"

Filling the wooden tub with warm water they carefully eased the shaking girl into the soothing depths and began to gently cleanse the battered body.

"Curly claims that once a girl leaves the tribe and then seeks to return, she must throw herself on the mercy of the tribal council. They will decide her fate, based on what she has done and who speaks up for her or against her. If they refuse to accept her back into the tribe and no warrior wants her as a wife, then she is turned over to the squaws as a slave. They can do anything they want with her and no one will interfere."

"Anything? Like this?" Mildred asked.

"Yes, a warrior may beat his wife but it is vengeful squaws who mutilate like this."

Kalee remained silent and indifferent as the ladies went about gently bathing the dirt from her body. She stood, head down, as they patted her dry and then led her to a bed. They quietly applied dressings to the open wounds, each woman deep in thought.

Sheathed in one of Pauline's flannel night gowns and under warm blankets, Kalee had quit shaking and seemed to drift off to sleep.

As they cleaned up after the bath, Pauline suddenly asked. "Slavery yes, I can understand that, but why this torture, this maiming?"

"Undoubtedly, to show their contempt," Juanita answered. "Kalee made a horrible mistake by going back to the tribe after marrying a white and pregnant with his child."

"Do all Indians react this way?"

"I guess not, but Curly said the Blackfeet are the cruelest of all and the squaws are no exception. They probably marked her up to brand her for life and make her unattractive to any warrior as a wife. Bucks will use such squaws for pleasure, at will, even rape them, but none will marry them."

"She's no longer pregnant, that's obvious," said Mildred.

"Any wonder. Did you see the bruises and scars on her abdomen," Pauline said, with a shudder.

"I wonder if she will tell us about it?" Juanita said, half to herself.

"I doubt it," Pauline replied. "She hasn't said a word yet. Maybe she will talk to Viola when she gets here tomorrow. I'll try to get her to eat when she wakes up. She's half starved, I'm sure."

A cold wind blew from the Little Belts when, well bundled, Bryce, Viola and Wendy arrived mid-morning the next day.

Intercepting the family, Clayton related the previous day's events. "She eaten a little but hasn't said one word. Maybe you can get her to talk, Viola."

The icy blue darts flashed again in Viola's eyes as she learned of the abuse Kalee had endured and, reading the signs, Bryce pulled her close.

Kalee clung to Viola and for the first time allowed herself to be hugged. The proud resistance to affection, so distinct before, was now replaced by an abject defeatism. Try as she might, Viola could not get Kalee to say a word.

Viola observed, "I can now begin to see the huge gulf between the Indian and white man's culture. It will take a long time. At least four generations of pain and struggle before we are melted into one people."

Not seeming to want Viola out of her sight, Kalee was moved to the bunkhouse where she could be nearby night and day. Appearing to find comfort in this nearness, Kalee nonetheless never offered to speak again.

On the third day the Girouards awoke to find Kalee gone. She had slipped out in the middle of the snowy night and disappeared. A frantic Viola aided in searching the ranch for the girl until a yell from Curly drew their attention.

"Here are her tracks," Curly yelled. "They're headin' straight toward the mountain up Big Baldy."

As Curly followed the tracks on foot, the rest of the men hurriedly saddled mounts and the search began. Up the gradual slopes of the Little Belts, the small tracks led to a spot where Kalee had chosen to end her confused and beleaguered life.

They found her cold and lifeless body in a sitting position against an ancient fir tree. She sat beneath the spangled boughs, the bruised and battered, yet smiling face turned to the east—to the east where the great spirit would arrive riding the mighty war horse of dawn to claim his lost maiden.

The grim cowboys constructed the traditional Indian burial bier where Kalee would be safe from predation, leaving her with her face turned toward a gray and snowy east.

It was a silent and somber group, facing into the driving snow, as they descended the slopes of Big Baldy. Each felt pain in his own way for the little Native girl who could not rise to the white man's standards of culture. Were they wrong to expect so much of Kalee? Could one of them have made the sacrifice so crucial to Kalee's survival?

Questions never to be answered.

CHAPTER XIV
SHADES OF RED AND SCARLET

It was with great difficulty that the C-Bar-M and the Q2 continued with preparations for the coming winter. The tragic and dramatic episode with little Kalee Querring left everyone emotionally drained and it was with only the greatest of effort that each individual went about his or her daily routine.

It was Bryce, with Viola's support, who finally made sense of the incident and helped salve the hurt and guilt in each. Bryce broke the ice by recounting his and Clay's loss of Michelle and their deep pain. For the first time, he shared Viola's poem and the deeper meaning within, explaining how it had opened his eyes to an inevitable destiny with greater meaning and purpose than earthly wants.

Once the curtain of individual hurt, shame and guilt was lifted, everyone entered into candid discussion about the tremendous gulf between the Caucasian and Indian cultures.

"I can see now that what happened to Kalee and ourselves is only a small but tragic step towards the blending of the two ways of life," Pauline said. "Our Gods, although addressed differently, are one and the same. That 'Someone' has taken Kalee for a reason not totally understandable now, but it is part of the plan for us all. Kalee is now in the kindest of loving hands and we are all enriched from knowing, loving and losing her."

Heads nodded in agreement and Viola, clutching Wendy to her breast, softly said, "Eloquently spoken, Pauline. Kalee's trials in this world are over but we are here to carry on for her. There will be more tests of our strength and we must keep our faith in the Lord and His ways or we will fall by the wayside, having failed to contribute anything to the healing of the many maimed souls among us."

"One of those maimed souls," Clayton said, "is Jimmy Day over at the Q2. Rob Querring says he is guilt ridden and despondent because he so rudely rejected Kalee. He feels he's to blame for her death and that maybe he should have been kinder and maybe even married her."

"I know what Jimmy's going through," Calvin said. "Although I tried to explain to Kalee that I loved her as a sister and would always be here to help her over the rough times, I couldn't marry her just because that was traditional in her Native culture. She became very hurt and angry with me and you know how she could cuss a person out. Wow! But maybe I can see the cultural gap better than Jimmy. I don't think that kind of marriage to any of we single men had a chance of survival."

"That's the way Doreen looked at it too," Pauline said. "She realized Marvin was infatuated with Kalee, but she told me she just didn't see how it could work out over the long haul."

"I seen a number of white men that was married to Injun squaws," Curly interjected, "and they all treated 'em just like an Injun buck would. They beat hell out of 'em once in a while and worked their asses off all the time. They said if you didn't do that, the squaw would lose respect for you and just run off."

Steve Lytle added, "It seems one of the two has to adopt the others way of life. Like there just isn't any in between."

"Well, aren't you folks overlooking the fact that both Juanita and Bryce are from mixed- blood marriages with Indian blood involved?" Viola spoke out rather testily.

"Yes, honey. My mother was Cherokee Indian," Bryce quickly cut in, as the blue darts sparked in Viola's eyes, "But they were far more advanced and civilized than these plains Indians, even before contact with whites. They'd also been exposed to the European culture for over one hundred years before Mama and Papa married and she'd been through a white man's school. My Papa was strictly French and it was Mama who educated Missy and me. She was very intelligent."

"Well, what about you, Juanita?" questioned Mildred. "How did your parents' relationship work out?"

"Not always good. My mother was half Spanish and half Apache Indian. There were many disagreements and like Curly said, Mama just wouldn't back off until Papa beat her a bit. Then, she would go about her household chores, singing and happy as could be for a while. Papa told me once that those crazy Indian squaws just didn't feel loved unless their husbands beat them every so often. He said he didn't have to beat her hard, just kinda' go through the motions so that she believed he was doing right and then everything was lovey dovey for a while. Papa said if he waited too long without a beating, Mama would get ornery and start a fight over nothing just to get him to do it. Papa always pleaded with me not to adopt Mama's ways and I haven't. I beat hell out of Curly once though, when he came in drunk and two days late."

"Boy, that's no shit!" Curly bellowed. "She beat me over the head with a skillet. I sure never done that again!"

The huge ranch house rocked with laughter and everyone relished the release of tension, now that the subject was candidly in the open.

A typical Montana winter descended on the C-Bar-M, flirting with cold snow and wind only to warm up pleasantly on the wings of periodic Chinook winds. Viola chided the group about their dire predictions of a Montana winter saying, "These little cold spells are no worse than we had in Missouri. I think you've been pulling my leg about the blue northern blizzard."

"I don't know, Viola," Steve said. "When Kalee was with us she told of a winter about four years ago when many of her people froze or starved to death, along with many buffalo, elk, deer, antelope and their own ponies. She said it snowed and blew for one moon, which I guess is about a month, with no let up."

"That's right," Clayton added. "That was the winter of '80/'81. I arrived in April of '81 with my first trail herd and there were rotting carcasses everywhere. The smell was unbelievable. That's why I'm emphatic about preparing for a once-in-a-while bad one."

"Clay's right," Curly joined in, "Me and Juanita got up here with the first trail herd for the Winnecook spread, I guess about the middle of May, and they was dead cattle still a layin' all over the place, getting' ripe in the sun and smellin' like hell."

With the slackening of fall chores and the coming of cold weather, the crew of temporary summer help scattered like fallen leaves. All migrated to warmer quarters in town or down the cattle drive trails to the south, leaving just a nucleus of shareholders and their families on the ranch.

The Montanaweather continued its fitful ways into early November and the chores fell into rather boring monotony. The cattle and horses still fed well on range grasses, requiring hay only during the sudden, but short, snow squalls.

It was on just such a day that the Girouard family slowly wended towards the C-Bar-M, as was routine each Friday morning. The wind blew in gusts and little spirals of powdery snow pinwheeled ahead and to the sides of the horse and buggy as the family huddled together under a big comforter.

Suddenly a series of blood curdling screams screeched through the hiss of wind-blown snow. Six mounted Indians charged at the group waving rifles and spears. In the distance, ghostly through the veil of snow, more Indians, some mounted, some on foot, could be seen.

Wendy started screaming uncontrollably as Bryce reached for the rifle and pulled the rig to a halt.

"It's all right, Wendy, it's all right," Bryce said to the hysterical girl as he pushed her to Viola's side and threw the comforter back to free his rifle and gun hand. "I won't let them hurt us."

The group of dark eyed riders drew up and stopped in front of the horse and rig. One, more profusely feathered than the others pulled slightly ahead to glare down at the family.

As they sat their horses in silence, Bryce said to Viola, "This is one time I do the talking. Do you understand me, Viola? Not one peep from you, no matter how the talk goes or what happens." Viola nodded silently as she pulled Wendy close.

Finally, the obvious leader of the rag-tag group spoke.

"Hah, we have rich white man. Fat horse, fancy wagon, much nice blanket. We proud Blackfeet, lose land, buffalo, hunting ground to white man. Now we take away from white man. You give us these things or you die."

"You call yourselves proud Blackfeet, yet you frighten women and children and try to steal like a mangy Crow? I don't see proud Indians. I see only chest beaters and squaw beaters who do not want to die from this white man's bullets as many of you will if you try to harm us or steal from us."

"Ho, listen to the boastful white man. What can one weakling white man do against me and my warriors?"

"I can draw my pistol and kill four of you before you can raise your rifles," Bryce spoke clearly. "You have heard of the fast gun that shoots arms and hands off outlaws? Well, I'm that man. Which four of you wants to die for a tired horse, and one blanket and buggy you could not use on Injun trails?"

The tight group of warriors began chattering and arguing in their native tongue as Bryce stood poised, Winchester in his left hand, his right suspended over his pistol.

Finally the leader turned to say, "You call us cowards and thieving Crows when it is the white man that has made us this way. Where are the buffalo? All gone. White man kill them all. Where are the wapiti and the lemei? All scared and running away so arrow cannot reach them. We have few guns and few bullets. My people are cold and hungry. White man did this to us and white man should pay for this."

"Yes, you are right, warrior of the Blackfeet. The white man has changed your life and you now suffer, but is it too much to ask of proud warriors to talk to this white man about trading for food, clothing and blankets?"

"We have nothing to trade. You have left us with nothing to trade. You have left us with nothing but a few teepees, buffalo robes and ragged buckskins. Even our dogs are all gone so we could eat." The group now sat their mounts in dejection, guns and spears lowered, a pitiful sight to behold.

"You have the sharp eye of the eagle and the stealth of the panther. These are good things to have when guarding the white man's horses and cattle. It would be worth a fat beef, some beans, rice, flour and a warm place to sleep if you and your people would watch over the C-Bar-M herds this winter," Bryce said.

The Blackfeet again gathered to mutter in their guttural, native tongue. A few curious squaws had left the family group and now stood in the blowing snow, ragged shawls and robes pulled about their shoulders. Black eyes shone like onyx marbles from under their head shrouds as they quizzically surveyed these strange events.

"All we have to do is camp and look at white man's cows and you will give us these things?" the leader asked.

"No, you must keep the hungry bear, panther, wolves, coyotes and the human coyotes from killing our cows." Then as his brain clicked on, Bryce added. "When the big snows come, you must lower the poles so that our cows can eat from the hay stacks we have piled up. The wapiti and deer will come to feed on this same hay and you and your people will get fat and warm with meat and hides."

"But we have no bullets for our guns and most of them are broken. How can we kill game without guns?" the warrior plaintively asked, revealing that they had little or no fire power to carry out their initial threat if the bluff didn't work.

Bryce felt a deep pang of pain for this pitiful band of once proud people now huddled in three small ghostly groups amid increasing wind and snow.

"I will give you my Winchester and some bullets now. Take your people two valleys to the north where we have built some long sheds. Use them for shelter from the wind and cold. You may kill one of the cattle with long horns for your people to eat. Do you understand what I am saying?" Bryce asked as the warriors stared at him in disbelief.

"You will do this for us? Why? Is this another white man's trick?"

"Half of the blood flowing in my body is of your people," Bryce said. "I will not trick people of my own blood. Four days from now, you of the Blackfeet chief, come alone to the C-Bar-M and I will keep my promise. You will lead me to your people and I will have guns, bullets, food and blankets for you in a wagon. You keep your promise and I will keep mine."

"This is good. I, Chief Strong Bull, will do as you say. Without your help, many of my people will die this winter. This will be a winter of the big snow. The signs are right for this and the signs don't lie."

"Good," said Bryce as he groped under the buggy seat for a box of 44-40 ammunition. He handed the rifle and bullets to Strong Bull, and the Girouards watched as the Indians regrouped and faded away to the north through wavering curtains of blowing snow.

Bryce clucked to the Morgan and the little family continued towards the sanctuary of the C-Bar-M as Wendy burrowed under the protective arm of her foster father and hero.

The buggy wheels made little sound and the horses hooves only clicked occasionally where the wind had blown away the snow. Not a word was said but Viola continually cast long, quizzical looks at Bryce as they rolled along. The normally vociferous little lady was so quiet that Bryce finally turned to her. Their eyes met and he could read the wonder and admiration there as she continued to stare.

"What are you looking at, dear?"

"A wonderful, kind, man, that's for sure. Beyond that, I don't know. Every time a new and difficult situation arises I see another equally wonderful side of you. Will I ever get to really know you, darling?" Viola asked.

"You're a fine one to talk, little lady of many faces, voices, talents and temperaments."

Viola had no retort and remained silent until the buggy pulled to a stop before their temporary bunk-house home.

It was with some dissension that all involved accepted the deal Bryce had made with the hungry Blackfeet group. Curly had a deep ingrained hatred of all Indians and understandably felt repugnance at the nearness of the Blackfeet.

With uncanny insight, Clay defused this first ever difference of opinion among the corporation members. He rightfully placed the bulk of the responsibility for working with the Blackfeet on Bryce's shoulders with the understanding that in his absence, only he would make contact.

It had been an emotionally tense and tiring day for all and Bryce was not surprised when Wendy, snuggled close to his side in her long flannel nightie, began to nod. He had been reading that night's chapter of *A Tale Of Two Cities*. Wendy was fascinated with the story as he read to her each evening, but tonight she was clearly out of it.

Gilt Edge Town

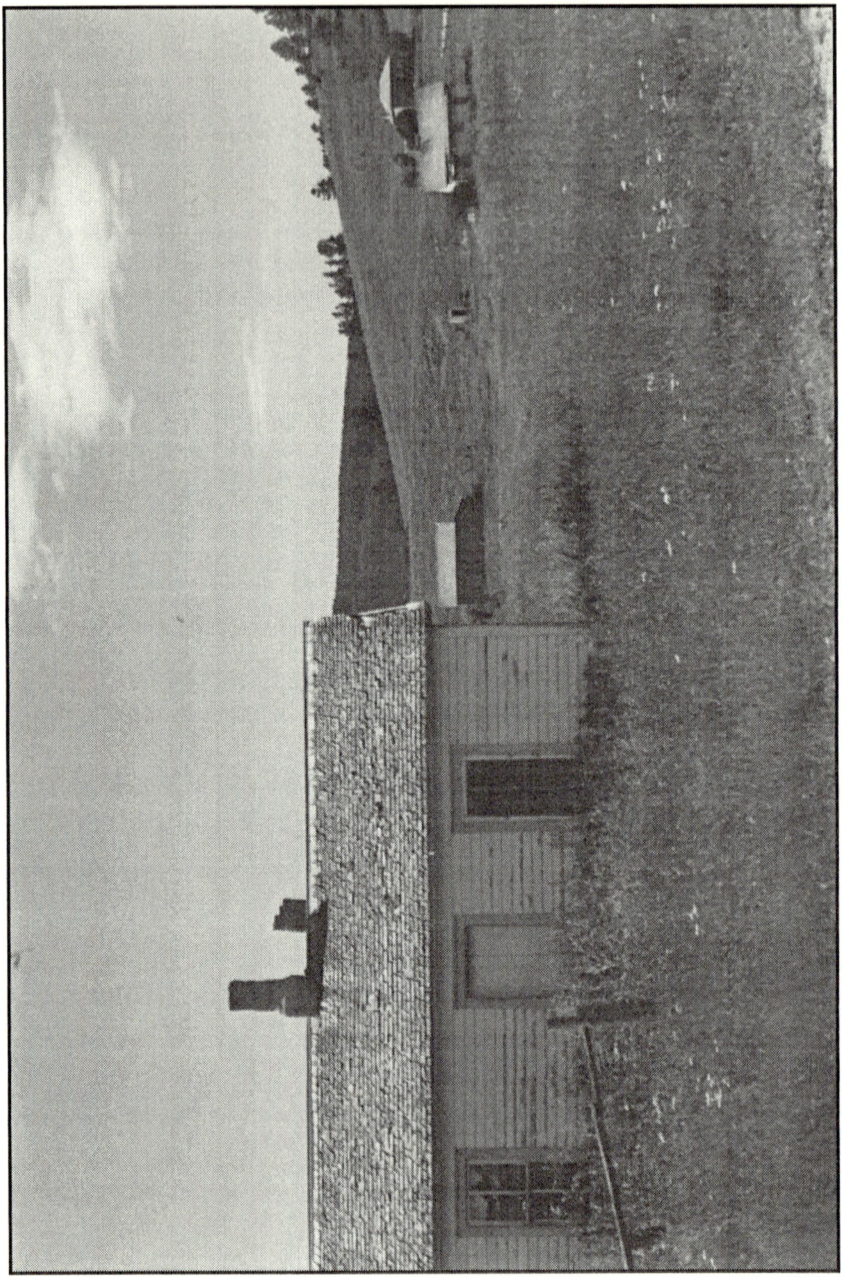

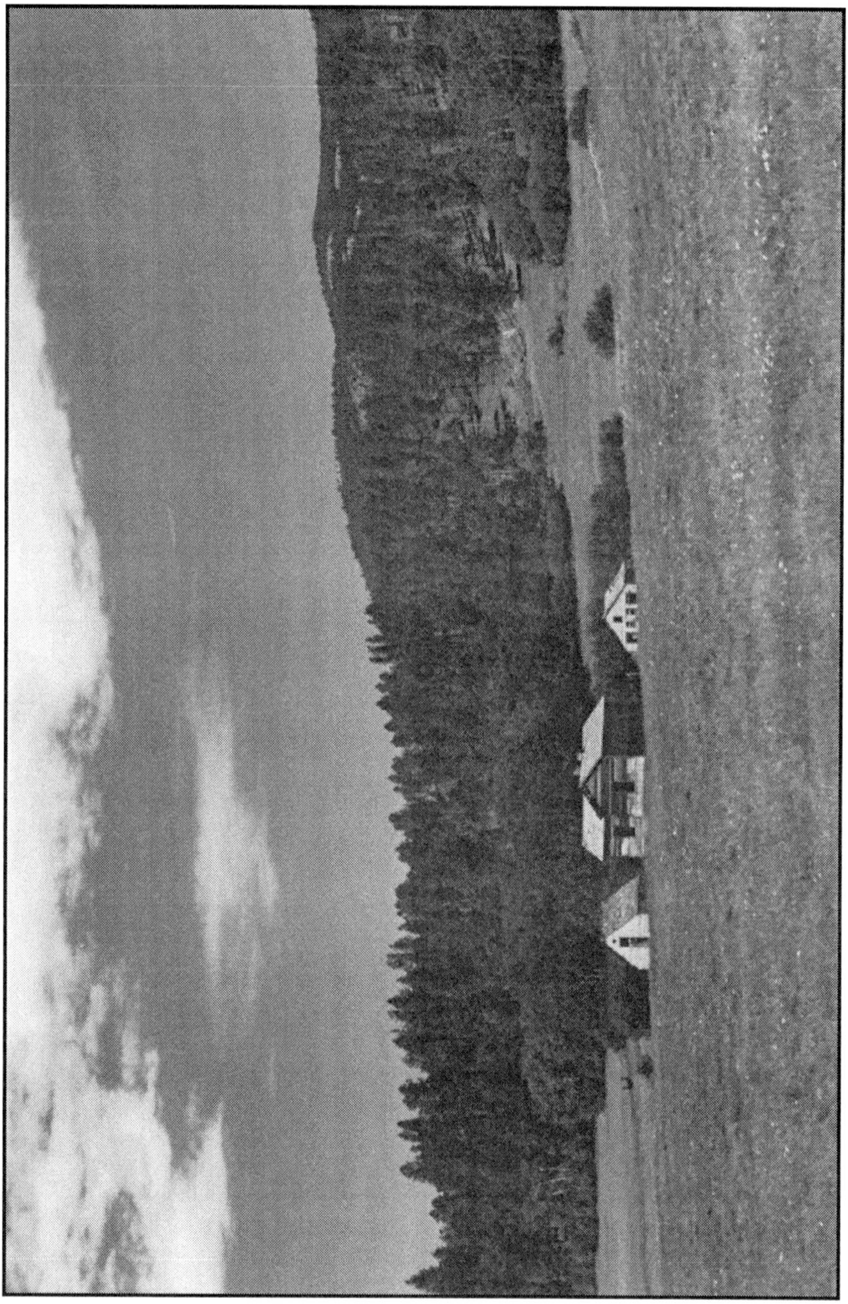

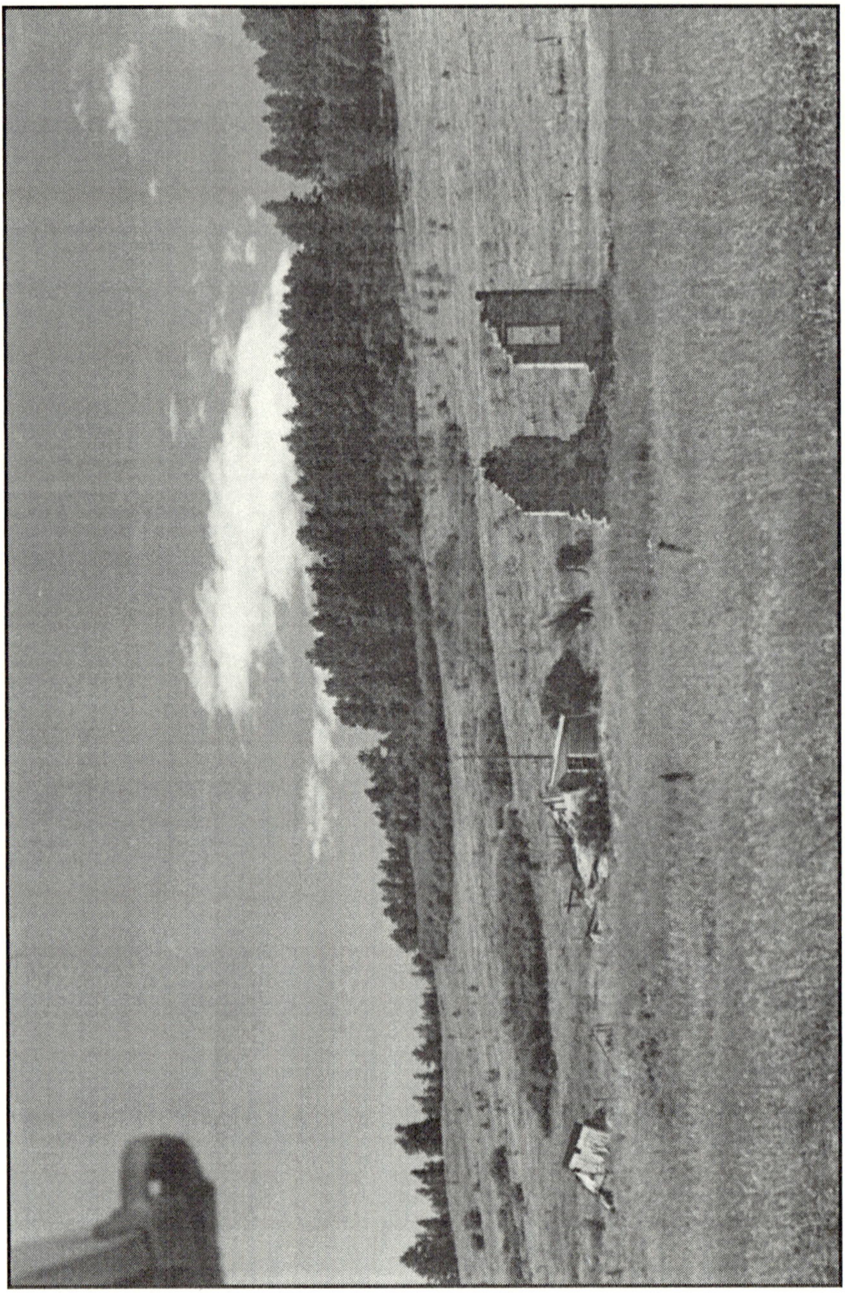

Wendy snuggled away in her bed, Bryce pulled a galvanized bath tub from its peg on the wall and placed it on a huge bath mat Viola had placed on the floor in front of the radiant stove. Together, they filled the tub with buckets of hot water from an oblong boiler on the stove. A dash or two of icy water from the bunk house cistern and Viola indicated it was just right.

As Bryce sat down at the table where he was working up an appraisal for another possible ranch purchase, Viola went about preparing for her bath. She placed her slippers on the seat of a chair pulled close and hung her robe over the back. Undressing, she lifted a leg to stick a toe in the water.

"Just a minute, honey," Bryce said as he leaped to his feet to help her step into and ease into a sitting position in the water. The dainty body now carried their child and he was not taking any chances with a fall.

He returned to his calculations until Viola called, "I'm ready for a rinse, sweetheart." Bryce mixed hot and cold water in a big bucket until the tepid mixture was just right and carried the bucket and ladle to the tub.

First, rinse the hair, then the upturned face, shoulders, arms, back and then the breasts, a routine, done many times before. Helping Viola stand, they clasped hands as Bryce ran rinse water over the pronounced swelling of their child to be, the buttocks and legs, then dropped the ladle into the bucket and turned to go so Viola could complete rinsing the more discreet body parts.

But Viola did not release her grip on Bryce's hand. The small fingers wrapped tightly around his did not relax a bit. A sharp pop on the well rounded bottom brought about an 'Ouch' from his wife and a momentary release of her grasp as he pulled away and walked back to his paper work.

He grinned from the table at the pouted lips turned his way and he had no more than started writing, when again Viola called out, "Honey, will you hand me that towel over on the chiffonnier?"

You little devil, Bryce thought to himself, you have a hundred, seemingly innocent, ways to lure my hands to your beautiful body when you're like this.

Retrieving a big jersey towel from the dresser, Bryce walked to his stark naked wife and began drying the honey and cream skin of

Dexter C. McPherson

her back. He took the towel and wrapped it tightly around her arms and shoulders, lifting her easily by the elbows to stand her on the bath mat.

Bryce crossed to the table and closed the tablet, knowing any ranch business was done for the night. Instead, he started dipping hot water into the used and sudsy water for his own bath, as many times before.

As he bathed and rinsed, Viola sat at the mirror fussing with her hair. First one way, then another as she obviously stalled for time. Like a cat sneaking up on a mouse, Bryce thought as he dried himself and wrapped the towel around his waist. He looked down at the tub of bath water. To hell with it, I'll empty it in the morning, he thought as he cast the towel on the back of a chair and proceeded to the big comfy bed.

He settled back on the pillow, his hands behind his head. He heard a poof and the room fell into darkness. Soft steps padded towards the bed. First one slipper, then the next, went sailing off to plop randomly on the floor, followed by the hiss of a falling robe and a young and eager body slipped under the blankets Bryce held aloft.

"Hold me close, darling," she said. "Oh, I love you so and need you so." Bryce pulled the young body close to him and could feel a firm breast and erect nipple against his chest as Viola snuggled within a protective arm, one slender leg wrapped around his.

"I'm sorry for the way I have reacted to guns in the past, honey," she said, "I see now, that the need to carry a gun in this part of the world is not just to kill another man."

"I'm also sorry for the way I had to tell you to be silent," Bryce replied. "There just wasn't time to explain. I didn't mean to be harsh."

"No, no, I could never be angry with you over that. I'm so proud of you and how you protected Wendy and me from those Indians. If you had not been armed and able to counter their attack, I'm sure we would all be dead now."

"I find more reasons to love you each day," Bryce whispered into the soft head of hair he was nuzzling and kissing. He could feel the soft bulge of their soon-to-be-born child across his waist as the warm and searching body rolled onto his.

Winter had rolled into mid-December when Bryce, Viola, Wendy and Tommy drove into the C-Bar-M one Wednesday afternoon. As everyone rushed to meet this premature return, Viola gathered them together to say, "Scarlet fever, we've got an epidemic started it looks like. Several of the Dayley kids got sick today and by the time I'd diagnosed it as scarlet fever, they'd had contact with most of the other children. How many are exposed, I don't know, but it is highly contagious."

"Scarlet fever! Oh, my God, that's deadly, isn't it?" gasped Pauline, her hands to her cheeks.

"Oh no, Pauline. Full blown scarlet fever can be dangerous but there are many shades of the disease. Some children just get light cases called *scarlatina,* some so light they are only sick for a few days. Father says that's because the mother has had the disease and passes on some immunity to the child."

"Oh! Well, I had what the doctor called *scarlatina* when I was about ten," Pauline said. "I thought it was a different sickness."

"No, it's all the same disease, so Rebecca and Tommy should be partially immune," Viola said thoughtfully. "But we don't know about Wendy. I had scarlet fever also when a child, but that won't protect Wendy. What about you Mildred? Do you remember ever having anything like this?"

Mildred knitted her brow in thought and finally answered, "No, I don't recall anything like that. I just never seemed to catch those things. I guess I had the German measles is about all. I've never even had the mumps, chicken pox, or any of the usual kids' illnesses."

"Then it's best you isolate yourself and little Lorena from the rest of us until we see what happens, Mildred. If Tommy and Wendy come down with it, it will be within three weeks. Until then, we must keep the children separated," Viola said. "The medical people aren't even sure how it's spread. Sometimes it will spread like wildfire, even when there doesn't seem to be any contacts. Maybe through pets, or insects, like mosquitoes."

"Pets? What about Lorena's cat, Flossy?" Mildred asked.

"You'd probably better keep Flossy out of the house. I wouldn't take any chances."

"It's going to be tough keeping Lorena away from the others," Pauline said. "They're so close."

"Well, if any of the children come down with it, I can help out," Juanita said. "I just about died from scarlet fever. I didn't get it until I was a young lady and was terribly sick. I turned purple and my skin all peeled off as I was recuperating. It itched like blue blazes. If anyone is immune, I should be."

The C-Bar-M families all drew apart to wait out the incubation period.

For an uneasy two weeks the families went about daily tasks, hoping against hope that none of their loved ones had been exposed to the ravages of scarlet fever. But the inevitable arrived one morning as Pauline beat on the bunk house door.

"Viola, Viola! Tommy doesn't feel good and he has a fever."

Viola met an anguished Pauline at the door to let her in from the cold.

"What other symptoms does he have?"

"He says his head aches and he has chills."

"Does he have a red rash?"

"No, I didn't see any."

"Look on his chest. It usually breaks out there first. It looks like millions of tiny red dots. I'll be down in a minute. Wendy seems kind of droopy this morning too and we may have two to care for."

True to form, it was soon obvious that both Tommy and Wendy had scarlet fever. Under Viola's direction, the children were bathed on the forehead and neck with damp cloths to keep the fever down.

"Father says if you can keep the fever down to 103° there is little danger of brain damage. Smaller children can even tolerate fevers of 104° for short periods without any permanent effects," Viola explained. "There isn't much else we can do until we find out if they have some natural immunity and it is only a mild case."

As was typical with scarlet fever, both children turned a brilliant red and were racked with fever and headaches, but on the third day Tommy shocked Pauline by announcing he was hungry. Turning eyes heavenward, Pauline breathed a "Thank you Lord," and rushed to warm up some chicken broth.

Pauline left the hungry boy sitting up and sipping broth to admit Viola. "Oh, just look at him. Look at him. Isn't that wonderful?"

Viola gave Pauline a hug and responded, "Well, just looking at him, he doesn't appear all that good. He's sure turning purple, but if he's hungry he has to be recovering."

"How's Wendy?"

"I think she's over the hump too. The fever is gone and she's sleeping soundly for the first time. I believe we can safely say that our children had the mild form called *scarlatina*. They'll never have scarlet fever again and their children will inherit the immunity."

"What about Rebecca?"

"I don't think there's much chance of her coming down with it. Father says nursing babies seem to have a built in immunity to childhood diseases. Especially if the mother has passed on her own immunity to the child. Rebecca may contract *scarlatina* later in childhood, but I don't think now."

"Oh, thank God," Pauline breathed gratefully.

Wendy recovered much the same as Tommy. An outrageous purple hue tinted her already dark skin, but Wendy couldn't care less. She was hungry and headache free. Return to a normal childhood was at hand.

Suddenly, the Montana winter exposed its harsher side. Temperatures dropped from 28° to minus 30° in a matter of hours. Winds shifted to the northwest and fine, powdery snow began to blow over the Highwoods and Little Belts to cartwheel across the Judith Basin.

Visibility was near zero as Bryce pushed his buckskin down the lee side of a drift fence towards the hay meadow and the Blackfeet camp.

Finally locating the band of Indians, he was amazed to find them doing quite well. They had timbered up the ends of part of a loafing shed, stretched teepee hides across the front and were all clustered together in the shelter of this 'long house.'

Accepting their warm invitation, Bryce entered the smoky interior. The back wall was lined with buffalo robe pallets, each one sporting warm Hudson Bay blankets provided by the C-Bar-M.

Strings of dried jerky and pouches of dried fruits and nuts hung from the ceiling and the dark-eyed people all appeared to be in good health and humor.

Strong Bull boasted how his people had killed many wapiti, lemei, antelope with the firearms provided and sure enough, they had killed one grizzly bear they found feeding on a fresh- killed calf.

Strong Bull proudly displayed the string of three inch long claws as he related how they had killed the huge predator. "Big guns blow bad bear down as many times as I have fingers," he boasted, holding up the five fingers of one hand. "Bad bear then lay down and speak to Blackfeet. 'Take me to your lodge, oh great warriors, for we are truly brothers and of the same blood.'"

His eyes wide with the impact of his narration, Strong Bull fell silent. There was no sound but a low moaning as all the warriors nodded and rocked in agreement.

Bryce, wisely remained silent until the Chief chose to speak again.

"This is how it was." And nothing more was said. Apparently to the Indians the subject was closed.

Riding towards home, Bryce mulled over the advice and orders he had given the Chief. Had he covered it all? Stay away from all whites until he told them the bad medicine was gone. Be sure to open enough hay stacks so the cattle don't jam up and injure each other. When the animals eat back into a stack, be sure to pull the over hang down so it doesn't collapse and smother some of the stock. Keep all the horses, including their own, confined to one area of haystacks. Hungry cattle and horses don't mix. He didn't want any cattle with their ribs kicked in or horses with their sides ripped open.

God, I hope I got through to him, Bryce mused. You just don't know, because they don't change expressions. If this blow continues, we'll have to rely on them entirely.

He groped his way through a white out of blowing snow, giving the buckskin its head, trusting that it would take them home. Just when Bryce had about given up hope of finding their way, Hoodoo stopped and nickered softly. Staring through a screen of white, Bryce could vaguely see corral rails.

"Bless you, Hoodoo, you did know where we were," Bryce said as he slid stiffly to the snow-covered barnyard. As he turned towards the barn, he heard the big door creak open and Curly call out. "Over here, Bryce. Come on, get your ass outa' the cold."

The buckskin undressed and rubbed down, Bryce scooped in a feeding of barley and the two men followed the rope Curly had stretched between his house and the barn.

Over a hot cup of Juanita's sassafras tea, the two men warmed their hands to the ever-moaning sound of the storm.

"By gadfry, if this don't let up pretty soon, we're in for trouble. You sure those worthless Injuns is gonna' take care of our stock?" Curly asked.

"I think so Curly. They seemed to be content and more friendly than ever. They've got a lot of elk, venison, and antelope meat hanging around to go with their dried berries, roots and nuts. Hell, they seem happy as if they had good sense. Even if you and I couldn't live that way, it seems fine to them and they appeared to be proud to have earned what they've got."

"I sure hope so. Did they say how many head we've lost?"

"They said only two. One longhorn yearling to a grizzly and one old steer that they blamed on some Flatheads from over west."

"Probably et 'em both themselves," Curly snorted.

"Well, maybe one, but they did show me a string of big grizzly claws and told how it took five 44-40 slugs to bring him down. I think that was honest Injun talk."

"Horse manure!" Curly retorted, "they ain't no honest Injuns."

"We'll just have to wait until this storm blows out and then go see," Bryce said as he moved his smoking britches away from the stove with a, "Jesus, Curly, you build a hot fire."

Two days later the wind died down and the skies cleared to reveal a wonderland of drifts, bald slopes and cornices of crystalline ice and snow behind every building and fence. The temperature dropped to minus 46° that first, still night, but the next day's sun brought warmth and a promise of thaw.

Welcome news came in twos that day as Bryce returned from the Indian camp to report they could only identify three missing head of cattle. Deputy Griffing also showed up at the C-Bar-M to notify Viola that banker Sutherland had a ten-thousand-dollar voucher there for Bryce.

"Hey, darlins, we can start our new house as soon as the weather allows," Bryce said, as he gaily swung Viola and Wendy off their feet under each arm.

"And plenty to buy all the furniture we'll need too," Viola added.

"And a typewriter for me, huh, Dad? Please, Dad!" Wendy implored.

"Honey, if all you're asking for is a typewriter, you surely shall have it," Bryce gasped through the chokehold of small brown arms around his neck.

"How about some pretty new clothes for you, also, Wendy?" Viola asked.

"Well, if there's enough left over. We have to buy some clothes for my baby brother, too."

"Bryce! you've got her completely convinced that we're going to have a boy," Viola scolded. "You shouldn't do that."

"Why? It's the truth you know. The way that little fellow kicked me last night, I just know he's a boy."

Viola only shook her head in exasperation.

"Did you see the floor plan Steve drew up for our house?" Bryce asked. "It's just like you wanted it arranged and we can always build another wing if the family keeps growing."

"When can we start building?"

"Steve says we can lay the corner stones just as soon as the ground thaws and then the foundations. After that, when the lumber gets here from Bozeman, it will only take about two days to frame, sheet and roof it, if we all pitch in. All we need is weather and materials."

"Viola, Viola!" Juanita called as she ran towards the bunk house. "Both Mildred and Lorena are complaining of sore throats and a headache. I think they've got a fever, too."

A quick look at swollen throats and bright red tongues pretty much made the diagnosis positive without a thermometer. "How could they get it?" Juanita asked. "We kept them completely isolated until Tommy and Wendy were well over it."

"We don't know, Juanita, but it's plain they both have scarlet fever and it's going to take all three of us ladies to care for them. Lorena probably doesn't have any genetic immunity and may get much sicker than Wendy and Tommy did. Someone will have to be with them day and night."

"What can we do?" Juanita asked.

"Just keep the temperature down to 103° or below and make sure they get plenty of water so they don't dehydrate, which is sometimes hard because their throats swell so badly."

The ladies all pitched in to care for the Lytles and each began to show exhaustion as worry and lack of sleep took its inevitable toll.

Curly had taken on the job of caring for Wendy, Tommy and even little Rebecca, although it was Wendy who changed the diapers and washed the fat little bottom.

"I can carry in a scoured doggie, but I sure can't change no dirty diaper," Curly exclaimed as he would hand Rebecca to Wendy whenever a wet sleeve or obnoxious smell indicated she needed a change.

Tommy held the safety pins and the cornstarch for Wendy but he, also, quickly adopted Curly's attitude about dirty diapers, turning his nose away during the process..

Bryce returned from checking on the herd, late one day, five days after the Lytles had fallen ill. Pushing through the heavy door and turning to close it against a chill wind, he heard sounds of sobbing from across the cold room.

Turning quickly, he crossed to where his tiny wife sobbed loudly as she held an also crying Wendy to her breast.

"We lost her, Bryce, we lost her. I did all I could but we lost her."

"Lost who?" Bryce asked as he pulled the two close.

"Lorena, Bryce. She's gone. I couldn't save her, even though I cut a hole through into the trachea, like I've seen Father do. She couldn't breathe and I couldn't get an air passage open quick enough."

"Honey, you did all you could," Bryce said, "You did all you could."

"If I'd only known her throat was swelling shut sooner. I should have known. I just drifted off to sleep I guess and when I heard her wheezing, I woke up and she was already blue in the face. It was too late. Her heart had already stopped." The small bodies shook uncontrollably in his arms as Bryce tried to calm his wife and daughter.

"Now you listen here, you two. We must be strong. You recall how you said after we lost Kalee that we must all be strong because the Lord will surely place other tests of our faith before us. Do you recall, Viola? This is one of those tests. It was time for Lorena to go and the Lord has to love you for the devotion you've shown for His children, but this is His will. It was not your decision to make whether Lorena stayed here or went with Him. Don't you see that, sweetheart?"

"Yes Mother, Dad is right," Wendy implored, as she squeezed Viola's waist with one arm and Bryce's thigh with the other. "We have to be a strong family, Mother. Our little boy will need us to be strong. A family he can lean on until he is big enough to care for himself. We will need to be strong for the Lytles too, Mother. They will need us now."

This very mature observation from a young child, prematurely aged by the sudden tragedy in her own life, seemed to be the catalyst to calm Viola. Her sobbing subsided and she relaxed in Bryce's arms.

He led the ladies of his life to an old rocker by the wood heater, eased them down and covered them with a big comforter.

"We have all lost some of those dear to us and somehow life goes on and we must persevere," he said. "Now you two just sit there and remember Lorena as she was and realize she is not really gone. Only in a different and better place, waiting for the time we are all together again. Now, I'm going to build a nice hot fire and then I'll warm up what's left of that shepherds stew we made last night. Say, how does some double fried, homemade bread with choke cherry jelly sound?"

Bryce whistled as he banged around, laying pitch curls and kindling for a quick fire. The rocking chair creaked as Viola rocked Wendy on her lap and the fatigue and strain showing on the small face brought a lump of compassion to his throat as he set about lighting lamps.

Food and pans warming, Bryce walked to the back of the rocker and bent over, soundly kissing the two precious creatures he called his own.

The next few days were quiet and tentative as Juanita showed her strength. She refused to let either Viola or Pauline share in caring for the deathly ill Mildred Lytle. Steve Lytle, shattered by the loss of Lorena and the tiny thread of life his wife still clung to, saddled up and disappeared into the folds, ridges and meadows of the Little Belts.

"Maybe, I should saddle up and go after him," a concerned Calvin said. "He shouldn't be alone at a time like this."

"He ain't alone, son," Curly responded. "The One he wants to talk to is up there in them hills. Sometimes a man just has to go to the right place before he kin reach who he wants to talk to. He don't need none of us right now. He'll come back when he's a ready to."

This piece of wisdom, rendered by the tough old wrangler, exposed a religious side heretofore well hidden behind a callous, gruff façade.

The next morning Juanita came to Pauline. "Mildred's coming out of it. Her fever is down and the swelling is gone from her throat. Her tongue looks like a sheep skin but she was able to drink a glass of water."

"Oh, thank God," Pauline said. "Did you tell her about Lorena yet?"

"Funny thing, the first thing she said was, 'Lorena's gone.' I asked her how she knew that and you know what she said?"

"No, what?"

"She said an Angel came to her and told her she was taking Lorena with her. She said the Angel told her she would take good care of her until they were together again. Mildred seems to be at peace with that. She seems to be able to handle Lorena's death better than any of us. Especially poor Viola."

"That's weird, Juanita."

"Yes, I know, but by golly, there must be something to it. I tell you she's as peaceful as can be with the truth."

"Who's with her now?"

"Bryce. He's been so good to fill in and just won't let Viola give any more of herself to this thing. Let's go talk to Viola now, maybe this will make her feel better."

The two stately ladies, a generation apart, but equally beautiful, walked hand-in-hand towards the bunk house.

True to Curly's prediction, Steve Lytle rode into the C-Bar-M the next afternoon, but the redness around his eyes told a story of his struggle with fate. He went straight to Mildred's bedside and the two were left alone to share their inner hurts and love.

As per the Lytles' request, little Lorena was buried on her favorite hill where the prairie flowers bloomed each spring.

Preacher Cleve Jones rode out to perform the graveside service on an unseasonably warm day, after which Viola read the memorial she had written.

Dexter C. McPherson

IN MEMORIAM

Died December 18, 1883 of Scarlet Fever, Lorena, little daughter of Mr. and Mrs. Steve Lytle, aged two years, two months and sixteen days.

Our hearts are sad and lonely.
For the one we see no more;
For the little feet that pattered
ceaselessly upon the floor.

For the little voice that gladdened
Many a sad and weary hour;
For a little life that faded
Like a pure and fragile flower.

Here lies a broken plaything,
There a tiny well worn shoe,
Here the prints of baby fingers
Thro' our tear dimmed eyes we view.

And they're scattered all around us
Sad reminders everywhere,
E'en the silence seems to whisper
Of an empty crib and chair.

And a mother's heart is breaking
For the babe she loved so well,
And a father's heart is aching
With a grief he cannot tell.

But above, in Heavenly whiteness,
Safe upon the Savior's breast,
While Angel choirs sing hallelujahs
Sweet Lorena is at rest.

Peaceful rest, replete with meaning
To those whose hearts are torn with grief.
To those who watched her labored breathing
Thankful when death gave relief.

And we bow in sweet submission
Tho' we miss our cherished one,
Yet our lips are oft repeating
"Blessed Christ thy will be done."

"Thy will be done" oh blessed Master.
Grant us faith that we may see,
Thro' the gloom that gathers round us
To a bright futurity.

And when at last we reach the river
And peer out across the foam.
We shall hear Lorena's welcome
And safely cross to home sweet home.[2]*

The spring of 1884 turned to early summer with a flush of blossoms. Buttercups, spring beauties, grass widows, wild onion and garlic gave way to other blooms. As little Lorena would have wished, her grave was surrounded by purple bee balm and asters growing amid hair bells, daisies and sun flowers. One narrow trail led to the granite stone where any step to the side could violate the existence of some of these beauties. Even the bare and rocky slopes were dotted with the fluorescence of red phlox, yellow sedum and orange Indian paint brush. This was surely a time when thoughts are kind, young hearts turn to love and the romantic wax poetic.

It was on the late afternoon of a hot day in June when the sky darkened, the wind came in gusts and shafts of lighting danced across the horizon. A typical prairie thunderstorm descended on the C-Bar-M and humans scurried for the sanctuary of their homes. Windows and shutters were closed as an eerie twilight shut out the late sun. Wind, rain, hail, jagged lightening and tremendous claps of thunder assailed the cluster of homes and out buildings that identified the remote ranch. Mothers rocked and soothed frightened babies and youngsters watched

---

2   * Written by Sarah Viola Millay (McPherson). Altered in names and date to fit story line.

for the shafts of lightening, trying to guess where the next strike would come.

As rapidly as it arrived, the storm moved away, a pale pink light glowing in the west as the wind died to a whisper. One by one, the inhabitants began to emerge and pick their way along the plank walks towards the McMahon ranch house. Little by little the group on the verandah grew as the storm clouds retreated, leaving only layered wisps of white, fluffy cloud's.

Bodies rapidly filled the chairs and benches as the sun dipped behind the clouds towards the horizon. The fluffy layers turned golden, emitting shafts of silver sunlight that glittered from every wet surface. Silver to gold, gold to pink, pink to red as the sun dipped below the horizon. The only sounds were the oohs and aahs of two youngsters as they watched the display turn violet, then magenta and finally purple, heralding darkness.

Rocking chairs squeaked as mothers continued to rock babies, a tomato can rang with the splat of a well-aimed quid, and a pen knife rasped as it reamed the spent ash from a pipe to later be rap-rapped out on the leg of a chair. From the meadow and creek came the hoarse gargle of sandhill cranes, the creee-creee of magpies and the clear two-note call of red wing and yellow-headed blackbirds.

Slowly, the Queen of Day closed her soft, golden lashes and upon retiring, pulled back the curtain of night to reveal a spangle of sparkling stars. The wings of night hawks whistled as Wendy pointed out the Big Dipper and Orion and Tommy found the Milky Way and the North Star.

A magnificent night in the Judith Basin.

Utica Town

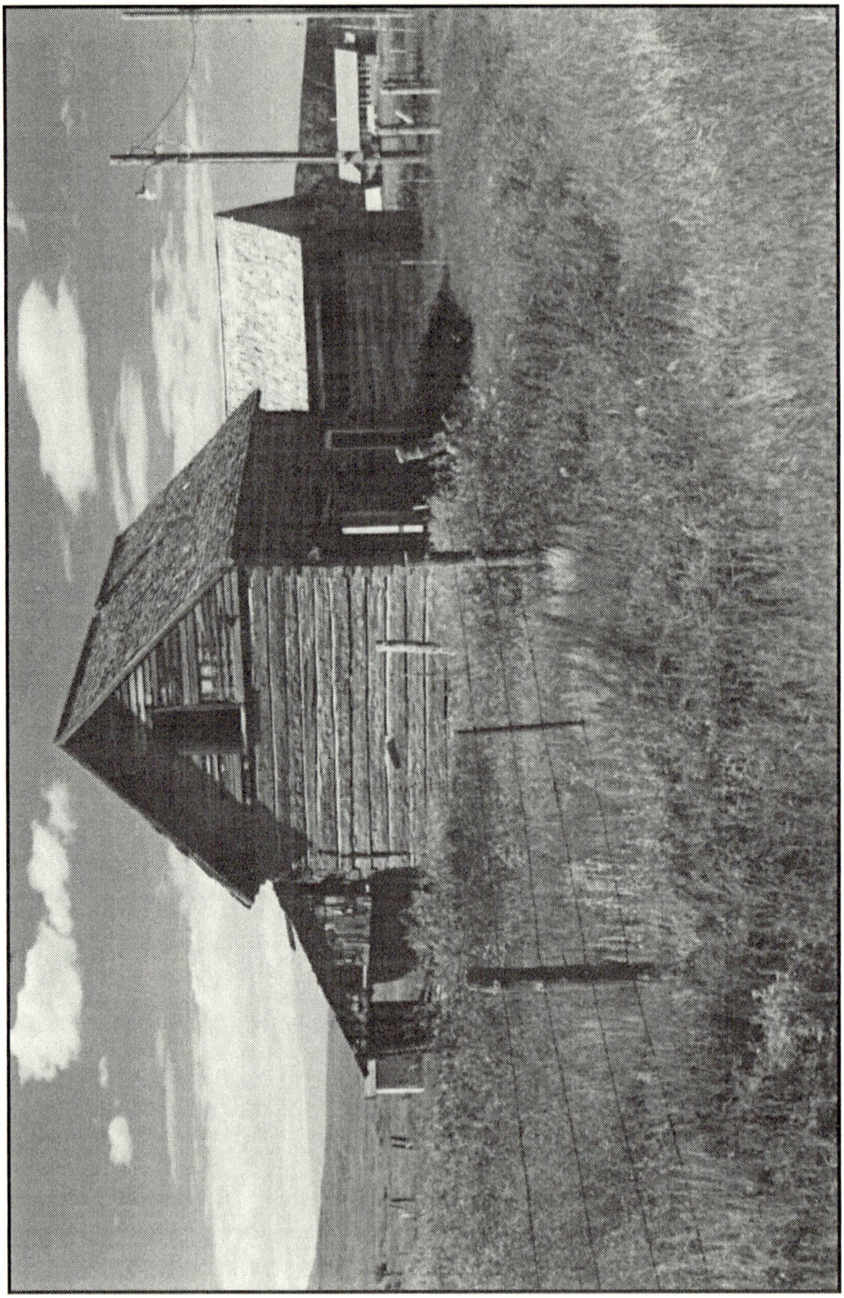

Judith Mountains

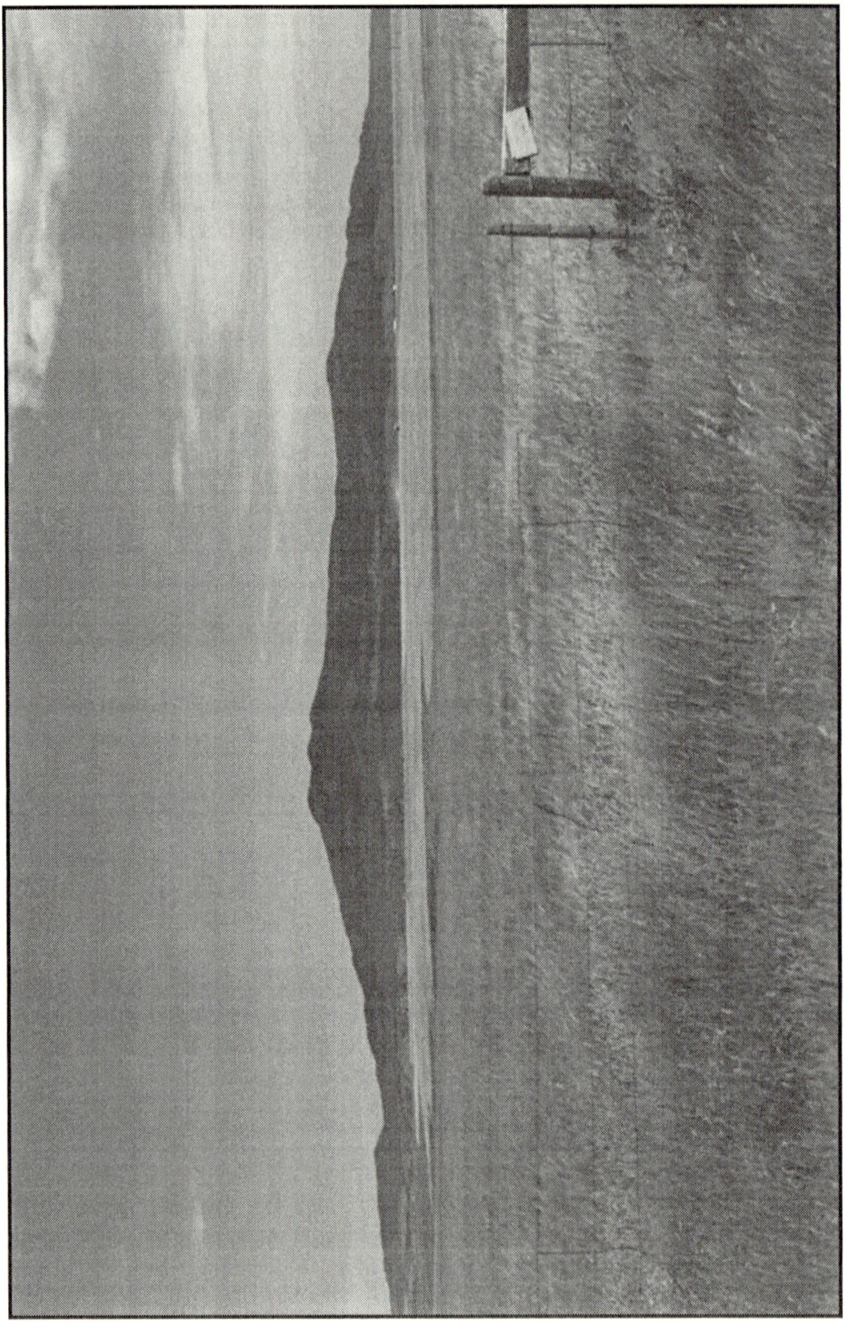

Thunderstorm and Sunset

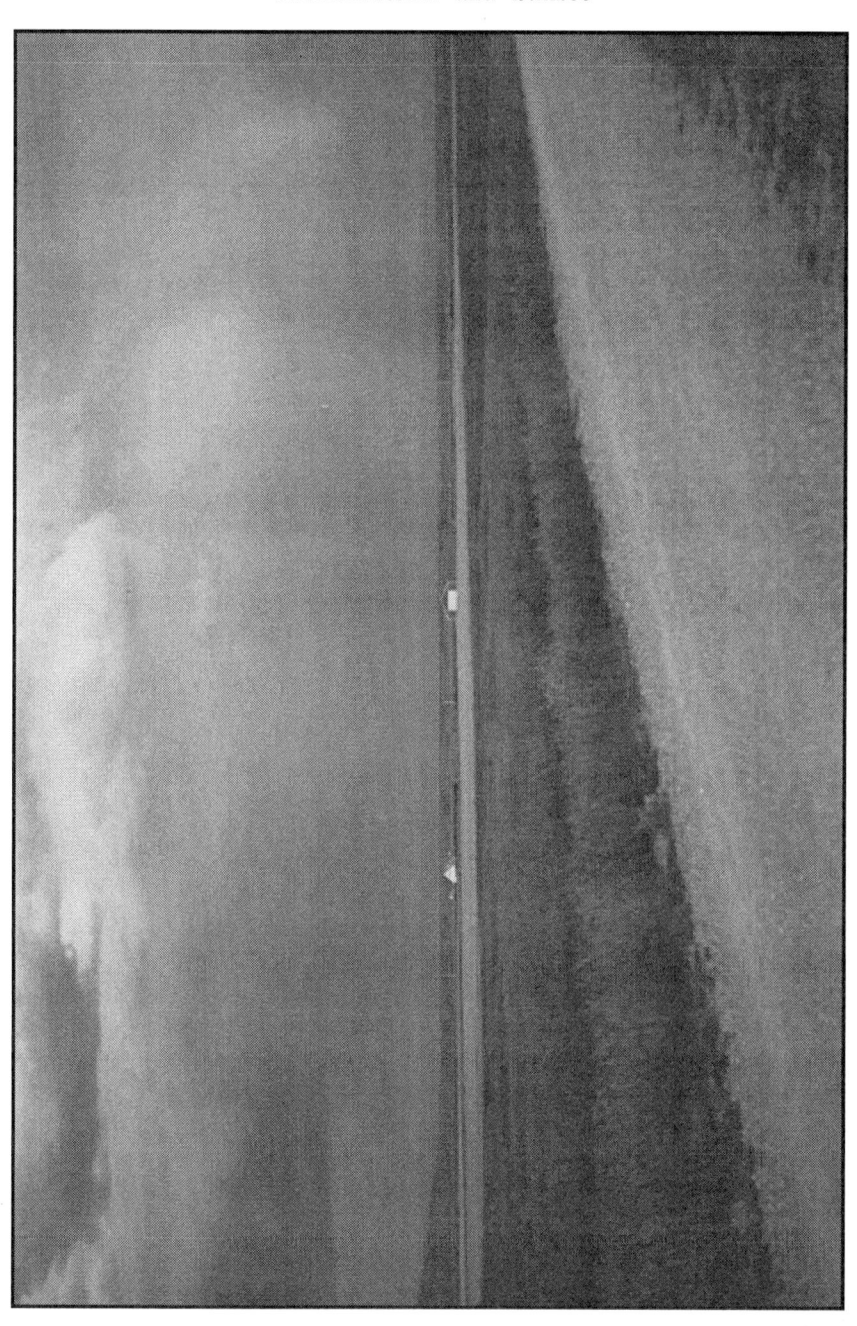

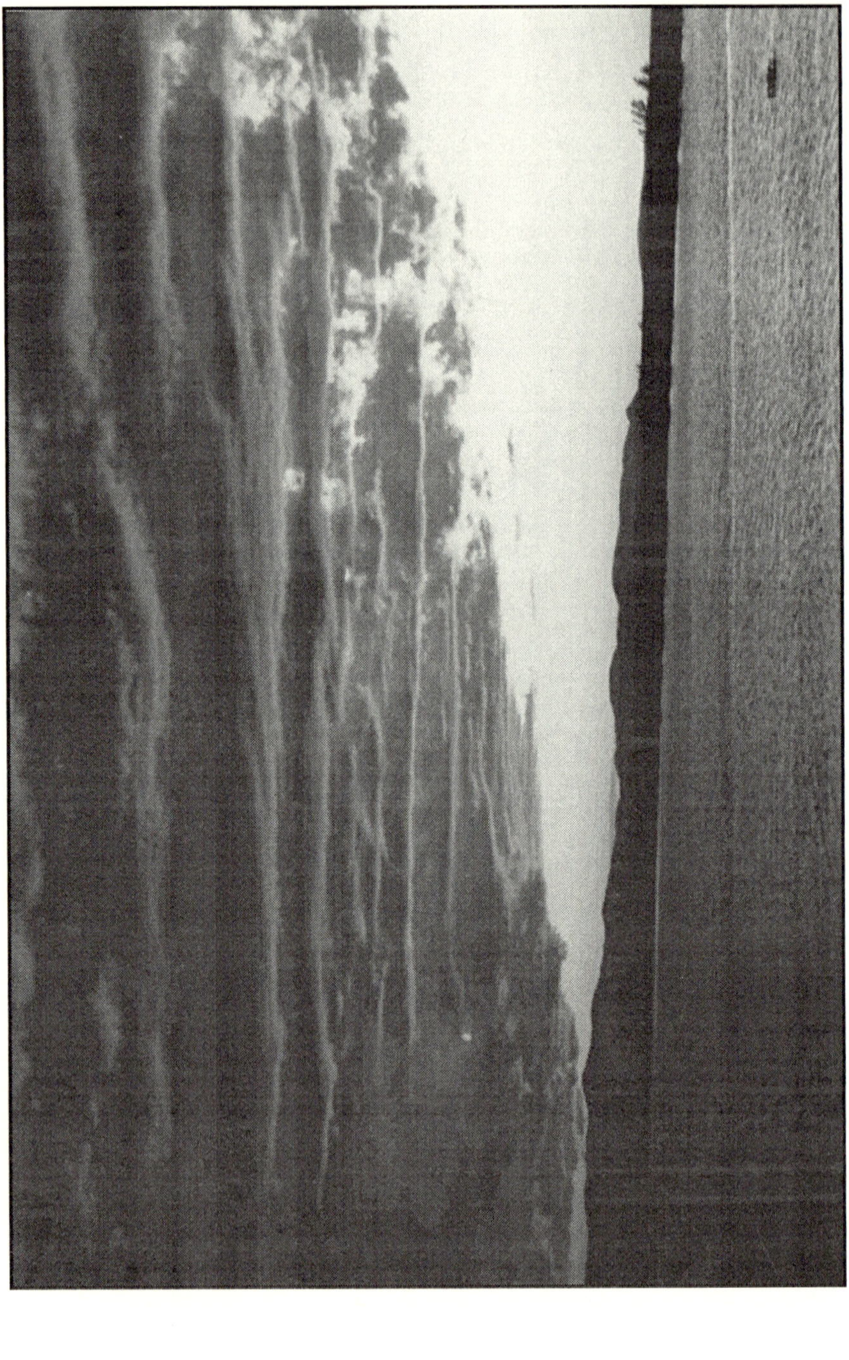

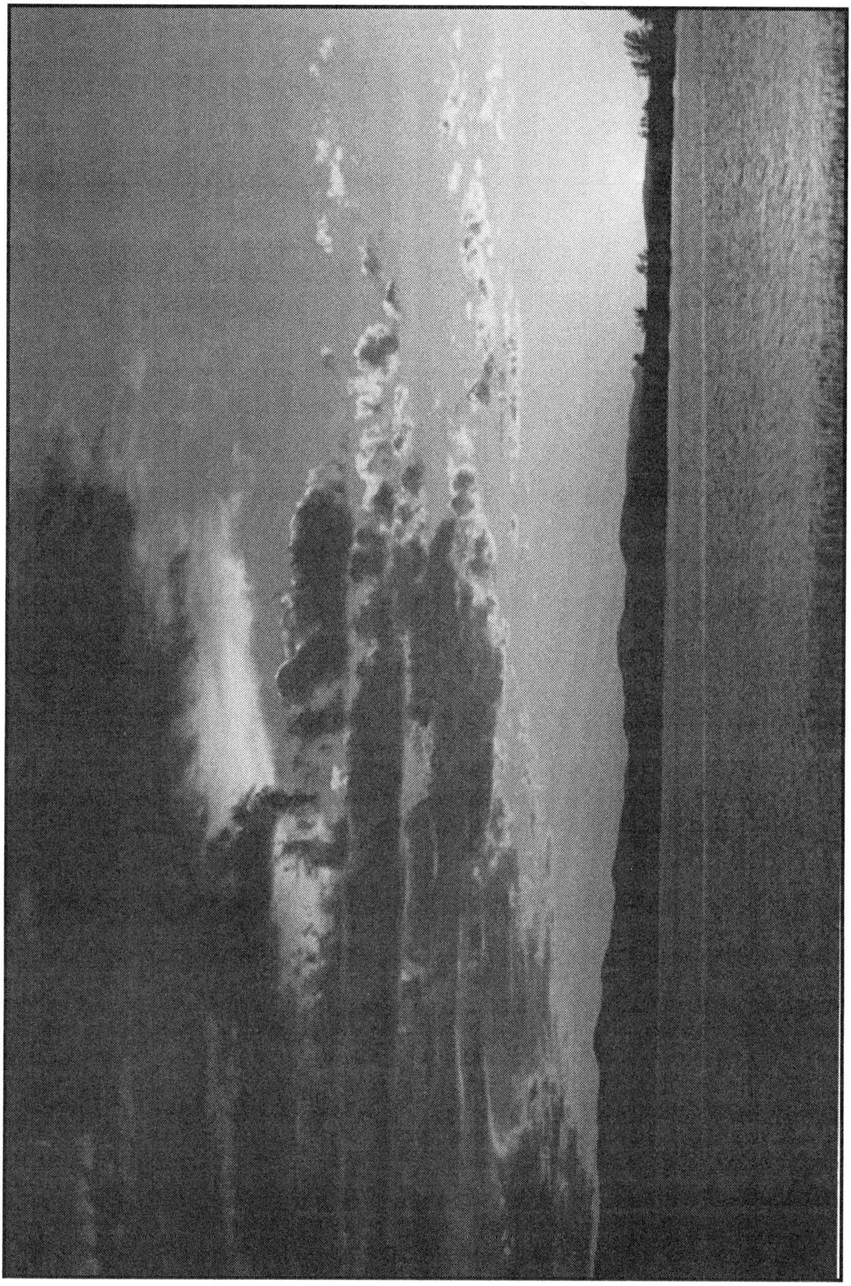

EPILOGUE

Although the saga of the Judith Basin Cattle Company is not patterned after any specific ranching operation of that time, there were many fledgling cattle and sheep operations in Central Montana during the 1960's.

Some of these ranches would survive the devastating blizzards of 1965 and a few would grow to become very large spreads, several which are still in operation today.

On the C-Bar-M, the Girouards build their new home, Viola gives birth to little Preston, the Lytles announce Mildred's pregnancy, and Calvin Millen and Richard Ochs return from Missouri with brides to set the stage for a new generation of ranching stewardship. The Angus crossbreeds survive the winter of 1965 and multiply into thousands, which carry on the biological/botanical process of grazing, fertilization and renewal such as once performed by the American Bison.

During his residency in Montana, the author was fortunate to meet many of those in the ranching community and as depicted in *Two Trails to Judith* dialogue, he encountered the same warmth, sense of family, and basic honesty as so written.

As *Two Trails to Judith* emphasizes, only the most futuristic and best-managed operations would endure.

It is the writer's vision that the Judith Basin Cattle Company would be one of the large ranching enterprises still viable to this day.

Dexter C. McPherson